"Sasha, I feel as if I've never made love before," Miles confessed, his voice hoarse.

"You haven't," she whispered, smiling. "Not to me."

Sasha's innocence touched Miles. Scared him. "I want to make this good for you, but I can't remember what kind of lover I was," he growled.

Her lashes fluttered. She met his gaze with her dark, steady eyes and smiled dreamily. "That doesn't matter. I'm not someone from your past. It's only you and me now. Follow your instincts." Her smile widened. "I plan to follow mine."

She lifted her arms to draw him down. And Miles gave up the last vestiges of regret that he couldn't recall his past experience with other women.

Sasha was unique.

All that mattered was the present...wasn't it?

Dear Reader,

Special Edition's lineup for the month of July is sure to set off some fireworks in your heart! Romance always seems that much more wonderful and exciting in the hot days of summer, and our six books for July are sure to prove that! We begin with bestselling author Gina Ferris Wilkins and *A Match for Celia*. July's THAT SPECIAL WOMAN! goes looking for summertime romance and gets more than she bargained for in book two of Gina's series, THE FAMILY WAY.

Continuing the new trilogy MAN, WOMAN AND CHILD this month is Robin Elliott's *Mother at Heart*. Raising her sister's son as her own had been a joy for this single mother, but her little family seems threatened when the boy's real father surfaces... until she finds herself undeniably drawn to the man. Be sure to look for the third book in the series next month, *Nobody's Child*, by Pat Warren.

Father in Training by Susan Mallery brings you another irresistible hunk who can only be one of those HOMETOWN HEARTBREAKERS. Also continuing in July is Victoria Pade's A RANCHING FAMILY series. Meet Jackson Heller, of the ranching Heller clan, in *Cowboy's Kiss*. A man who's lost his memory needs tenderness and love to find his way in Kate Freiman's *Here To Stay*. And rounding out the month is a sexy and lighthearted story by Jane Gentry. In *No Kids or Dogs Allowed*, falling in love is easy for a single mom and divorced dad—until they find out their feuding daughters may just put a snag in their upcoming wedding plans!

A whole summer of love and romance has just begun from **Special Edition!** I hope you enjoy each and every story to come!

Sincerely,

Tara Gavin
Senior Editor

Please address questions and book requests to:
Silhouette Reader Service
U.S.: 3010 Walden Ave., P.O. Box 1325, Buffalo, NY 14269
Canadian: P.O. Box 609, Fort Erie, Ont. L2A 5X3

KATE FREIMAN
HERE TO STAY

Silhouette®

SPECIAL EDITION®

Published by Silhouette Books
America's Publisher of Contemporary Romance

With thanks to my intrepid critique partner,
Doretta Thompson, for her insight; to my agent,
Alice Orr, for her wisdom; and especially to
Mark and Ben, for their love, which
transcends all those pizza dinners!

 SILHOUETTE BOOKS

ISBN 0-373-09971-1

HERE TO STAY

Copyright © 1995 by Kate Freiman

Books by Kate Freiman

Silhouette Special Edition

Jake's Angel #876
Here To Stay #971

KATE FREIMAN

began creating stories with happy endings even before she could read or write, after the old movie *Frankenstein* gave her nightmares. She believes she holds the record for rereading Louisa May Alcott's *Little Women*, and, of course, grew up wanting to be Jo, the writer.

A casual meeting with one of Kate's graduate professors—to discuss a book, of course!—turned into true love, marriage and immigration from Connecticut to Toronto, Canada. Her husband, Mark, became a lawyer, and they have one teenage son, Ben, who can usually be found with an open book in one hand.

Kate received the Romance Writers of America "Golden Heart" Long Contemporary Romance award in 1990. She says, "I love the optimism of romance novels. I feel it reflects the strength and courage of everyday women, the real heroines." Readers can write to Kate, c/o Silhouette Books, and include a S.A.S.E. for reply.

* * *

"Ms. Freiman's creative daring and impeccable romantic sensibility make her an outstanding addition to the Silhouette family."   —*Romantic Times*

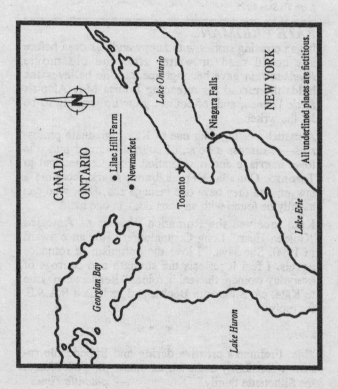

CANADA

ONTARIO

• Lilac Hill Farm
• Newmarket

★ Toronto

Georgian Bay

Lake Huron

Lake Erie

Lake Ontario

• Niagara Falls

NEW YORK

All underlined places are fictitious.

Prologue

Being dead shouldn't *hurt* so damn much, he thought grimly. Therefore, he probably wasn't dead. What he was, however, was trapped, freezing and in pain. Especially his left shoulder. Just breathing hurt like the devil. Willing himself to stay awake, to stay calm, he tried to sip in air in a way that didn't make everything feel worse. If he could stay in control, he had a chance.

He opened his eyes and saw nothing. Dear God, was he blind, too? Fear chilled him. He forced his eyes to stay open in spite of the weariness, willing them to work. As shadowy forms took shape, he realized he wasn't blind. Relief flooded through him like brandy. But for the light-absorbing darkness, he could see.

Immediately his relief turned back to fear. The dark reached out to swallow him. He couldn't move. His arms, his legs, tied, trapping him in the dark. Helpless again.

No! Don't lock the door! Turn on the light! Please? I won't tell! Promise! He struggled to free his hands.

Suddenly the voice in his head faded. A jagged pain started in his shoulder and ripped into his lungs, bringing the present into sharp focus, erasing the dim past. Defeated, he peered into the darkness until he could make sense of the shapes within the shadows surrounding him. It was night and he was pinned inside a crumpled car... somewhere.

He couldn't see because there were no lights, not even from the stars or the moon. No other cars. And no houses. No one to find him until—*maybe*—morning, whenever that would be. He had no idea what the time was. His watch was pinned under him, and the dashboard clock was dark.

What the hell had happened? All he could remember was...nothing? *Nothing*. Not where he was, or who he was, or why he was...wherever he was. He closed his eyes, trying to think. Trying to remember. He sifted through his thoughts, finding nothing to answer his questions. His mind worked, but it was like having a blank tape in the machine. *Who was he?*

The need to sleep overwhelmed him. Maybe he'd wake up and find it was all a dream. With his eyes closed, he drifted again, letting the dark wrap around him.... But sleep wouldn't take him.

God, it was cold. *He* was cold. The wind blasted him through the broken window. Bone-rattling, biting cold. He shook from it. Every tremor smacked him into the bent interior of the car. The pressure sent pain knifing through his ribs and into his head. The searing pain in his shoulder screamed for relief. With an odd sense of distance from his own condition, he decided his shoulder was dislocated.

Suddenly alert, he listened for signs of life. Nothing. Only the night. How long had he been there? Asleep. Unconscious. Cold.

He tried to move, to reach for the denim jacket on the seat beside him, to ease himself out from the twisted mess of glass, metal and steering wheel. Pain slammed him back down, humbling him, making him gasp for breath. In the frigid air the pain felt hot. It played no favorites, assaulting him with blinding force everywhere.

He closed his eyes and tried to wait the pain out. Better. If he could get to his jacket and trap what was left of his body heat, maybe he would just sleep for a while, gather his strength. Night couldn't last forever. Someone was bound to find him.

He tried once more to move. Breathing in slowly, past the fire in his chest, he pushed to free himself. The pain that ripped through him sucked the breath from his lungs. A starburst of colors flashed in his head, and then...nothing.

Chapter One

No one could have walked away from that crash. Sasha hugged herself against the bitter wind and made her way cautiously to the mangled red-and-white vintage Corvette lying in the ditch. The light from several flares and her lantern sparkled on the road's surface, but even knowing the black ice was there didn't prevent several back-wrenching slips. She'd called the Ontario Provincial Police from her car phone the moment her lights had picked out the wreck. Now, shaking with cold and dread, she had to find out if the ambulance she'd requested would be too late.

The silence of the cold night was almost spooky. She listened for sounds from the car. A call. A groan. Anything to reassure her that whoever was inside was alive. With a sick feeling, she let the beam of light play along the crumpled car until she found the shattered left side window. The driver would be trapped inside, but alone or with a passenger, she couldn't tell. A dark shape inside absorbed the light. Sasha inched closer. A low moan came from within.

Sasha's heart leaped. Someone was alive! She moved too quickly on the deceptive surface. Her thick-soled boots found no traction, and with a jerk she forced herself upright. Heart pounding now, she shuffled to the side of the wreck and took a deep, steadying breath, then bent and reached through the broken window until her searching fingers and the lantern light found the same thing: a shoulder in a soft, dark sweatshirt studded with broken glass sparkling like deadly sequins.

On another quick breath Sasha prayed for calm, for objectivity, for knowledge. She brushed lightly at the chunks of tempered glass, then slid her fingers toward the person's neck, seeking a pulse. At the same time she aimed the light farther into the car. Seeing no one in the black leather passenger seat, she turned her complete attention to the driver.

Judging by the size and hardness of the shoulder and neck, the person inside was a man. A big, strong man. His pulse was weak, and his skin under the sweatshirt felt cold. The flashlight reflected the man's thready breath hanging in the frigid air, mingling with her own as she slowly exhaled.

He moaned again, very softly, obviously feeling pain despite being unconscious. Sasha wanted to offer him some comfort, but she had to get back to her truck to warn the OPP they'd probably need an emergency task force truck to pry the man out of the twisted driver's seat.

As she shuffled back over the hidden danger of the slick black ice, Sasha prayed fervently that help would arrive in time.

He felt it again, a light touch on his shoulder, too light to hurt, enough to get his attention. He fought to wake up. When his body refused, he groaned.

"Easy, now." A low voice filtered through his haze. A woman's voice. "Don't try to move. The police will be here soon. They'll get you out and take you to a hospital. Any minute now." The voice was soothing. He decided he could trust the speaker. Hell, did he have a choice?

He tried to talk, to ask her where he was, and what had happened, and who she was, but his first word came out as a croak. Searing pains followed the sound. He took a cautious breath and tried again, fighting to open his eyes. *He needed to know.*

"Shh. Everything will be all right. I'll stay with you until the ambulance comes. You just relax." Her touch lifted from his shoulder. "It's very cold. I'm going to get a blanket for you from my truck. Then I'll stay with you."

She's staying. The sense of panic he'd been fighting suddenly faded. This time, when the darkness rose up inside him, he sank into it gratefully, somehow certain he was safe now.

Sasha wrapped her arms around herself, unable to stop the shivering that came, not from the biting-cold night air but from deep inside herself. She stood to the side, appreciating the efficiency and skill of the ambulance attendants and the police rescue experts, watching with a strange sense of emotional detachment. She understood why, of course. It was an instinctive survival tactic that allowed humans to cope with the most horrifying reminders of their own mortality.

The rescue team worked on the bent and twisted side and roof of the car, freeing the man inside a little at a time. He must be badly injured, she mused. He had stayed unconscious during most of the rescue. The medics had looked her way often, reassuring her that his vital signs were strong enough. She knew they understood the odd connection between strangers when one person sat comforting, touching, reassuring another while waiting for help.

Finally the man was freed. His groans cut to her heart as the medics eased him onto the stretcher. She felt drawn toward him as the stretcher moved past her to the rear doors of the ambulance. She gazed down at him while the medics adjusted the stretcher to slide it into the ambulance. He was covered by blankets from his chin down, and his face was too bloodied for her to know what he looked like.

Sasha wanted to reach out, to touch his shoulder one last time in reassurance, but she knew it was a foolish, useless gesture. He was now in far better hands than hers, and she might hurt him rather than comfort him.

As if he sensed her presence, the man opened his eyes and looked around without moving his head. In the light from the interior of the ambulance she could see his pupils were dilated, but she couldn't tell the color of his eyes. Oddly, that made her even sadder.

Then his eyes met hers. "Stay," he whispered hoarsely. As if sensing something important, the ambulance attendants paused.

Tears burned behind Sasha's lids. "I can't." She swallowed hard. "You have to get to the hospital, and I have to move my truck out of the middle of the road. Don't worry. They'll take good care of you."

"Stay," he urged again in that hoarse whisper. "With me."

Sasha touched his shoulder lightly and offered him a wobbly smile. "I'll come to the hospital to see you. But you have to go now. Let the doctors take care of you."

His eyes fluttered almost closed, then opened again. "Promise...you'll come." It was a demand, not a request. She almost smiled. Despite his injuries, he retained a sense of personal power. She guessed he was a man used to command.

"I promise. Now go. Let them help you."

The man's eyes closed again, breaking the contact between them. The medics slid the stretcher into the ambulance and within a minute the ambulance was creeping down the slippery, winding road. Sasha let out a long breath. It hung in the air, clouding her vision. When the vapor floated away she found herself face-to-face with a youthful, serious-eyed Ontario Provincial Police officer holding a notebook. His name tag said he was Constable Dave McLeod.

"From the looks of the car and the side of that tree," he confided, "I'd guess he spun out on the black ice and bounced off the tree before ending up in the ditch. Hell of a time getting him out, eh? The car's a write-off. Too bad. A classic Corvette like that's collector quality. Well, the driver's lucky to be alive, eh? Florida plates. The guy probably thought winter was over up here." He sighed. "The engine's stone cold. He must have been here a while before you found him."

Absently Sasha nodded, but she really had no sense of time. It had seemed to take forever to free the driver from the wreck, but she'd never once glanced at her watch. Her own discomfort had seemed of little concern compared to his safety. It certainly wasn't the first time she'd been exposed to the elements to deal with an emergency, although never one like this.

"I'll just take your name and address, ma'am, then let you go. You look like you're freezing. You've been out here a couple of hours, I think. Hard to believe it's spring, when it's this cold at night."

His words made Sasha realize how chilled to the bone she was. Gratefully, she nodded. "My name is Sasha Reiss." She gave him her address and home phone number, as well as her pager and car phone numbers. He wrote the information down in his notebook, his black-gloved fingers gripping the pencil awkwardly. She imagined he wasn't much warmer than she was, having been on the scene only a short time less than she had.

"Occupation?"

"Equine veterinarian." She saw his pencil stop moving. "Horse doctor."

Constable McLeod looked up from his notes. "What brought you way out here on a dirty night like this? I sure wouldn't be out here in the middle of the night unless I had to be." His quick smile was frankly flirtatious.

She gave McLeod a brief, weary half smile, agreeing. "I have a client about thirty-five miles east," she told him. "They have a local vet for routine things, but they call me for special needs. One of their mares slipped on ice and needed stitching. She's a fussy mare, doesn't like men very much."

He shook his head as he closed his notebook. "Sheesh! Now we've got feminist horses, eh?"

Sasha smiled, suspecting that, like many of the men she knew, Dave McLeod had old-fashioned values he felt were under attack by newly independent women. "Not really. But this one had a few unfortunate experiences with men, so she assumes they're all dangerous."

The young constable nodded. "I guess it all depends on your point of view, eh? Are you really going to go to the hospital? You don't have to, but that's really nice. Let me write down the guy's name for you." He grinned. "Then get yourself home and under an electric blanket." The playful expression on the constable's face faded. "You did fine tonight, Doc. This guy probably owes you his life."

Numbly, Sasha nodded and took the piece of paper on which McLeod had written. She didn't look at it until she was back in the cab of her truck. As the heater and the defroster fought the damp, cold air, she opened the paper and read by the roof light the name written in neat, square letters: Miles Kent. The name itself meant nothing to her, but she tucked it into her inside breast pocket as if she vicariously could lend him some of her strength.

Sasha shifted into first gear and gingerly drove past the wrecked sports car. Within a short distance the road ran straighter and dry. Her body ached with cold and fatigue, but her mind stayed focused on the stranger on his way to the nearest hospital.

Some people thought medicine was all chemistry and mechanics, but she'd been a healer long enough to know there was a spiritual element that could work miracles. In the past she'd focused her energies on healing her equine patients. Now she prayed that even her little bit of spiritual effort would help Miles Kent walk away whole and safe.

The next day Sasha phoned the hospital before and after her barn calls, to ask about Miles Kent. He was in intensive care, but the nurse assured her that she could visit briefly, since they hadn't located any next of kin, and her presence might help. Twice daily in the following two days she made time in her hectic schedule to stop at the hospital.

It felt so odd to sit by the bedside of a stranger, holding his good hand and telling him about her day. Although she was a doctor, there was something unsettling about being surrounded by the high-tech machines that measured Miles's progress while his body healed itself in silence. He was a big man, so unmoving that she found herself wiping tears after each visit. His hand lay limply in hers, not even twitching when she stroked his skin as if he were someone dear to her.

On the second day a doctor stopped by to thank Sasha for her visits, and confirmed that the police still hadn't found a close relative. It distressed her that Miles Kent was so alone, even as she cautioned herself not to care too much about a man she didn't know. He might be the nicest guy in the world, or a loony... a Nobel Peace Prize nominee, or Jack the Ripper's third cousin.

Her mind continued on in silent debate—common sense advised her to keep her distance, and compassion demanded that she offer him whatever comfort she could until he was well enough to leave. Then again, common sense warned her that he had been in so much pain he probably didn't recall extracting a promise from her. But compassion wouldn't let her shake her feeling of connectedness to Miles. Besides, didn't her mother always say she had more guts than brains?

As she had every day for the past three, Sasha phoned the hospital after noon, even though she'd been there in the morning and planned to go again in the evening. This time the nurse told her Miles was awake and off the monitors, and had been moved to another room. Sasha spent the afternoon wondering what it would be like to talk to a lucid Miles Kent, and if anyone had told him she'd been hanging around holding his hand for three days. Would he be pleased? Or irritated that she'd been with him when he hadn't known? Would he read too much into her attention, or understand she'd keep the same kind of vigil for an injured horse?

After finishing her rounds for the day and showering, Sasha took a soft teal woolen dress from her closet, then thought about what she'd just done. *Why on earth was she primping for a stranger stuck in a hospital bed?* She so seldom wore a dress, even on dates, and this certainly wasn't a date. Quickly she put on a pair of clean, well-worn jeans and a golden turtleneck sweater that skimmed her hips. With her hair in its customary single braid down her back and her bangs freshly fluffed, she pulled on black suede fringe-trimmed boots. Although she wore no makeup, she sprayed on her favorite cologne, *just because* she liked to smell like something other than a horse. Then, grabbing her jacket, she went out to her truck and made the short drive to the hospital.

The door to Miles's room was open just a sliver. Suddenly nervous, Sasha hesitated. This could be awkward. For all anyone knew, he didn't have a clue who she was, and probably wouldn't want a stranger hovering over him while he was in pain.

Her thoughts were abruptly interrupted when the door swung inward and a nurse hurrying out nearly ran into her. It took Sasha a few blank seconds to realize she knew the woman. Emmy Dunne was the mother of twin girls in the Pony Club Sasha advised.

"Well, hi, Doc!"

"Hi, Emmy."

"What brings you here?" Emmy tipped her head and studied Sasha with the bright interest of a sparrow.

Sasha felt her cheeks grow warm. "I, uh, I was the one who found Mr. Kent. I promised I'd stop by to see him."

"Oh!" Emmy gave her an odd look.

"What?" she demanded softly, immediately uneasy. "Is something wrong? I thought he was doing well."

Emmy shook her head. "He's doing better. Come on in. I'll introduce you."

Puzzled by Emmy's guarded tone, Sasha followed her into the room. The first of the two beds was empty, its linens stripped. In the second bed lay a large figure of a man, his head partially wrapped in a white bandage. His closed eyes gave Sasha a moment to study him one more time. This time, however, she was aware of him as a man, not an inert body with a battered face and limp hand.

Miles Kent's face had been badly bruised, but under the shadows of stubble, welts and purple blotches lay the strong bones of a handsome man. His shoulders seemed to stretch the width of the bed, the right one bare and heavily muscled, the left wrapped in an elastic bandage. His left hand was hidden by the light blanket draped over his large body, but his right hand rested above the blanket, lying across his abdomen. She decided she'd better keep her interest in anatomy limited to horses and not speculate about that flat belly.

"Mr. Kent, you have a visitor," Emmy said with quiet cheeriness. Sasha watched his long-lashed eyes flutter open. "This is Sasha Reiss, Mr. Kent. She's the one who found you after the accident."

Judging by the scowl on Miles Kent's mouth, Sasha doubted he was overjoyed to have her there.

"Go on, Doc." Emmy lowered her voice to a confidential murmur. "He's having some trouble recalling the events, and his injuries are making him a little cranky." Emmy grimaced. "Well, very cranky. Maybe your lovely presence will mellow him out a little. You've got a few minutes until the painkillers take effect."

"Doc? My doctor?" Miles muttered in a gravelly voice.

"Not unless your name is Trigger," Sasha told him, approaching slowly. Emmy laughed and gave Sasha a little push toward the bed. "I'm a horse doctor," she added at his blank look.

"For all I know, my name *is* Trigger," he growled.

Sasha cast a worried glance at Emmy, who merely winked back. "Gotta go. Press the buzzer if you need anything, Mr. Kent. 'Bye, Sasha!"

The door whooshed shut and Sasha found herself alone with a stranger who was studying her intently. She'd place his age as mid-thirties, although with all the bruising and swelling, it was hard to tell. His eyes were hazel, she discovered. Golden hazel. For some reason, that knowledge made her glad she'd come to visit.

"You found me?" Miles asked, his voice sounding weary, rusty. She nodded. "I can't remember.... Did you see what happened?"

"No. I'm sorry. You'd been there a while, I think. The engine was pretty cool."

"I can't remember anything except waking up in the ditch. How the hell could I total my car without any reason?"

"Black ice. It coats the road, fills in the cracks and grooves until the surface is as slick as a wet skating rink, and at night it's invisible. I noticed you're from Florida. You probably aren't familiar with northern driving conditions. Black ice is terribly treacherous. One touch of your brakes can send you off the road. Even people who know what to expect can get caught. Some winter mornings up to a dozen cars spin off the 404. The towing companies put numbers on them, like at a coat-check counter, because they can't handle them all at once."

He didn't smile at her mild joke. "This isn't winter," he muttered. "Is it?"

"No, it's spring. But even without snow, there's enough moisture to cause havoc if we get a cold snap. It makes driving like playing Russian roulette."

His cut lips curved into what seemed to be a smile, a bitter, ironic smile, she thought. "Looks like I lost the game. The cops told me my Corvette is history."

"But you aren't, Mr. Kent. Isn't that the important thing?" Impulsively she reached out to touch his shoulder in reassurance, but the way he glanced at her hand made her pull it back. This was not a man who would accept comfort easily. She hoped no one had told him that she'd been holding his hand for three days.

"Do me a favor, Doc? Stop calling me 'Mr. Kent.'"

"But they told me that's your name. Is there something else you'd prefer me to call you?"

"They told me that's my name, too, and I haven't a clue if there's something else I'd prefer," he growled. "If they told me I was Napoleon, I'd have to believe them."

Sasha bit her lip and clasped her hands together. Why hadn't Emmy told her what was going on before she put both feet into her mouth?

"Oh," she managed to say.

"Yeah."

"I ... I'm sorry," she murmured, wishing she had more than that inane expression to convey that she really was sorry. She raised her hands in an open, helpless gesture, then lowered them, feeling extremely inadequate. She knew what to do when a client needed comforting over bad news about a horse, but she'd never encountered anything like Miles's situation.

As if he could read her thoughts, his lips moved into a smile that had none of the bitterness of his earlier one. Despite the bruises, Miles Kent was a very handsome man.

"I can't tell you about me until the cops get their report from Florida. So why don't you tell me about you? Do you live around where you found me?" Without the bitterness in his voice, he sounded rather nice. Gruffly persuasive. She was intrigued.

"No. I was out on an emergency call. I actually don't live far from here."

"And where the hell *is* here?"

"Newmarket."

"Newmarket." He echoed her exact tone, as if the town's name didn't mean anything to him.

"Ontario? Canada?" she prompted, wondering how much he'd blanked out. "About twenty-five miles north of Toronto."

"So they tell me. I seem to have forgotten, remember?"

She gave him an apologetic little smile. "Touché."

"I wouldn't fence with you, Doc," he murmured, his eyes meeting hers in a way that sent warm tingles up and down her spine.

Sasha couldn't think of a thing to say, clever or otherwise. All she could think of was that, whoever he was, bruises and all, Miles Kent had more than his fair share of charisma and sex appeal. She found him very attractive, more so than any other man she could think of, even though he was trussed up in a hospital bed. Not that it mattered. He'd be gone as soon as he could travel.

"You live on a farm, Doc?" Miles's voice was starting to fade. Whatever Emmy had given him for pain was finally starting to take effect, but Sasha could see he was fighting it.

"Yes."

"Tell me about it tomorrow."

Sasha smiled to herself. He was a very confident, assertive man, apparently used to getting his way. Even in this condition he took charge, and he probably wouldn't take well to frustration. She could understand why Emmy had warned her that he was a little cranky. She'd be pretty cranky herself, in his situation. More than that, she'd be angry, frustrated and scared. Miles Kent also must be, she reasoned, but being of the male persuasion, he'd probably rather die than admit it.

His eyes closed. "Right now, need sleep," he mumbled. "'Night."

Ordinarily, Sasha was a toucher, and she never hesitated to stroke or caress her patients or her friends. But now that he was awake, Miles was a different case. Sasha fought the urge to touch him, to brush her fingertips over his brow or lay her hand gently on his unbandaged shoulder. The last thing she wanted to do was make him more uncomfortable than he already was.

"Good night."

"Hey, Doc." Miles opened his eyes again, but Sasha could see he was out of focus. Their eyes had barely met before he shut his again. "See you 'morrow," he muttered.

He fell asleep smiling. Oddly touched, she left quietly, waving at Emmy as she walked toward the elevators. Only when she was opening the door of her truck did she think of giving Emmy a piece of her mind for setting her up like that. Too late now, and not really important, she told herself. She probably wouldn't be seeing Miles Kent much past tomorrow. He looked like the robust type who healed quickly, and she'd already seen how little he liked being fussed over. She'd bet he'd be on a plane for Florida within a few days, and she'd be just a memory in his vacation from hell.

Chapter Two

Miles stared at the photo on the United States passport. It was more or less the same face that had stared back at him from the bathroom mirror, but it wasn't one he recognized. The description on his driver's license didn't help, either. Brown hair. Hazel eyes. Six feet two inches tall. One hundred and eighty-five pounds. Age thirty-four, unless he'd also forgotten how to subtract. Address, Secret Island, Florida, wherever the hell that was. No street, just an island and a zip code. Maybe he was a beach bum.

Except he didn't think beach bums drove classic cars and carried gold credit cards. At least, not all current, valid and in the same name: Miles Kent. Same name as on the Social Security card. If he was a beach bum, he probably wouldn't have the wad of cash the police had found in his wallet, along with charge receipts from places in Canada he had no recollection of visiting. In fact, the cops had found a whole paper trail in the wrecked Corvette, leading from the Gulf Coast of Florida all the way up past the Canadian border.

Interesting, since he also had no memory of driving for two days, or of going through the Canadian border checkpoint.

Then again, he had no memory of anything prior to waking up in the mangled Corvette.

The cops hadn't found anything else in the car, except a small leather suitcase packed with several changes of clothes and basic toiletries. No illegal substances, thank God, but nothing of value to him right now, either. No address books or letters or agendas or anything to hint at where he'd been going, or why he was here. No clues to who he was. Only a name—supposedly his own—that meant nothing to him.

A staff shrink had come in earlier, a tall, lanky man in rimless glasses, whose laid-back manner had made Miles think of a cowboy, not a psychiatrist. This Dr. Simmons had asked him if he wanted a chance to talk about what had happened, in particular how he felt about his "memory deficit." He hadn't.

Before he left, the shrink had suggested that Miles think about how he felt, anyway. Well, hell, he knew exactly how he felt. He was confused, frustrated and angry, and he didn't think talking about it with a total stranger was going to change that. The shrink's theory, that his brain was shutting out something he couldn't deal with emotionally, didn't wash. There had to be a better explanation for this than that it was all in his head. Miles might not know who he was, but he was pretty damn sure he wasn't crazy.

But what did he really know about himself? So far, all he knew for certain was that he hated being helpless—and eating hospital food.

With a groan of raw frustration Miles gathered up the cards and the license and stuffed them back into the envelope. He handed them back to the young pup of a cop, McLeod, and shook his head. McLeod shrugged.

"We've requested help from the Florida state police. I should have more information for you later today. Tomorrow morning at the latest. I tried phoning that fancy restaurant you have receipts from, but they must not be open this early. I'll have to try a little closer to dinnertime."

"Whatever you get, let me know." McLeod nodded. "As soon as you get it," he added, not certain the cop understood his sense of urgency.

McLeod just looked at him for a moment. "When are you getting out of here?" he asked finally.

The change in topic didn't surprise Miles. They'd been vying for dominance. The kid had his badge, but Miles didn't feel like someone intimidated by authority figures. Other feelings simmered under the surface when he thought about cops and bureaucrats, but awe wasn't one of them.

"I think they're stalling to make sure they get paid, just in case I'm a deadbeat." The thought left a bitter taste, a vaguely familiar feeling, as if maybe that had been a problem at some time in his murky past. But if that was true, then where had he gotten all those credit cards, all that cash? Could he have mugged the real Miles Kent and stolen everything?

Including his face? Nah. One more theory down the pipe, but one theory he didn't mind flushing. Thinking of himself as a thief felt more than a little uncomfortable. What would he do if he turned out to be some high-wheeling crook on the lam?

"Hey, don't sweat it," McLeod told him, grinning. Sure. He could grin. He knew who he was. "We'll know soon enough."

"Not soon enough for me."

McLeod stood and shrugged into his shiny blue winter jacket. "Don't play detective. Leave it to the professionals."

Miles couldn't resist needling the pompous puppy. "What if I *am* a professional?"

McLeod snorted. "Save that one for the movies." He picked up the envelope of credit cards and cash that the police were keeping in their safe and nodded before heading for the door. With his hand on the handle, he stopped and turned back. "By the way, did Sasha Reiss visit you?"

For some reason Miles felt caution settle into place like a mask. The nurses had mentioned that his rescuer had visited him almost every day he'd been unconscious, but he was still processing how he felt about that. Was there some connection between McLeod and Dr. Reiss? Whatever the cop's reason for asking, Miles didn't like him being in his face.

"What if she did?"

"Nice lady. I sure wouldn't mind her coming to my rescue," McLeod said, grinning smugly. Then he turned his back and walked out the door.

Miles glared at the door as it closed slowly, shutting him in alone with his thoughts. And one of those thoughts was that Constable McLeod was too damn young for Sasha Reiss.

Not that it was any of his business.

Sunday evening, when Miles answered Sasha's knock, she noticed immediately that his voice was much stronger than the day before. She took a fortifying breath and pushed open the door. Miles was lying propped up in his bed, his battered face clean-shaven. The sheet and blanket bunched just above his waist, exposing a powerfully muscular chest so bruised that he looked as if he were wearing camouflage. The mat of hair covering the upper half of his chest was the same sable color as the hair spilling rakishly over the bandage on his forehead.

Sasha swallowed hard, then summoned a smile to answer his. It wasn't fair, she thought, for him to be so attractive. She didn't know if he was married or involved, and the awful thing was, neither did he. She'd just have to pretend he was a horse. An old, swaybacked, flea-bitten, knock-kneed nag.

Just the kind of horse she'd find herself adopting because no one else wanted him. No, better think of him as a man she didn't know from Adam.

"Hey, Doc. I thought you'd stood me up for some four-footed rival." Miles's golden eyes met hers. He sounded gruff, but she saw that he was trying to smile. His mouth looked so sore she could almost ignore the temptation to speculate about how mobile and expressive it must be. Good Lord, what was the matter with her?

"I usually don't work on Sundays unless I'm on a call, but I had a special job that ran late. A shipment of—" She broke off at the way he watched her speak. No, she couldn't tell him.

"A shipment of...?" he prompted. "Horses?"

Inexplicably, heat rose to her cheeks. "No. It was nothing."

"C'mon, Doc. Your nothing is better than what's been going on here. I'm too full of painkillers to focus on the paper, and the soap operas don't do anything for me."

She studied the light fixture above Miles's bed as if it were a piece of fine sculpture. "A shipment of stallion semen was delayed at the airport in Montreal. By the time the mare's owner picked it up at the Buttonville airport, between here and Toronto, it was late afternoon."

"So you were playing Cupid by proxy?"

She nodded, wondering why she was having so much trouble looking him in the eye when she'd given public lectures on artificial insemination to rooms full of strangers.

"I don't think I'd like being a stallion," he said solemnly.

Sasha glanced at him and he winked. She laughed, suddenly more comfortable with him. And yet, not comfortable at all. Instinctively she recognized that Miles Kent was not the kind of man who'd be a woman's buddy. He'd be a lover, maybe a business associate, but not a chum. There was too much raw vitality, too much pure sexuality emanating from him to let any woman relax completely. It was the kind of reaction she'd longed to feel for that one "right man," which Miles, a stranger just passing through her life, definitely wasn't.

"Some stallions are luckier than others," she told him, firmly tamping down her awareness of him. "But distance makes some relationships difficult, if not impossible. Not everyone can afford to ship a mare and board her for a month or more at the stallion's farm. A couple of hundred years ago stallion owners would travel with their horses. But that's pretty tough on the stallion."

Miles raised his dark brows. "Puts a new spin on the concept of cruising, doesn't it?"

She smiled. "At least these studs don't have to pay for drinks."

Miles started to laugh, coughed, then groaned and pressed his hand to his taped ribs. "Oh, God! Don't make me laugh," he wheezed.

She took a step forward, then hesitated. "I'm sorry. Should I call the nurse?"

"No. I'll be fine as long as you aren't funny." His bruised lips quirked up into an infectious grin that sent warmth spreading through her. "Tell me about your farm."

"I can do better than that. I brought some pictures."

She dug the packet out of her huge leather purse and handed it to him. When Miles took it, she noticed again how strong his hands were. She realized she didn't have any idea what he did for a living, but she knew that at some point in his life Miles Kent had worked with his hands. If she was an artist, she would want to sketch hands like his. If she was a romantic fool, she would imagine what hands like his would feel like on her body.

Doc Reiss was a very attractive woman, Miles decided. Striking, not pretty. Those dark eyes of hers were beautiful, and gentle as a doe's. Her features were strong, and her body taut, athletic, graceful. He'd bet there were honest muscles, not shoulder pads, under her sweater. And her hands. God, her hands were incredible. Long, slender fingers, narrow wrists, short nails. They were hands that looked sensitive and gentle. Hands that had held his when he'd been unconscious. Competent hands that would soothe a skittish patient, hands that might tremble when they stroked a lover.

The rush of heat to his gut warned him that such thoughts could very well embarrass him much more than their brief discussion of artificial insemination had embarrassed her. Besides, what did he know about Dr. Sasha Reiss, except that she was a softie? Even though she didn't wear any rings, she could be married, and mother to a small brood of kids. Hell, he didn't even know if he was married. Frustration made him grit his teeth.

Miles took the packet of photos from her, careful not to let their fingers touch. Then he looked into her face until she finally met his eyes. Was she shy? The idea amused him. He had a feeling he didn't meet many shy women.

"C'mere, Doc. Stand over my shoulder and tell me what I'm looking at."

It was a reasonable request, but her effect on his senses wasn't anywhere near reasonable. She smelled soft. When she moved, she moved softly, sounded soft. In self-defense he took out the photos and looked at the top one, an aerial shot of a rambling stone farmhouse and stone barn, with rolling green pastures neatly fenced. The dark blobs were probably horses. Oblong blobs, he guessed, were of baled hay or straw scattered in adjacent fields. Two white horse trailers, one small and one large, a white pickup truck and a red tractor stood parked between the house and the barn. On the far side of the barn stood a large warehouse-style structure.

"A friend of mine took that from his plane," she told him.

"How many acres?"

"Forty-five. I lease twenty acres to the farmer next door, and he provides me with hay."

"Looks nice."

Her smile looked a little misty. "Mmm. It was my grandparents' farm. My mother's parents. Actually, it originally belonged to my great-great-grandparents. Granddad was a hobby breeder. Canadian Hunters. I inherited the farm from him."

Her pride in her ancestors made him uncomfortable. Why? he wondered. Was there something about his family that he was less than proud of? Or was it just that she knew who she was and who'd come before her, while he was stuck

with a passport photo that looked like him but didn't ring
any bells?

"What's this thing here?" He pointed to the warehouse.

"The riding arena, for riding in winter weather."

"It's winter weather now," he muttered. "The calendar
says it's the middle of April."

Sasha laughed softly. He wanted to say a dozen more silly
things to make her laugh, just to hear the sound. He wanted
to untie her braid and let that dark hair slip free over his
bare skin. He hoped he was free to do so. He hoped he
wasn't the kind of man to feel this way if he was married.

"You know what they say about the climate in Canada?" she asked. "Nine months of winter and three months
of lousy skating."

And lousy driving, he could have added, but he didn't
want to spoil the moment by making Sasha feel sorry for
him again. He forced a smile, which made his face ache.

"Seems like it." More to himself than to Sasha, he went
on, "I wonder what the hell I was doing up here? Seems I
have credit card receipts from a restaurant somewhere near
the Quebec border, but damned if I know why I was there."

She stared at him with those dark eyes that made him
think of Bambi's mother. Just when he was sure she was
going to get serious on him and make him regret his un-
guarded speech, she smiled.

"I imagine you were having dinner," she said.

His smothered laugh came out in a snort.

A voice burst out of the speaker in his wall, announcing
that visiting hours were over for the day. Sasha started to
move away. He fought a sudden wave of panic. She was a
stranger, but she was the only person he knew. The only one
he *knew* that he knew, anyway. He hadn't known his own
face in the mirror. But he knew Sasha's face, her voice, her
scent. He didn't want to lose that connection, no matter how
flimsy.

"Leave the pictures, okay? I want to hear more about you
next time." He tried to smile, but he suspected he looked like
Quasimodo.

She hesitated, then said, "Sure. I can come back tomorrow evening."

He didn't want to let her see he was pleased. And he knew he shouldn't let himself count on her. But at the moment she was all he had, besides a plastic bag full of stuff, and a name that was supposed to be his.

"What's your husband going to say about you visiting me?" He had to ask, but he found himself dreading the answer.

"I'm not married," she told him. "Except to my work." She smiled. "Sleep well."

He watched her leave and knew that the last thing he was going to do was sleep well. For someone whose memory seemed to be wiped clean of anything significant, he had an awful lot on his mind.

Sasha stood in front of Miles's half-open door, trying to catch her breath after sprinting across the parking lot. Visiting hours would be over in less than ten minutes, but at least she'd made it in time to say hello. After thinking about him all day, whenever she wasn't concentrating on a patient, it would have been too ironic to miss visiting hours altogether. It had been her thinking about Miles—as well as a tough medical case to puzzle out—that had caused her mind to wander while she'd driven to the wrong farm. Driving the extra distance back again, to the right farm, had cost her almost an hour at the end of an already full day. She was pushing exhaustion, but she'd given her word.

She knocked and pushed the door open a little more at the same time, calling his name softly. Miles was sitting in one of the wooden chairs, a frown on his battered, handsome face. He wore what looked like beige pajama bottoms and a black robe belted at his waist. His feet were bare, his left ankle wrapped in an elastic bandage. The top of the robe gaped open, revealing the dark curling hair across his chest.

Sasha said his name again, but his scowl stayed in place. "Hi. Sorry I'm late. I didn't even have time to shower and change, so I smell like a horse," she told him as she stepped inside.

"You've obviously got enough to do without these extra little errands of mercy." Miles's low voice vibrated with anger. Sasha didn't know what she'd done wrong in his eyes, but she'd had too long and hard a day to pursue the matter. She did know she didn't deserve his sarcasm.

Sasha reached for the door handle, her eyes level on his. "You don't know me well enough to speak to me like that," she told him quietly. "Good night." She turned away, her hand touching the door.

"Wait!" he bellowed, then groaned. The sound of the chair legs scraping the floor made her turn back. Miles was trying to stand and clearly not having an easy time of it. "I don't know *anyone* well enough, not you, and not me, damn it!" His anger came out strained through his effort to speak.

Instantly her irritation evaporated. Of course he was angry. He was in pain, inside and out, physical and spiritual. How insensitive could she be? If he was one of her patients, he'd probably kick or bite, taking it out on whomever was handy. She'd been on the receiving end of that kind of behavior often enough to recognize it, although usually it was from four-footed types.

Nothing personal—that was the important thing to keep in mind. Miles was in pain and she wasn't. She could certainly deal with that. She stepped back into the room and waited.

"Sasha, I'm sorry," he said, the softness of his tone surprising her. He met her gaze, half standing, gripping the back of the chair. "Damn! I hate this!"

The anguish in his hazel eyes brought her to his side in a second. Carefully reaching past the tapes and bandages, she slid one arm around his waist and braced herself so he could lean on her shoulders. His arm rested heavily on her. His warmth sank into her. The musk of his skin invaded her senses, reminding her acutely of one of the questions that had needled her all day. Was Miles married? Did he know yet? Was he the kind of man who would tell her the truth, or try to take advantage of her compassion and her proximity?

Those weren't the most useful questions she could be asking, she realized. Miles was clearly in need of real help.

"Bed?" she asked.

"I take it that isn't an invitation," he drawled, but his voice was still strained despite his attempt at humor. She tried not to smile but failed. "Bed, if you can. Chair, if you can't. I don't want to hurt you."

But in spite of Sasha's resolve to be dispassionate, to treat him as if he were a patient, Miles already had hurt her, irrational as it was. She decided it would be best for both of them to keep things light. He had enough to deal with without her feelings getting in the way.

"What do you weigh, one eighty?" she asked.

His unbruised eyebrow arched. "My ID says one eighty-five. Why? You planning to sweep me off my feet?"

She tilted her head to smile up at him. "Miles, most of my patients weigh upward of twelve hundred pounds and aren't nearly as good with English as you are. Compared to them, you're a featherweight. But just like you," she added, "they're seldom reasonable when they feel cranky."

He snorted. She blinked in mock innocence.

"If you put your mind to it, you probably could be reasonable." His smile told her he understood her strategy and would accept her help. "Let's go. One foot in front of the other."

She could feel the effort it cost him to move back to the bed, a step at a time. His muscles bunched, and he hardly drew a breath until he was sitting on the mattress. He was a powerful man, but obviously he was terribly sore. He sat for a moment, head bowed, then looked up into her eyes.

"You do smell like a horse," he drawled. "I like it."

His crooked grin was pure, totally unexpected, totally unapologetic devilment. Sasha felt herself smiling in response. When he wasn't carrying on like a wounded bear—which he was, in a way, of course—Miles Kent could charm the spots off a Dalmatian. She needed some distance to let her keep her objectivity. She needed to turn his attention away from her.

"Did you learn anything more about . . . ?" she started to ask, breaking off when she couldn't think of a tactful way to continue.

His grin faded. "Who I am?" He looked straight into her eyes and she could feel him measuring her response as he said, "Yeah. For one thing, I'm not married."

He studied the doc's reaction. One eyebrow went up a fraction of an inch and she said, "Ah," very thoughtfully, as if he'd done nothing more than given her the answer to a tough math problem. Cool. Uninterested. Impersonal. She might have carried it off if she hadn't blushed.

He was tired of being a body, a patient, the "mild head injury," the "memory deficit case," a room number. Whoever he was, he was a person, a male person, and he was damn glad Sasha had noticed.

She cleared her throat. "Do you need help lying down?"

"Under the circumstances, I wouldn't turn down your offer," he told her, playing shamelessly on her compassion just to keep her close, to keep her strong hands on him. After the impersonal probing and poking of doctors and nurses, Sasha's firm touch felt so good. Still, he couldn't come right out and ask her to keep touching him. He wanted to, but something beyond the fact that he hardly knew her made him bottle up that need.

"Tell me what you want me to do."

Oh, Doc! he thought. *What a loaded question!* But the truth was, what he wanted from her had very little to do with the delayed realization that made her blush again. He wanted some of her strength, her calm, her inner peace, because he couldn't find any of his own. He didn't even know if he'd ever had his own. Judging from the bare facts he'd learned about his life earlier, he suspected not.

"Can you support my shoulders? I can do the rest."

Sasha smiled, the way he'd hoped she would. "Okay. Just lean back into my hands."

She stepped closer to the side of the bed, facing him, and slid her hands under his arms to cup the backs of his shoulders. She bent toward him until her head was almost beside his, giving him a jolt of awareness. God, she smelled good! Earthy. Sexy.

"Trust me, Miles. I can hold you," she murmured, her breath warming his neck.

He was weaker than he wanted to be. She was stronger than he'd guessed. Miles didn't like it. He resented having no control over this bizarre situation. Whoever he was, he thought, he wasn't someone who asked for or accepted help easily. He didn't like being forced to now, much as he liked being this close to Sasha. He hoped to hell he was a fast healer.

Sasha took much of his weight as he drew his legs up onto the mattress, then eased down onto his pillows. Every injury screamed in protest until he stopped moving. When he realized he'd inadvertently pinned her hands beneath his back, the pain no longer seemed important. She stayed there, trapped into a mock embrace, her breasts inches from his chest, her soft mouth within easy reach if he just lifted his head a few inches. Instead of trying, he shifted until she could free her hands and straighten. She moved away as if nothing had happened.

But he had seen it in her eyes. She'd been on the same wavelength. Aware. Oh, yeah, aware. Curious—but cautious. Especially cautious. She didn't know him. He couldn't blame her. What could he say to reassure her? He didn't know who he was.

He should do something to ease the tension, at least for her. His tension seemed to be an integral part of him and he felt like an overwound clock, ready to spring loose at any time.

"How'd you break your nose, Doc?" he asked. He wanted to trace the line of her nose, over the little bump, softly teasing her, making her think about kissing him. He didn't, but he wanted to.

She smiled, making him glad he'd lightened the mood. She was all he had. He'd come too close to jeopardizing that tenuous connection already once tonight.

"One of my very first patients took exception to having his teeth floated," she told him.

"Floated? You mean like some old grandpa with his teeth in a glass?"

Her laugh was like magic. "No! The file used to rasp the sharp edges of horses' teeth is called a float. None of them like having it done, but some can be pretty piggy."

"You're lucky you didn't get your face broken."

"Don't I know it." She shrugged. "All occupations have hazards, but mine tend to think for themselves."

The thought of her being vulnerable to physical danger made him uneasy. Impulsively he caught her hand in his. "Be careful, Doc."

She looked down at their joined hands. "Thanks, Miles."

He liked the way she said the name, making him feel it really was his name. He wondered if any other woman in his life had said his name like that. "Thanks for what?"

"For worrying about my safety. I'm a pretty tough old bird, but it's still nice to have someone..." She shrugged again, and he saw the color rise in her cheeks. "You know. Express concern."

He didn't think that was exactly what she was going to say, but he understood her hesitation. How could someone care about someone else without knowing them? How could you know someone who didn't know himself? Miles rubbed his thumb over the back of her hand, feeling the steel under the silk, and raged inside at the silence of his memory. Who was he? Who was the man inside Miles Kent? Would he ever know?

A bored-sounding voice from the speakers announced that visiting hours were over. "I better go," she told him, tugging her hand out of his. "I still have chores to do before I can shower."

"You take care of the place alone?" He wouldn't be surprised. There was such a sense of competence about her—

and a sense of independence. Comfort with herself. He envied and resented her for it, even as he admired it.

"Not entirely. A couple of the nearby farmers' kids work for me part-time, and some of the Pony Club kids use my horses for their projects. But there's always something to do before I can lock up for the night."

And he was the reason she was going to be doing her chores late tonight. Because she felt sorry for him, she kept visiting him. Disgust at his helpless state, at his dependency, colored his words with pent-up fury and resentment.

"Don't keep coming back because you feel sorry for me. I don't want your pity!" he snarled, hating himself even as he lashed out.

Sasha shook her head. There were sparks in her dark eyes. "Compassion, Miles, not pity. I'm sorry you can't see the difference, but I'm not willing to be a target for your anger. You better get over it, or it won't matter who you are."

Chapter Three

"Stupid, insensitive, awful thing to say," Sasha muttered, her teeth clamped on the plastic cap from a syringe. She thumped the big gray gelding on the neck, then gave him a tetanus shot so skillfully that he didn't seem to notice. Too bad she hadn't been so skillful last night when she'd scolded Miles for having a bad attitude. He'd given her a look that could have frozen lava and told her she better leave before the nurses kicked her out.

She'd barely slept last night, tormented by visions of Miles trapped in his car. Of being within inches of kissing his mouth. Of holding his hand, unknown to him, willing him to heal. Of his crooked smiles and warm hazel eyes. And of Miles curtly telling her to go. The images refused to dissolve in daylight.

"Did you say something, Doc?" Donna, her longtime friend and the gelding's doting owner, asked from the other side of the big horse.

"No." Sasha took the plastic cap out of her teeth and recapped the syringe before tossing it in the garbage can.

"Just talking to myself. Bats in my belfry." She gave the gray a pat. "Casper's done. He's a good fella, aren't you, boy?"

Casper lowered his muzzle to blow against her palm, then swiped his big tongue across her hand. Smiling, Sasha reached up and scratched behind his ear. It was so much easier with animals. So much more straightforward. Most of the time, anyway. She'd known a few hard cases in her day. Almost as hard as Miles Kent. Those were always the ones she cared about most.

"Who do you want next?" Donna called as she led the horse back to his stall. "Sox or Elite?"

"Either one." Sasha crouched over her medical kit, a huge molded-plastic toolbox, to prepare the next shot. From the pocket of her jacket, which hung on a nearby peg, her pager beeped. "Hang on. I have to use the phone."

She phoned her service and picked up the message from her lawyer. A Humane Society seizure order against a local man who'd tried to get her, and several other vets, to destroy a perfectly healthy horse he couldn't handle had been upheld. In disgust, the owner had agreed to sell the horse to Sasha for a nominal amount. If she could load the horse into a trailer, he was hers. Elated, Sasha shared the news with Donna, who squealed with delight and hugged her.

"If you need help, let me know."

"Thanks, but it may not be the safest job you'll ever volunteer for. Desperado's pretty unpredictable. I'll probably have to tranquilize him. Even then, he could be a tough customer."

Funny, she mused, but whenever she thought of Desperado, she thought of Miles. A tough customer with attitude, who could have the most disarming moments of sweetness. The words *fascinating* and *captivating* also came to mind, but somehow, in both cases, they seemed to imply danger.

He was a brass-plated fool to care whether Sasha showed up or not. She was just another itch he couldn't quite scratch, like the memories that teased at the corner of his mind. He didn't want her, really, except that he couldn't have her. Literally and figuratively. And she only came to see him because she felt sorry for him. She was just a do-gooder.

He knew one more thing about Miles Kent now, although he didn't know why: he hated do-gooders.

So why the hell was he staring at the clock, for the third evening in a row, as if it could tell him anything more than that time expanded to fit the waiting?

That shrink had dropped by again. No pressure, the guy swore, just a few minutes of shooting the breeze—while he sized Miles up. Take it easy, the shrink had told him. Let the mind heal itself. But he'd be damned if he was going to force himself to sit around until his memory snuck up on him. He needed to *do* something to make it happen. But what? The harder he tried to think, the more his head ached, and the more frustrated and angry he got.

Miles grunted and turned his attention back to the two-day-old Canadian newspaper one of the nurses had given him. He'd automatically turned to the business section first. The small print made his vision swim, but he managed to focus on a piece about small Canadian companies seeking U.S. investors to bail them out of trouble. That set him thinking....

The knock on his door, when it finally came, made his heart pound as wildly as a blown piston.

"Yeah!" he snapped. He was mad at her for making him look forward to seeing her, and mad at himself, too. He didn't want to depend on anyone for anything. Another thing he knew for sure about the man called Miles Kent. Maybe one of these days he'd find out why.

"Hi," she chirped, as if she hadn't kept him waiting for three days. "I hear you've been charming the nurses," she said, a little too sweetly.

Miles refused to lower his paper immediately. Damn! He'd forgotten she had a friend on staff when he'd pitched a fit about not being allowed to shower or shave himself.

"They tried to treat me like a baby," he growled from behind the newspaper, but he felt his face heat up.

"You could stop acting like one."

He crushed the paper into his lap and glared, but her smile stayed sweet. It was getting harder to stay mad.

"How are you feeling?" she asked, serious now.

"Mean enough."

"You know what we do with horses who don't cooperate for treatment? We use a thing called a humane twitch. It's a short pole with a loop of rope at the end. We wrap the loop around the horse's upper lip and twist the loop to tighten it. It doesn't hurt the horse, but it gets his attention. Maybe I should have my Pony Club kids teach the nurses how to twitch snarky patients."

A sudden, brief image of small wrists bound tightly with graying rope flashed into his mind. A chill settled into the pit of his stomach even as he tried to answer Sasha's gentle teasing. Was he remembering something from his own life? Or a scene from some movie or book?

She moved into the room. He caught a hint of her perfume, something light and soft, and stopped trying to think. He watched her settle herself in the other chair and wondered if she ever wore anything besides jeans and sweaters. Not that they didn't do her justice. It was just idle curiosity about a beautiful woman who stirred his interest, that was all. Apparently his libido was healing faster than the rest of him.

She gazed at him with those dark eyes that had haunted his dreams. "So, have the police been able to get any more information for you?"

He lifted his good shoulder in a weak shrug. "Some. A few basic facts." Facts he wasn't ready to deal with yet. "Not enough to figure out what I'm doing here." The pity in her eyes prompted him to change the subject. "We never finished looking at those photos you brought."

She smiled. "I didn't think you'd still be interested."

"Hell, yeah. I feel like I'm in solitary confinement here. You're the only person I see all day who doesn't call me Mr. Kent and treat me like a collection of body parts."

He hadn't intended to make her blush again, but it was nice that she did. He reached for the packet of photos on the nightstand, pleased to note that broad movements hurt considerably less with each day.

She started toward the bed, then hesitated, her dark eyes suddenly as wary as a stick-shy dog's. His simmering anger at the situation turned against himself. He couldn't afford to alienate her. She was all he had linking him to reality, until he could make sense of what was supposed to be his identity.

"It's okay, Doc. I don't bite," he told her a little more gruffly than he'd intended. "Not hard, anyway."

"But you do bark," she teased, bringing her chair close to the side of his bed.

"I probably bay at the moon, too."

"A lone wolf?"

"Feels that way," he conceded. The information Constable McLeod had given him was more than proof that he was very much a lone wolf. "Who's this?" He pointed to the top photo of an older couple standing in the doorway of an old stone house, a golden retriever and a German shepherd staring up at them.

"My grandparents, with Midas and Schnitzel, about fifteen years ago." The smile on her face was so sweet, so sad. It made him uncomfortable, but he wasn't inclined to figure out why. He turned to the next photo, a middle-aged couple standing in front of a windmill. "My parents," she told him. "They retired a few years ago, and every year spend months traveling. Right now they're in Holland."

If he had parents, he couldn't remember. "What's this?" It was a slightly out-of-focus close-up of a pile of assorted fluffy kittens.

"My first litter of barn kittens. Their mother was dumped in a sack at the end of my driveway in the middle of February, a few months after I moved to the farm. I still have two of them. Friends took the other four, but there are always more being abandoned.''

''And this?'' A three-legged black Lab stood over a small goat.

''That's Topsy. Triceratops. And her pet goat, Gruff.''

''Triceratops?'' Miles laughed. ''Doc, you have a strange sense of humor.''

She chuckled. ''Not me. I let the Pony Club kids name the animals I adopt.''

''So how did you end up with a three-legged dog and a goat?''

''A hunter claimed he mistook Topsy for a deer—a black deer, right?—and her owners didn't want to pay big vet bills or care for a disabled dog. And Gruff was abandoned when she grew too big to be a cute Easter gift. They were inseparable right up until the day they died together in their sleep.''

He held up a shot of a dark horse that wouldn't win any beauty contests. It had a long face, a skinny neck and a sagging back, with a tail that looked like an old string mop. Sasha, standing beside the beast, looked gorgeous. Her face glowed with love, as if that ugly plug were her pride and joy. He wondered if there was something Sasha *wouldn't* take in.

''Okay. Who's this?''

''That's Houdini, a retired Standardbred racehorse. He's actually rather famous, but not for his racing career. He escaped from a truck on its way to a slaughterhouse in Montreal and crossed sixteen lanes of traffic on the 401 without a scratch. The slaughterhouse owner decided to let him go, if the Humane Society could find a home for him. I had an extra stall, so in he moved. The slaughterhouse agent said he admired the horse's spirit, but I'm sure he also had his eye on adverse publicity.''

He studied her face. She was beaming. ''You're a sucker for a sob story, aren't you, Doc?'' Like his, he thought.

She laughed lightly. ''Mmm-hmm. So it would seem. This next one is a family portrait of my pensioners.'' She pointed to a group shot of horses even uglier than Houdini, which he hadn't thought possible until he saw the evidence.

"They look like beggars."

"They are, in a way, poor guys. Three of these horses were retired, with nowhere to go. A couple were seized in raids. And these two smaller ones are mustangs, from the adoption program, whose owners got too old to keep them."

"No lady horses?"

She shook her head. "That's the way it's worked out lately, but it's just as well. Mares would drive the stallion crazy when they were in season."

He gave her a long look that made her blush. "You got anything you can put a saddle on, or are they all hard-luck cases?"

"Next one." The horses in this photo looked fit and glossy, standing in the sunshine in a green field. "These are the last three Canadian Hunters from my granddad's breeding program. They're magnificent." She beamed with pride.

"I can see that." He flipped to the next photo, of a spotted white horse in a small, dirty enclosure. The animal was rearing up, its eyes wild. "What the hell is this?"

Sasha's eyes sparkled. "That's Desperado. He's the leopard Appaloosa stallion I just bought."

The woman was truly nuts! "Why would you buy this maniac when you've got those hunters?"

"The owner approached me to put Desperado down, so he could collect on the insurance. The Humane Society issued a seizure order to prevent him from going to any other vet after I refused, so he sold the horse to me for a song."

Sasha was a compulsive soft touch, but she was obviously willing to play hardball when she believed in something. Instinctively he admired that, but he couldn't understand her making such a bad bargain for herself. "This thing looks homicidal."

"There's nothing fundamentally wrong with the horse. I won't destroy a healthy animal because the owner is incompetent. That stallion has fabulous conformation and bloodlines, and he should have an excellent disposition. But he had the bad luck to be bought as a weanling by a real creep. The guy abused him, then sold him to another creep. Desperado's been through four owners in three years, each one meaner than the last. He doesn't know how to trust or whom to trust. So he lashes out to protect himself, just in case."

A strange uneasiness crept through him at her words. It was as if something about this crazed horse's history resonated deep within his own silent memories, but he couldn't pinpoint anything that triggered a single specific memory or image. Disturbed, he kept his eyes focused on the picture. Sasha continued talking, saving him from having to look at her or comment. Just as well. He didn't want her to see his face just then. He didn't trust himself not to look pitiful.

"But now Desperado's mine."

"So what are you going to do with him? Sweet-talk him into being a good boy?"

She nodded, a dreamy smile on her face. "I'm going to try."

"What if he tries to attack you?" The thought made him clench his fists, as if he could fight the stallion to protect her.

"I'm sure he will," she said a little too cheerfully. Was she a glutton for punishment? "I'll just have to psych him out and be patient."

"Well, Doc, if anyone can, it's probably you." He flipped to the next photo, trying to dismiss the fear he felt that she could be hurt. She must know what she was doing. It was her profession. Anyway, it wasn't his concern.

He glanced down at a group shot on the first stairs of Sasha's house. Sasha's parents stood on the bottom stairs. Sasha stood above them, flanked by two men with their arms around her. All of them were grinning. The taller of the two men looked familiar. For a split second Miles felt the rush of adrenaline at the possibility that he'd found a missing piece of his memory. Then he realized why the tall guy looked familiar. He pointed to the image and looked at Sasha for confirmation.

She smiled without guile or guilt. "I see you've met Peter."

"I've met *Dr.* Simmons," he corrected, angry that neither Simmons nor Sasha had mentioned their connection. "The staff shrink. He's been by a couple of times to try to get me in touch with my feelings." One of which, if he was being totally honest, he'd have to admit was a touch of jealousy. "What's he doing on your front porch?"

"He's one of the kids my parents fostered. He still thinks of himself as my big brother."

Trying to sort out his reactions to her relationship to the hospital shrink, Miles handed the photos and envelope back to her. Sasha moved away to put the packet into a huge leather purse that looked as if she could use it to pack for a weekend. Then she slid the extra chair a little farther away from him and sat down. "Do you have any idea when you'll be able to get out of hospital?"

"A couple more days, from what they tell me."

"You had quite a concussion, didn't you?"

"So they say."

"And your ribs?"

"Four dented, nothing broken. Left knee and ankle slightly sprained. Left shoulder dislocated. Everything healing, except the hole in my memory." He blew out his breath in disgust.

The worry on her face made him feel like a jerk for being such a wimp. No wonder she pitied him.

"Miles, don't try to force it. Your brain is working on it, even if you don't think about it. The memories will come back when they're ready."

He snorted. "That's what your friend the shrink told me. Easy to say. He's not the one in limbo, is he? He knows exactly who he is, every day, all day—from when he wakes up to when he goes to bed. And so do you. Right?"

She was quiet for so long he thought he'd turned her off totally. He wasn't exactly acting like Prince Charming, but it would be fraud to try. He was frustrated by the situation, and apparently his way of dealing with frustration was to get angry. It didn't prove who he was, but it probably proved he was human.

Sasha's dark eyes stayed on his as if she could see right down to what he suspected was his rather black soul. "Would it help to talk about it?" she finally asked, her voice very soft, like a gentle touch to a wound.

Her gentleness made him feel vulnerable. Her compassion gave him permission to be weak, to give in to emotions. He didn't want to be vulnerable and sensitive. He wanted to get a grip on the situation, and get his life back on whatever track it had been on before the accident. He needed to be in control of his fate, and he needed his memory to do that. Pity wasn't going to make him stronger.

"No." She looked hurt by his bluntness. "Maybe later," he grunted at her, feeling vaguely uneasy.

"Anytime." She smiled. Irrationally, that made him feel better. "I'll leave you my pager number, in case you want to call me during the day. Just to, you know, say hello. Get a baseball score. Or a hockey score. Or both." She tipped her head to one side, that long braid swinging temptingly. "Would you like to borrow a radio? I've got one I could spare."

She was so eager to do something for him. He felt obligated to accept something. "Sure. Thanks." Her smile widened and her eyes sparkled. Suddenly he was feeling better than he had all day. Over a radio, for crying out loud! That must have been some bang on the head.

"Miles, don't dismiss Peter's help. He's a very good doctor."

"I'm not crazy, damn it!" he snapped, feeling rotten even as he vented his frustration. "I don't need a shrink. I need hard facts to hang something on, not touchy-feely psychobabble."

She opened her mouth, probably to argue, but a sharp knock on his door silenced her. A second later Constable McLeod walked in. He gave Sasha a smile like a kid at his first prom, then switched off his smile and made eye contact with Miles. A flash of another cop, stern, condemning, came into his mind. He felt himself tense.

"Hi, Doc! Good to see you. How are you doing, Mr. Kent?"

"What have you got for me, McLeod?"

"I should go," Sasha said, starting to get up.

"Stay, Sasha," Miles told her, not bothering to examine his motives for wanting her with him when McLeod dropped whatever bomb he obviously had ready. She nodded and sat down, and Miles felt some of his tension ease. McLeod's eyebrows rose. Miles stared back, daring him to say a word out of line.

"Your fingerprints checked out. Turns out the local police had them on record. You had a couple of break-in attempts at your house, and they needed yours to compare with the ones found at the scene. Other than that, I can't tell you much."

McLeod opened his black notebook. "You live on a private island off the Gulf Coast of Florida, and have an office on the mainland. You subscribe to the *Miami Herald,* the *New York Times* and the *Wall Street Journal,* as well as *Forbes* and *The New Yorker.* You have a housekeeper who comes over twice a week. Her husband does the ground work. They're paid by your office and you don't spend a lot of time chatting with either of them. Your meals come from a catering service. No wife, no live-in girlfriend, no kids, no pets."

The cop looked up from his notes and gave a quick glance at Sasha. Miles clenched his teeth. McLeod looked back at his notes. Miles let out his breath.

"You have one full-time employee, a Mrs. Eleanor Dobbs, who holds the title of executive assistant. She didn't report you missing after forty-eight hours. Presumably, she knew you were leaving, but not why or where you were going."

McLeod looked up again. "I don't think your Mrs. Dobbs trusted us. She refused to tell us anything except that she'll phone you tonight. She especially declined to describe the nature of your business." He gave a short bark of a laugh that Miles knew didn't have anything to do with amusement. "I'm going to assume it isn't anything illicit in nature."

He shrugged. None of it rang any bells. "What about the restaurant receipts?"

"You had dinner twice, and stayed two nights at a bed-and-breakfast nearby. You paid in U.S. currency. The owners shared a healthy portion of single malt Scotch with you on the first night, but couldn't get anything out of you except that you were from Florida and escaping from the usual rat race. The wife especially was disappointed." McLeod grinned. "She said they opened the B and B in order to meet new and interesting people, but you didn't exactly play the game."

Miles snorted. "Doesn't sound like I'm much of a party animal," he suggested wryly.

The truth was, it didn't sound as if he had much of a life. An existence, but not a life. All those facts and not a single thing that told him who he really was. Nothing he could hang an identity on. His life was like a glass mountain.

McLeod chuckled, but Sasha leaped to her feet, her dark eyes shooting sparks. *Now* what? Frustration made him shake his head, which set up a series of sharp pains, as if someone had just sent billiard balls colliding in his head.

"How can you make a joke about this?" she scolded. "How can you laugh about the fact that no one seems to know you or care that you're missing? How can you go through life not touching anyone, not being touched by anyone, then shrug it off?"

"Hey, Doc, take it easy," McLeod said.

"Don't tell me to take it easy, Dave McLeod! This is serious. Miles is hurt and he's lost his memory. Someone has to care about him! Someone has to worry about him and try to do something! If you aren't going to do anything..."

Her voice broke and Miles realized she was about to cry. Cry over him as if he was some mutt that had been hit by a car. Damn it all! He was her flavor-of-the-month stray, and she was going to charge in and help him whether he wanted it or not. He glared at her, his free hand gripping the wooden arm of the chair as if to splinter it. He would have, if he could.

Sasha didn't seem to notice. "Dave, isn't there any way we can—"

"Back off, Sasha," Miles told her, his voice tight. "It's my life, even if I can't remember it right now. I don't need you to tell me how to feel, and I don't need you to organize a police investigation into my identity, just to make you feel like you're doing something useful and good." He managed to speak without exploding, but he was feeling dangerously like a volcano ready to blow.

She gasped, and stared at him. "But—"

"I don't need you feeling sorry for me, damn it! I don't need you treating me like one of your crippled strays. I don't have to know who I am to know I can speak for myself, and look out for myself. I don't need your help and I sure as hell don't want it! Got that?" he growled at her, his voice coming out like the warning of a junkyard dog.

Sasha backed away. The stricken expression in her dark eyes cut straight to his soul. Too late, he realized he'd attacked the only person who genuinely seemed to care what happened to him. In disgust, in shame, he turned away. He had to apologize, but his own stupidity made him speechless.

The shock of Miles's anger knocked Sasha's breath out of her. All she could do was stand there, her mouth agape, staring at him as her eyes filled with tears. She didn't want to cry in front of him, didn't want him to know how his attack had hurt her, but she simply couldn't make her arms and legs respond to her brain's commands to move.

Finally she gathered her wits. Grabbing her purse from the floor, she rushed past Dave. She kept the tears barely under control as she reached for the door handle. Sasha yanked open the door, pulled it shut behind her and then leaned against the wall beside Miles's door. Outside, in the hallway, nurses and orderlies passed by, intent on their jobs. Visitors wandered along, some beside shuffling patients, some appearing to search for a room number. No one seemed to pay any attention to her.

Sasha wiped hastily at her eyes and cheeks with the back of her hand, then adjusted her purse strap on her shoulder and headed for the elevators. Just as the doors opened, a heavy hand on her shoulder stopped her. Startled, she turned and looked into Dave McLeod's earnest young face.

"Are you okay, Doc?"

"I'll live," she said with a shaky smile. They stepped into the elevator and the doors closed behind them. Sasha was acutely aware of the other passengers and could tell that Dave wanted to speak, but not in a crowded elevator. She hoped she could slip away before he said whatever he thought he should say, intending to make her feel better, which would only make her feel worse. Bad enough to be stupid. Awful to have a witness.

Dave stuck by her side when the elevator came to the ground floor. "Come on. I'll walk you to the parking lot. Never know what kind of weirdos can be lurking in dark corners." He pushed open the front door and waited for her to walk through.

Hugging her jacket around herself as she strode across the parking lot a half step ahead of him, Sasha welcomed the sting of the crisp night wind on her damp cheeks. Dave cupped her elbow in his hand and lengthened his stride to keep up with her. When she reached her truck, she stopped and fumbled in her pocket for her keys.

"Listen, Sasha, I'm no psychologist, but I'm guessing Kent is hiding something."

His words almost made her smile. "He isn't *hiding* anything, Dave. He can't *remember* anything. There's a difference, don't you think?"

He shoved his hands into his jacket pockets and rocked back on his heels. "I mean *before* the accident. Were you listening to my notes? The only human being we could find who admitted she knew him refused to tell us anything. I can't tell if she's protecting him or afraid of him. And that bothers me. Watch yourself around him, eh? You know what they say about biting the hand that feeds you. And if you have any doubts, about anything, call me right away."

Dave withdrew one hand from his pocket and held out a business card. His suspicions about Miles disturbed her even more because they reflected her own. Still, she felt compelled to defend him.

"I think you're wrong about Miles being sinister and dangerous. But it doesn't really matter. I doubt I'll be seeing him after tonight. He made that pretty clear." She realized, too, that she hadn't had time to leave her phone number. Of course, he could look her up in the book, or ask Emmy. But she would bet her farm that he wouldn't do either. He was too angry, too proud, too stubborn and too hurt to ask for help. And some of that was her fault.

Dave shook his head. "You're a soft touch, aren't you, Doc? Hell, any guy in his right mind would love to have a woman like you fussing and worrying over him. I sure wouldn't mind." As if they had a will of their own, her eyebrows rose. He gave her a quick, almost apologetic grin. "Just being honest. Look, Kent's acting like a cornered bear, like he can't afford to let his guard down. You better not let yours down, either."

Now there was a familiar refrain. Sasha smiled. If only Dave knew how many times in her life someone—her parents, her grandparents, her teachers and mentors, her foster siblings and her friends and colleagues—had warned her to leave some wounded critter alone. She really wasn't as compulsive as they seemed to think. Occasionally, reluctantly, she'd even taken their advice and watched helplessly as the critter had slunk away to nurse its wounds alone.

But why would a man of Miles's looks, intelligence and wealth live such a desolate life? Was he hiding something, or hiding *from* something?

"You're a nice lady, Doc. Play it safe, okay? I mean, hell, just because Kent doesn't have a police record doesn't mean he isn't dangerous. Desperate men do desperate things sometimes. You stay out of his way. Okay?"

She smiled at Dave's earnest lecture. "Thank you."

He nodded. Taking the keys from her clenched fingers, he unlocked her door. "Go on. Drive safely. The roads are getting slick again. See you, okay?"

Sasha climbed into the truck and started her engine. Dave gave her a jaunty salute and she waved as she shifted into first gear and let out the clutch.

"Maybe Dave is right," she muttered to herself as she aimed the truck toward the parking-lot exit. "If Miles Kent thinks I'm mistaking him for a crippled stray, that's his business. I've got enough to keep me busy without wasting time on a man with the world's biggest chip on his shoulder. Miles Kent can go to hell, for all I care."

But she *did* care. She couldn't help it. Miles had touched something deep inside her, in the part of her heart where she was a woman first, and a doctor a distant second. Instinctively she recognized that, if circumstances were different, she could fall in love with a man like Miles.

The more she thought about his reactions, the more upset she became. What gave him the right to attack her for caring about people, even strangers, just because he lived like a hermit? The truck's engine protested her angry stab at the gas pedal. She barely managed not to tear out of the parking lot.

By the time Sasha reached the farm driveway, the hurt had faded to a dull ache. And she realized, with a little hiccup that was halfway between a laugh and a sob, that she'd gotten exactly what she'd deserved. She'd let her guard down around an unknown animal, and he'd struck out when he felt threatened. It would be a good lesson to keep in mind when she went to pick up Desperado tomorrow.

Chapter Four

Darrel Hogg shot another stream of tobacco juice into the mud near Sasha's feet. One more time, she thought grimly, and she was going to shake him by his bony shoulders until he swallowed the noxious stuff. She didn't have to glance at her friends Donna and Marie to know they shared her lack of enchantment with Mr. Hogg.

"I still don't see how you three little girls are gonna get this devil into that trailer," he drawled smugly.

Sasha met his beady eyes, trying for her best Clint Eastwood impression. "I suggest you move out of the way, Mr. Hogg. Desperado doesn't seem to like you."

The man snorted, then launched another stream of tobacco juice into the stinking ooze of Desperado's paddock. "That monster don't like nobody, sweetcakes. What he needs ain't TLC. He needs a two-by-four between his damn eyes. If you're too soft to do that," he added with a shrug, "least you can do is use a tranquilizer gun on him. Unless you girls would like to spend the night with yours truly."

The slimy creep had the nerve to leer. That did it! Sasha took a step closer, her hands on her hips. Hogg gave her a shifty-eyed look and shuffled his feet in the dirt.

"If anyone needs a tranquilizer dart, it's you. Now back off," she said, stepping a little closer. To her satisfaction, he backed up an equal step. "Right back to the porch would be a good idea."

She felt Donna and Marie step up behind her, one on each side. The appropriately named Mr. Hogg stepped back on his own. With good reason. At five foot nine, Sasha was the shrimp of the trio. She took another little step toward him, Donna and Marie sticking close beside her. Darrel Hogg swore under his vile breath and shuffled toward the run-down farmhouse across the muddy yard.

Donna smothered a snort of laughter. Marie indulged in some colorful phrases about Darrel Hogg's ancestry. Sasha turned and grinned at her friends. "Okay, *girls,* shall we convince Desperado he'll be much better off with TLC than a two-by-four?"

With the two women, both experienced horse trainers, working beside her, Sasha tried to coax the wild-eyed stallion into the trailer backed up to the only opening in the small paddock. Desperado let them come just so close, then reared, snorted and wheeled away, flinging mud from his ragged hooves. After a half hour, both Sasha and the horse were sweating in the chill, damp April afternoon. When Donna and Marie paused to grab a drink, Sasha joined them.

She took a long swallow from her bottle of spring water, thankful they'd had the foresight not to expect clean water from Darrel Hogg's well. His yard smelled like a swamp. God only knew what microorganisms were lurking in his water table, waiting to poison the unsuspecting.

"I will not let that beast get the better of us," Sasha muttered, head bowed against her forearm as she leaned on the cab of her truck.

"Which beast? Hogg or the horse?" Marie asked.

"Both of them," Sasha told her, but she suddenly thought of Miles Kent. She certainly could add him to the list of male beasts. He'd been as unpredictable, as potentially dangerous as the exhausted, frightened stallion now eyeing them from the far side of the paddock.

"Got any ideas?" Donna said. "I hate to desert you, Sasha, but I've got to get home before my kids do, or they'll destroy the kitchen making themselves snacks. They're into peanut butter banana melts this week, and that stuff is sticky."

Sasha gave her friend a weak smile as she pondered the situation. She studied the wild-eyed, muddy maniac staring at her across the paddock until a thought struck her.

"Let's try something different. I'm going to get the bucket of crunch and go in alone. You two climb out and try to stay very still, out of sight." She picked up the small pail of horse treats, then shrugged at her obviously skeptical friends. "Unless I yell for help. Okay?"

"Sure," Donna said, sounding anything but.

"Do they have shrinks at 911?" Marie joked.

Snickering softly, the two women retreated from the fence to hide themselves beside the trailer. Sasha shook the pail of treats, catching Desperado's attention. After almost a half hour of excruciating patience, he let her approach him, let her entice him toward the trailer ramp. To her amazed satisfaction, the huge horse followed her into the dark trailer, one step at a time. With the skill of long practice, Donna and Marie quietly shut the trailer door and secured the ramp while Desperado greedily stuck his head into the bucket of treats.

"That's it, son," Sasha crooned. She still had to snap the lead shank to his halter and get herself out of the trailer, but everything had gone so well that she couldn't resist lingering a moment with the stallion. Carefully, she reached out and stroked the crest of his heated neck. He blew into his treat bucket.

"Easy, pet. You're doing just fine now. I'm going to hook the line to your halter. Then we're on the way to your new home, and you won't have to see Darrel Hogg ever ag—"

The world exploded. Stars burst in front of her eyes. She fell back against the chest board, still clutching the bucket. Pellets of crunch hailed into her face. Her head banged on the metal partition brace. She started to sag to the floor of the trailer, unable to stop herself from sliding toward Desperado's lethal front hooves.

"Here we are, Mr. Kent," the volunteer following him around chirped. The woman was motherly, apple cheeked and exhaustingly cheerful. She was doing her best, but he couldn't wait for her to leave him alone. He was trying to be polite, but didn't want to be cheered up. Between the eerily empty police report on his identity and the memory of Sasha's hurt eyes when he'd yelled at her yesterday, he had plenty to be miserable about.

"Thanks," he managed to mutter as she took his elbow and stood waiting to help him ease down to his bed. He adjusted his grip on the cane. If he didn't know he'd lose his balance, he'd shake off her well-intentioned grasp. He knew he was pushing his luck, but he hated feeling dependent on anyone, especially someone who thrived on the helplessness of others.

"*There* you are!" That nurse who knew Sasha— Emmy?—the one who'd been such a tyrant about his shower, burst into the room. She fixed him with a look that seemed to be accusing him of something, but he really wasn't interested. He had enough on his mind.

"Oh! Hello, Mom," Emmy said to his volunteer and gave her a quick kiss on the cheek. "Mr. Kent, Sasha was just brought into Emergency. I thought you might want to—"

His heart felt as if it had stopped. "What happened?"

"I don't know. She's waiting for—"

"Get me down there," he growled at his volunteer. "*Now!*"

"Oh, dear! Yes, of course! Hello, Emmy. Excuse us."

This time he welcomed the woman's steadying grip. His knee and ankle protested the exercise he insisted on over-doing. He gritted his teeth all the way to the elevators. Damn! He'd been such a jerk yesterday, sending Sasha away like that. She'd only been trying to help. But he was so con-cerned about his pride that he'd slashed at hers.

If this was what he was really like, he didn't like himself much.

Everything took too long. The elevator wouldn't come. When it finally did, it stopped on every floor while people dithered about getting on or off. Then, when he got into the emergency room, there was no sign of Sasha. His volunteer made vague noises about not being allowed to wander around getting in the way. He stopped a doctor.

"I need to find Dr. Reiss."

"I don't think we have a Dr. Reiss on staff."

"She's a patient. Just came in. Emergency. I need to find her."

"Oh. Right. I know who that is." The doctor frowned. "Are you a member of the family?"

He didn't even hesitate. Glaring right back, he said, "Yes. Where is she?"

"You'll have to check with the admitting nurse. I have a patient to see. Excuse me."

"Mr. Kent?" His volunteer spoke up from behind him. "I asked about your Dr. Reiss for you. She's in examining room B. Would you like me to...? Yes, I suppose you would. Come with me." Suddenly that sugary voice didn't irritate him half so much.

"Thanks," he said a little gruffly, meaning a whole lot more. He didn't even mind when she patted his good shoul-der.

A nurse bustled out of examining room B just as he got there. His volunteer led him into the small room. "I'll leave you with your young lady. Here's a chair for you. If you need help getting back, have someone call me." He nodded and managed a half smile. She patted his shoulder again and left.

He leaned on the cane and stared at the woman lying on the examining table. She was filthy, and the odor of horse and hay was strong even over the smell of disinfectant. Her face was hidden by towels, but there was blood on her shirt and on her neck, and on her hands as she held the towels to her face. Dear God, what had happened? His gut twisted at the possibilities.

"Sasha?" he said, but the sound stuck in his throat. He tried again. "Sasha? It's Miles. What happened?"

"Oh, Miles!" she said softly, her low voice muffled by the towels. "It was nothing. Really."

"Sure. That's why you're in the hospital, covered with blood." He stepped closer to the side of the examining table.

She removed the towels from her face. He braced himself. What he could see of her face didn't look bad. Dirty and bloody, but not cut up. Then she turned her head and met his eyes. The left side of her face was swollen and raw, as if she'd been beaten with a club. His stomach clenched.

"Oh, God, baby!" he gasped. "What happened?"

"Desperado tried to kiss me," she murmured.

He reached for her hand. She let it rest limply in his. The strength he'd found there before was gone. Impulsively he lifted her hand to his face and pressed his lips to her knuckles. Her dark eyes met his steadily, widening a little in surprise when he kissed the back of her hand. Hell, he was surprised, too. But it felt right. In fact, it was the first thing he'd done in this whole nightmare of his that did feel right. He was trying to offer comfort, but he really wanted to cling to Sasha's hand as if it were a lifeline, and he a drowning man. Somehow, he had to make her understand what he himself didn't.

"I'm so sorry, Sasha," he said, holding her hand against his own battered cheek for a long, silent moment.

"How touching," a man's voice teased from the doorway. "Hello, Sasha. Mr. Kent." Miles wasn't especially surprised to see Dr. Peter Simmons, Sasha's foster brother, grinning and shaking his head. "Don't tell me you broke your nose again?"

Miles wanted to grab him by his lab coat and make him apologize for taking her injuries so lightly, but a tiny laugh escaped Sasha's bruised lips before he could say anything. "Good news travels fast around here," she muttered.

"It's been a slow night," Simmons answered. As he walked closer, Miles could see the concern behind the grin. Reluctantly Miles conceded that maybe the guy was joking to hide his real feelings. "How's the head?"

"Hard," she muttered.

Simmons snorted. "Tell me something I don't know." Then he looked at Miles and all traces of humor left his eyes. "Am I leaving her in good hands, Kent?"

Sasha's fingers tightened briefly in his. Miles looked back levelly. "As far as I know." It was as much of the truth as he knew. If he was some kind of monster in his past life, there didn't seem to be any evidence of it to fill in the blanks in his memories.

Simmons nodded. "She's a lousy patient."

"Peter, go shrink somebody's head!" Sasha scolded, her voice just a little slurred. "I hate it when you treat me like a child."

"Then don't act like one," Simmons told her, winking. "I'm off in three hours. If you need anything, get me paged, or call Marla at home. Promise?"

Sasha sighed. "Promise. Give Marla and Jimmy my love."

The door closed again behind Simmons's back. Miles looked down into Sasha's eyes, sick at the sight of the bruises on her beautiful face. Her wobbly smile didn't do a thing to reassure him as he drew her hand to his cheek again. It felt cold.

"Sasha, can you forgive me for being such a jerk yesterday?"

She gave him a soft smile. "Yes, I forgive you for being such a jerk yesterday." Then her smile faded. "How are you feeling today?"

He squeezed her hand gently. "I'm fine," he told her, dodging the unspoken question about his memory. "The important thing is how you are. Do you think anything is broken?"

"Not this time," she said. "I'm glad you're here. It's kind of scary being alone and hurt, isn't it?"

Again he evaded her silent reference to his own circumstances. He wasn't ready to face that yet. But he could offer Sasha some of the comfort she'd given him. "I'll stay with you, if you want."

She sighed. "Thanks. I'd really like that."

A very young-looking doctor barged into the little examining room. "Sir, you'll have to leave while we treat Ms. Reiss," he said brusquely.

He turned to the man. "This is *Dr.* Reiss. And I'm not leaving unless she says so."

The doctor's mouth opened and closed, like a fish. Then he sighed and nodded. "As long as it's all right with the patient."

"Gentlemen? I appreciate your concern over protocol, but I'd really like to get cleaned up and go home. I've still got chores." Sasha sounded amused in spite of the way her words slurred slightly.

Miles felt his face get warm at her gentle scolding. The doctor's baby face turned the color of new brick. "I'll send in a nurse to clean you up while I take another look at your X rays. I'd like to keep you overnight for observation," he told her pompously.

Sasha smiled as if dealing with a very persistent child. "I can't. I have my own patients waiting for me."

They batted the question back and forth like a Ping-Pong ball until the outmatched junior doctor shrugged and gave up.

Miles waited for the other man to leave before giving in to a protective urge. "Sasha, he's right. You shouldn't go back to the farm alone. And you shouldn't do chores tonight. If you can't afford to stay overnight in the hospital, I'd be glad to—"

"Don't be silly. It's covered by my health insurance. What I can't afford is for anything to happen to any of my animals because I'm not there to take care of them. I've got some friends lined up to help as soon as I get home." She smiled, and he could see the stubbornness behind the sweetness. "I promise I won't do the heavy stuff. But I have to be there to make sure everyone is okay."

The door swung open again. "I hear you're being cooperative as usual," Simmons commented as he stepped inside. He crossed his arms over his chest and shook his head. "Since you insist on going home tonight, I called Sam to pick you up. He won't let you do anything stupid, no matter how hard you try."

"Thank you so much," Sasha muttered, while Miles wondered who Sam was. "When is he coming?"

Simmons glanced at his watch. "About an hour, maybe less."

"I'd rather take a taxi, Peter. You know I hate hanging around hospitals."

Miles thought fast. Now that he'd gotten this reprieve from his own stupidity, he intended to maintain contact with Sasha as long as possible. "I'll take her back to my room and keep her out of trouble until this Sam comes."

"Good idea," Simmons agreed.

Sasha sighed noisily. "Hey, guys, I'm not a piece of furniture."

"Humor me," Miles told her. "I don't need my memory to figure out I like being in control of a situation."

Her dark eyes sparkled, even though the left one was almost swollen shut. "I could have told you that," she said.

"Okay," Simmons said, a speculative look on his narrow face. "That's settled. You're responsible, Kent. See that she behaves until Sam can take over." With a quick wave, he walked out and left them alone again.

Sasha gave a tiny sputter of a laugh. Miles squeezed her hand gently. "Who's Sam?"

"My other foster brother." Her voice came out more slowly, as if her face was hurting more than before. "He's a master cabinetmaker and single dad. His place is on the next concession road north of mine, so he exercises his big-brother privileges even more than Peter.''

A nurse bustled in and began fussing over Sasha's face. She grimaced and a tiny moan escaped her lips, and he squeezed her hand to tell her that he was with her. When she squeezed his hand back, as if seeking strength from his, he felt something in his gut he couldn't quite identify. Something oddly satisfying, yet somehow unsettling. Maybe it was the tug of being needed, even a little, by this special woman.

The antiseptic cleanser stung and the light pressure of the wet cotton pads on her bruised face hurt more than she expected. Sasha felt like a baby for moaning, but she'd gotten used to the numbness, and the pain caught her by surprise. That was the way with pain. Even when you anticipated getting hurt, the actual sensation was always a shock. She closed her eyes and tried to brace herself.

When Miles squeezed her hand, offering her comfort, it took her a moment to realize he really was there, really was willing to lessen her pain with his strength. She squeezed back, weakly, just trying to let him know she appreciated not being on her own this once. When the nurse was finished, she repeated the doctor's warning that a night in hospital would be prudent. Sasha simply thanked her, needing to save what little energy she had left for getting home and doing chores. She sat on the edge of the examining table, waiting to gather enough of her strength to step down.

"Take it slow," Miles said in his low, gravelly voice. It was a voice that invited confidence, intimacy, desire. He looked down at her, looming tall despite his own injuries. She tried, unsuccessfully, to shake the confusion of feeling desire at the same time as feeling as if she had kissed a moving vehicle. She needed a distraction.

"I have to call my friends who brought me in—"

"You mean they just dumped you here and split?"

His swift anger on her behalf puzzled her. "No, of course not. They brought me here after we trailered Desperado home and unloaded him. But Donna is a single mother and Marie works evenings, teaching riding, so they couldn't stay. I wanted to take a taxi here myself, but—"

"You took the damn horse home first." He shook his head, then stepped back a few inches. "Come on. Let me take you back to my place," he said in that seductively low voice. He grinned, a wickedly slow grin, that hinted at tempting possibilities. Now that he didn't look quite as battered, he was one very sexy, rather cocky male. Heaven help her if he got his memory back before he left. Miles Kent at full wattage would be one dangerously attractive man.

Her cheeks stung with heat at the thought of being alone with him. Would he put his arms around her, offering comfort?

Whenever she or any of her foster siblings had been hurt, either physically or emotionally, her parents and grandparents had always had a lap available, or a hug and a special treat once they got too big for lap sitting. She'd been a caregiver herself for so long that she'd forgotten how sweet it could be to receive comfort.

But she wasn't so naive as to think a hug from Miles would be particularly comforting. It would be like pouring kerosene on a fire. Miles Kent was disturbing, and embracing him would be a highly...arousing experience.

"You must have been a hell-raiser as a kid," she muttered.

For a brief second his expression darkened. Had she awakened some unhappy memory? Like Desperado, Miles's life was not exactly an open book. She would always have to guess about the abuse the horse had suffered, and somehow, prove to him that she would never mistreat him. Miles, too, would have to guess about his past, until he regained his memory. Unlike Desperado, however, Miles didn't have to be a slave to his past, whether he remembered it or not. She hoped he realized that.

"I imagine there were some who considered me the devil's own," he drawled. "But, as they say, success is the best revenge. And apparently, I'm some kind of success."

His resolute tone when he mentioned revenge sent a little chill up her spine. Had he remembered something? Or was he simply making a statement? Dave McLeod's warnings came back to her. She couldn't deny her impulse to heal whatever wounds Miles had suffered. But would he be as dangerous as Desperado? She might never find out, she realized with some regret. He was hardly the stereotype of a homeless, confused amnesiac who needed shelter. He'd be going home to his private island as soon as the doctors were satisfied with the progress of his injuries.

Sasha eased herself off the examining table until her feet touched the floor. Then she waited for her head to clear, aware that Miles was watching her. Although he was the one leaning on a cane, she had the distinct impression that if she started to keel over, he'd have plenty of strength to catch her. The thought made her smile.

"What?" he asked.

"I was just thinking that this is a new spin on the blind leading the blind," she told him. Gingerly, she stepped toward the door. A wave of dizziness made her catch her breath. Or maybe it was the sudden feel of Miles's hand on her waist, supporting her. "Thanks. I . . . I'm not sure this is going to work. I think I was a little optimistic about my condition," she admitted.

"Let me get you a wheelchair."

She shook her head, which wasn't the best thing to do to her scrambled brains. Smothering a gasp, she said, "No. I have to get myself moving eventually."

Miles muttered something about damn stubborn women, but within a couple of minutes he had scared up—almost literally—a volunteer to help them both to his room. The woman who answered his call was the same volunteer who had delivered him to Sasha.

"My goodness!" the woman gasped when she walked into the examining room. "No wonder your young man was so worried. It was very impressive the way he demanded to be taken to you, like a knight rushing to defend his lady.''

Amused despite her embarrassment, Sasha glanced at Miles. He gave a shrug with his good shoulder, but the color that stained his cheeks belied his nonchalance. The volunteer took Sasha by the elbow. As they made their slow, awkward way toward the elevators, the woman introduced herself as Emmy's mother, Doris.

"So you're Caitlin and Hilary's grandmother,'' Sasha said, hoping to take her mind off the dizziness.

"I certainly am. I can't wait to tell the girls I've finally met you. They've been after me for ages to come to one of their meetings, but honestly, horses frighten me. They're so big. And they can be very dangerous.''

Sasha heard Miles grunt at this point in Doris's monologue and she knew he was thinking about Desperado. She hoped he wouldn't say anything to scare Doris about her granddaughters. "Most of them aren't dangerous,'' she said hastily.

"It only takes one,'' Miles muttered.

Sasha decided to ignore him. She was having enough trouble staying upright until the elevator stopped at his floor.

"You know,'' she said to Doris as they negotiated their way down the hall, "if you come to a meeting, you don't have to get close to the horses to watch the girls. Think about coming soon. They'd love it.''

"Maybe I will. The meetings are at your farm, aren't they?''

"Yes. Saturday mornings.''

Doris halted at Miles's door, giving Sasha a moment to grasp the doorframe while she led Miles into the room and settled him on the edge of the bed. Doris then turned to reach a helping hand to Sasha as she followed, a little queasy from the elevator ride. Gratefully, Sasha let the older woman help her into a chair beside Miles's bed.

"I think I will come to a meeting,'' Doris said firmly. "I'll tell the girls. It will be fun.''

"Great." Sasha remembered something Caitlin had told her. "And Doris? I've got a litter of the sweetest kittens I need to find homes for. Two of them are gray tabbies."

"Oh! Gray tabbies?" A sad look crossed Doris's soft face. Then she beamed at Sasha. "Yes, I think I know someone who would like two tabby kittens. I'll bring my cat carrier, if that's all right."

Sasha gave Doris's hand a quick squeeze. After she'd asked Miles four times if he needed anything else, Doris finally left them alone. Sasha couldn't help laughing at the bemused expression on Miles's face, even though her own face hurt with every change of expression.

"What?" he demanded.

"I think she likes you." He shrugged, but his expression seemed to soften a little. "I have a feeling you aren't used to being mothered quite so aggressively." He snorted. Sasha wondered if perhaps she'd accidentally hit on some truth about Miles.

Miles ran his right hand over his chin. "I suspect you're right," he said thoughtfully. "She really takes this helping stuff seriously, doesn't she?"

Sasha tried to nod but her head protested and her neck stiffened. Instead, she grunted agreement. "She's been a widow for a long time. The girls told me her old gray tabby cat died at Christmas, and Emmy says she's very lonely. That's why she volunteers here, and in a home for mentally challenged adults."

"What about emotionally challenged adults?" he asked, his crooked grin not at all convincing. "That's supposedly my problem. Your friend Peter thinks my memory is playing hide-and-seek over something I don't want to remember."

"Is that possible?"

"What could I be trying to forget? Think I did something horrible? Tax evasion, maybe? Maybe I'm a serial murderer. What do you think, Doc?" He studied her so intently that she felt her already painful face burn with a blush.

"I think you couldn't possibly be a murderer, or anything remotely like that. I think it's possible something awful happened *to* you, but I can't believe you would do anything horrible to anyone else."

"Do you always see the best in everyone?" he asked quietly.

Embarrassed, she shrugged. "I try."

"Aren't you ever wrong?"

"I keep hoping my optimism will be rewarded."

"And what about the monster who attacked you?"

She managed a somewhat painful, lopsided smile. "Desperado wasn't trying to hurt me. He just panicked when he realized he was in a trailer, and threw his head up. I happened to be in the wrong place at the wrong time. He could have trampled me after he knocked me down, but he stood like a perfect gentleman while Donna and Marie pulled me out from under him."

The color drained from Miles's face. He swore softly. "Do me a favor? Spare me the details." He moved himself closer to her chair. "On second thought, maybe I'm not a serial murderer. I seem to be a little on the squeamish side." His quick grin was rueful.

Sasha smiled as much as possible. "You do remind me a little of Desperado, striking out when you're scared."

He uttered a rude noise that made her smile broaden, despite the pain in her face. "I'm not scared. I'm frustrated, and that makes me angry. That's all."

"Oh. I see."

He leaned down toward her, trapping her in the chair. He gazed intently at her for a long, unsettling time. Her smile faded as she felt herself leaning upward toward him, as if drawn by some magnetism emanating from deep within him. His golden eyes did a leisurely sweep of her face, lingering on her mouth. She could feel the warmth of his breath caressing her battered cheek. She could smell faint traces of spicy cologne and his own masculine skin. Sasha realized she was shaking, tiny tremors that raced over her nerves, tickling her into a state of intense awareness.

Miles's hand reached out and cupped the unbruised side of her face. Slowly, irresistibly, he drew closer, leaning to meet her. The image of his face grew blurry. She closed her eyes. His warmth seemed to surround her.

Chapter Five

Gently, so gently that her eyes filled with tears, Miles touched her sore lips with his. "I just wanted to make up for Desperado's kiss," he told her, his voice husky and intimate. "From the devil you know to the devil you don't know."

Sasha swallowed. Slowly she opened her eyes to find Miles watching her, a guarded look in his eyes. "In comparison, Desperado does lack a certain finesse," she murmured.

His smile warmed her like very smooth, very expensive brandy. She was tempted to read more into that sweet, simple kiss than the comfort Miles was offering. Lord knew, the attraction was there, simmering between them despite their frequent misunderstandings. That mutual attraction might even be the cause of those flare-ups between them. After all, she was trying not to get involved, and so must he be.

She'd never felt this confusion of emotions over any other man. When she'd told Miles she was married to her work, she'd meant it seriously. None of the men she'd known had ever stirred her blood, totally distracting her, the way Miles did. The feeling was deliciously intoxicating, daring her to seek more without the safety of sober judgment.

It was time, Sasha decided, for a reality check. For Miles, that meant finding out who he was and making his way back to himself. For her, that meant her life would go on even after Miles left. His leaving was inevitable, and she'd be a fool to let herself pretend otherwise. Besides, if there was one thing she was good at, it was letting go.

"Did you hear from that Mrs. Dobbs who's supposed to work for you?" she asked, trying to sound businesslike despite the way her swollen face made her slur her words, and the way the effect of his kiss had turned her voice husky.

Miles lifted an eyebrow as if to challenge her change of subject, then settled back on the edge of the bed. "Yeah. She called last night, but she wasn't much help. She was suspicious that it was some kind of setup, she said. About all I could find out from her at first was my own phone number. She finally told me I play Monopoly with real money, buying and selling businesses, and holding large interests in some very profitable companies. She's been working for me for ten years. If I need outside help, I hire consultants."

Miles spoke about himself as if he were describing a character in a play. There was no sense of connection to the facts, no emotion behind his recitation. Except, perhaps, dislike for the man he might be. And if his detachment bothered her, she mused, it must be torturing him, even if he wouldn't let on.

She wanted to help him, but she was an animal doctor, and Miles had rejected Peter's repeated offers of human psychological help. What could she do? Sasha thought for a moment. Nothing, really, she concluded, except to offer moral support. But there was someone who might be able to do something real to help Miles regain his memories.

"Your Mrs. Dobbs seems to be the only one who really knows who you are. Maybe she can give you some clues that will help jog your memory."

Miles frowned. "Like what?"

Sasha thought again. "Like photographs," she exclaimed, a little muffled by her sore jaw but excited by the possibilities. "Even under ordinary circumstances, people forget things, and then they see a photo and it reminds them of a person or an event or a place. It's worth a try, isn't it?"

Miles gaped at Sasha. It was so simple! Why hadn't he thought of it when she'd been showing him pictures of her life? Well, the answer to that question was simple: he'd been trying not to make a fool of himself over his awareness of her. Maybe a monk could think logically with Sasha sitting next to him, but Miles sure wasn't a monk. As a red-blooded male, his hormones ran riot when every breath brought her scent to him, every glance discovered some part of her he wanted to explore further with his hands and his mouth. Just remembering the brief taste of her lips made him wish he could forget.

That last thought almost made him laugh. Here he was wishing he could forget something, when he'd spent the past week ranting and raving about having amnesia.

Hoping Sasha couldn't see how his hands trembled, Miles reached toward the nightstand where a black phone sat toadlike beside his water glass. "You're a genius, Doc," he muttered, picking up the phone and punching in the phone number written on the pad on the stand. A woman's voice, soft and Southern, answered on the second ring. "Kent Associates."

He smiled grimly at the name of his company. Ironic, wasn't it, he thought, when he apparently didn't have any associates. "Mrs. Dobbs? It's Miles. Miles Kent." The name still sounded strange on his tongue.

"Oh! Miles! Of course. It's Eleanor. I'm so glad you called," she drawled, that hint of the South making him frown. He searched for a memory that hovered at the edge of his mind, teasing him. Was it Eleanor Dobbs he was trying to recall, or some other woman's honeyed voice? He forced his attention back to the phone. "I was afraid I hadn't been much help to you last night," she went on. "But

I didn't want to call back and take the chance of disturbing your rest. How are you feeling today?"

"Better, thanks."

"Do you know when you'll be able to come home again?"

"I'll probably get out of the hospital in the next couple of days," he told her, trying desperately to picture *home* and failing miserably. "Will you be able to handle the office until I get back?" Especially since he probably wouldn't know what to do himself. He tried to visualize his office, unable to see any mind's image that felt like *his* office. He couldn't meet Sasha's eyes, knowing she was watching him, wanting to help him, and knowing he was failing.

"Of course I can. You have a few dozen messages, but nothing urgent, so it's business as usual. Is there anything special that you'd like me to do?"

Unsure how much his gracious and competent-sounding assistant understood about his predicament, he drew a deep breath. "Yes, uh, Eleanor. I'd like you to take photos of my house and office, and anything else you think I should remember. Shoot off a couple of rolls of film, get them developed right away, then book yourself a flight to Toronto and bring them to me. I need to talk to you. I'll give you directions—"

"Oh, dear!" Eleanor's gasp came out almost as a sob. The sound cut his words off. "Oh, Miles! I didn't want to believe that Canadian policeman when he told me over the phone that you'd lost your memory, but I do believe him now. I'm so sorry, but I can't possibly do what you've asked, although I can arrange for someone to do it for you. Would that be all right, instead?"

Avoiding Sasha's curious eyes, he swallowed hard. His chest felt as if something very heavy was pressing against it. "Eleanor, can you tell me why you can't do it yourself?"

"I hardly ever leave my apartment. It's so hard for me to get around, even with this beautiful wheelchair you provided for me. Don't you remember that you work out of an office in your home, and that your office and mine are linked by all the latest technology? All the bells and whistles, you like to say. There are fax machines and computers and phones, and of course, we often use courier services.''

While he frantically tried to picture any of what his assistant described, she chuckled softly. ''My goodness, I guess you don't remember how petrified I was about the fax machines when you first had them installed. You spent hours with me, helping me. Just the way you did when we switched over from that electronic typewriter I thought was complicated enough, to a computer. You hired a computer teacher to come to my apartment and we ordered lunch from the deli, and then pizza for dinner, because it took all day for us to learn everything you wanted to learn. It was nice to work with you face-to-face, instead of by remote.''

He heard the unmistakable excitement in Eleanor's voice as she talked. He wondered bleakly why she was confined to a wheelchair, and why he himself lived like a hermit. At least, from what his assistant was saying about their relationship, he wasn't some kind of ogre. Not all the time, anyway.

''I... I'm sorry, Eleanor. Nothing personal, but I really don't remember any of that.'' From the corner of his eye he saw Sasha's face. Shock, and worse than that, pity. Damn! ''You said you can hire someone to take photos and get them up here. How quickly can you do that?''

''Well, it depends on who you'd prefer me to... Now, what am I saying? I guess you don't remember, but my son, Jonathan, likes to take pictures. After all you've done for him, it would be his pleasure to do you a favor. I'll phone him as soon as we finish here, and have him contact you for instructions, if that's satisfactory.''

''It is,'' he said, wondering what he'd done for her son. It was all so blank. ''Thank you. And would you do me another favor?''

''Anything, dear boy. I feel so bad for you. What is it you'd like me to do? Do you have enough clothes and money?''

Her maternal fussing almost made him smile. "Yes, I do. What I'd like is for you to keep this confidential until I get the situation under control. You understand."

"I surely do, Miles. But you don't have to worry. I'm used to keeping your business confidential. That's why I didn't want to tell the Canadian police anything, even though they were very polite. I hope that won't get either of us into trouble."

He did smile then. After reassuring his assistant that neither of them were in any kind of legal trouble, he thanked her and said goodbye. Then, with his emotions on spin cycle, he turned toward Sasha. She was watching him, those big eyes of hers full of pity, but the sight of her battered face made him add one more confusing feeling to the mess inside his head. He wanted to take care of her, despite the fact that he could hardly take care of himself.

"It sounds like you hit pay dirt," she said, her voice stiff, as if speaking hurt. Recalling how sore his own face had been for days after his accident, he was sure it did.

He smiled. "From what I can piece together, I'm apparently just a fanatical recluse, not a serial murderer." Briefly he recapped what Eleanor Dobbs had told him, and her suggestion to have her son take photos and send them to him by courier.

Sasha frowned. "But by the time he does that, won't you be ready to leave? Wouldn't it make more sense just to go home and let your memory come back once you're in familiar surroundings?"

"Probably," he finally conceded. He knew she was right. But something visceral, something instinctive, kept him from wanting to leave. He had no reason—not even a lame excuse—to stay. He just couldn't shake the feeling that if he left too soon, he might never find himself. Or maybe his reluctance to leave had more to do with the way Sasha made his pulse race. Had he ever felt like that about another woman? Was it something as trite as loving and losing that had turned him into a hermit?

"But if your shrink friend is right, maybe my going home will have the opposite effect," he added, thinking out loud, grasping for straws. "Maybe I need to get away to remember. When I think about it, that must have been what I was doing when I drove up here. I used to do that a lot when—" He stopped, realizing he'd had his first real memory.

Sasha leaned forward. Her eyes shone with gentle eagerness. "What, Miles? You just remembered something, didn't you?"

He nodded. "Yeah. I used to drive an old beat-up rattletrap along back roads—somewhere. I don't know where. Just aimless driving and thinking." Miles raked his fingers through his hair. "I'm tempted, but I can't keep driving around, going nowhere." He gave a disgusted snort. "That won't solve anything."

At least she didn't say something lame to try to make him feel better, he thought bitterly. The silence stretched between them, while he tried to chase a memory that was already out of reach, and wondered once again what he'd been trying to escape. Finally he gave up and shook his head in frustration.

"Miles, instead of driving around aimlessly, you're welcome to stay at my place," Sasha offered softly. "I mean, until you feel better about going home." He felt his jaw start to drop and snapped it shut. Her unbruised cheek turned pink. "It's very peaceful on the farm and I have plenty of room, so..." She let the words trail off and shrugged.

It didn't make a single shred of sense to stay here a day longer than necessary. Whatever his life was, it was on Secret Island, Florida, not on a farm for strays and cripples in the boondocks of southern Ontario. Running away, staying away, was a coward's decision, and that wasn't the sort of truth Miles wanted to learn about himself. But then, what kind of man hid on an island, except a coward?

More important, Miles didn't know if he was the kind of man who could do the right thing when he was already very, very attracted to Doc Reiss. It was too tempting to think of the two of them alone together, with no past and no future between them to complicate the relationship. He might be that kind of man, but Sasha wasn't that kind of woman.

Better to walk away from her now, when it was still easy. Well, easier.

"Doc, I shouldn't take advantage of you," he murmured, intending to turn her down gently. But somehow he ended up saying, "But you just made me an offer I can't refuse. Only on condition that I pay my way," he added.

"That's not necessary."

"It is to me. I won't insult you with cash, but there has to be something I can do to repay you. I'm not a deadbeat."

"There's always something to do around a farm."

"Then it's a deal. But it's not indefinite. Just till I get on my feet. A few days, maximum. Okay?"

He watched her beautiful, battered face, searching for a clue that she'd changed her mind as suddenly as she'd made the offer. All he saw was a smile that must have hurt. It was a lot like the satisfied smile she'd worn when she'd told him about saving that vicious stallion, Desperado.

That really was all he meant to Doc Reiss...another needy case. The thought sent a wave of anger surging through Miles. He wasn't a pathetic foundling, damn it! Regardless of what had happened to his memory or his ribs, he was a man, and that's what his instincts wanted her to see.

The problem was, if he even hinted at what the sight, the sound, the scent of her did to his libido, she'd take back her invitation faster than he could blink. His memory had taken a hike, but his logical mind was functioning again. No sensible single woman who lived alone would want a randy stranger coming home with her.

"Aunt Sasha! Aunt Sasha!" a child cried as his door swung open. A little girl, about five or six, he guessed, flew across the room and practically launched herself into Sasha's lap, burrowing close. All he could see of the kid was her back, and long, dark hair in braids tied with rawhide thongs.

He winced when he heard Sasha gasp. Another one of those brief flashes of memory slid through his brain, an image of a woman wearing a red lipstick frown and pushing someone... *him?*... off her lap. And then he was back in the present, expecting Sasha to push the child off her lap to protect her injuries. Instead, she closed her arms around the little body.

"Easy, Magpie," a man's voice said from the doorway. "Aunt Sasha is hurt, remember?" A tall, powerfully built man with Native Canadian features followed the little girl at a much slower pace. The man, dressed in jeans and a plaid flannel shirt under an open denim jacket, looked at him steadily, sizing him up. Miles looked back, letting the other man know he was doing his own sizing up. This must be Sam, the other foster brother from Sasha's photographs.

Another image, this time of a faceless man in a plaid shirt, smashing open a door, hand raised, fist clenched around something—a belt?—about to descend. He felt himself cringe away from the image, and gripped the arm of his chair.

"Hi, Sam." Sasha's voice steadied him as surely as her touch would have. "I'm okay. Maggie missed the sore spots." Sasha gave her foster brother a smile that told Miles she was very fond of him. Miles wondered about Sam's single-parent status. Was there something between him and Sasha? After all, a lonely man and a motherless child were right up her alley.

"Sam," Sasha said, "this is Miles Kent. Miles, this is Sam Hunter. And this is Maggie-Magpie Hunter." Her arms around the little girl said without words that the child was very special to her.

Sam leaned over and held out his hand. Miles reached up and shook it, automatically assessing the man's grip. Strong, self-confident, with nothing to prove.

"You two have a bus-kissing contest?" Sam asked, grinning. Little Maggie giggled infectiously. Sasha gave a tiny laugh, then groaned. He couldn't help grinning back, himself.

"Does it hurt, Aunt Sasha?" The adult-sounding concern in the childish voice touched Miles in an unexpected, inexplicable way.

"A little, honey. Not enough to keep me down, however. Sam, thanks for coming to get me. I think my jacket is still in Emergency."

She set Maggie down beside her and started to get up. Miles saw her sway, saw the color drain from her face. He tried to stand, to support her, forgetting how ludicrous that was given his own condition. A second later Sam was gripping Sasha by the elbows and holding her up. Sasha smiled slightly. At that moment Miles couldn't say if he was jealous of the other man's closeness to Sasha or furious with his own helplessness. Probably both. What he did know was that Sasha was leaving. That was going to leave an empty feeling he didn't want to dwell on—but knew he would.

Still leaning on Sam, she asked, "When do you think you'll be getting out?"

"Probably tomorrow, day after at the latest." He waited for her to tell him that, on second thought, she couldn't have him at the farm. In some far corner of his mind Miles wondered why he kept expecting her to reject him, when she'd been going out of her way to help him. Perhaps the reason was buried in his lost memory.

Sasha took a deep breath, then moved out of Sam's supporting grip. She took a card out of the back pocket of her mud-spattered jeans and put it into his hand. "Call me. I'll probably be able to pick you up myself. If not, I'll figure something out."

"What's this?" Sam asked.

"I invited Miles to spend some R and R time at the farm."

"Oh, yeah?" Sam's black eyes focused on him. Miles read the warning, the suspicion, in that silent look.

"You know how good nature is for healing," Sasha said, and Miles could see that she didn't have a clue what was going on between him and Sam. Just as well. No point in making her nervous. Sam looked as if he already was doing plenty of worrying on her account. Sasha smiled sweetly before taking Maggie's hand and starting toward the door. "If I don't answer the phone, call the pager number. I'm hoping I can do my rounds tomorrow as usual."

"Don't push your luck," Miles advised.

"I was going to say the same thing," Sam said, giving him another one of those narrow, warning looks.

Chapter Six

Two days after the Desperado incident Sasha parked her truck close to the front doors of the hospital, turned off the ignition, then sat, gathering what little reserve energy she had left. Of all the Sundays to be on rotating emergency call! All day her head had ached and her face had hurt. She'd popped so many ibuprofen that she suspected she'd rattle if she shook herself, except she was too sore to try.

It had been a perfectly awful day so far, and the rest of it didn't promise any improvement. The weather couldn't decide what to do. It was mid-April, but while nights still brought frost warnings in rural areas, the days were either unseasonably hot or cold. Today the weather had alternated between gray, heavy, cold and damp, then hot and muggy. Full of spring fever, her patients had been silly, skittish and uncooperative. Some of their owners hadn't been much better. Now she felt sticky from sweating, then getting chilled when the sun retreated, and she needed a shower in the worst way. But she'd driven straight from her last emergency call to the hospital, foolishly eager to bring Miles home while there was still daylight left.

Now that she'd stopped moving, however, exhaustion made her limbs feel too heavy to move. With a sigh Sasha pocketed her keys and climbed out of the truck. How Miles was going to get himself up onto the front seat, she couldn't guess. She should have thought to borrow a car from Peter's wife, Marla. Irritated with her inefficiency, Sasha strode toward the front doors, ignoring the curious glances at her battered face from people passing her.

"Yeah?" Miles barked in answer to her knock on his door.

Summoning a stiff smile, Sasha pushed open the door and stepped inside. Miles stood in the middle of the room, a cane in his free hand, scowling. He looked as if he could chew quarters and spit nickels, as her grandfather used to say of his gardener when any of the animals feasted on the shrubbery.

He also looked very, very good, in a soft, black cotton sweater, faded blue jeans and a denim jacket. His left arm was in a sling under the jacket. Miles looked much better than he probably felt, judging by his tone of voice. If his aches had reacted to the damp as hers had, she couldn't blame him for being grumpy.

"Hi," she said as cheerfully as she could.

Miles met her eyes and the scowl disappeared. In its place was a wariness that made her wonder what *he* was wary about when *she* was the one facing the unknown.

"It's not too late to change your mind," he said, his gruff tone challenging, as if he expected her to revoke her invitation. Or perhaps hoping she would back out to save him the hassle of telling her he'd changed his mind.

"Are *you* having second thoughts?"

He leaned forward against the support of the cane, his gaze steady, probing. Sasha felt as if he were stripping away the layers of herself that protected her softest, most vulnerable parts. What was he looking for?

"Nothing a few seconds out of this place can't cure," he drawled. "I can't remember being in any hospitals in the past, but I think it's safe to say they don't bring out the best in me." He gave her a crooked grin. "Your friend Emmy was mumbling about cattle prods earlier."

A tiny laugh sputtered out of Sasha. "She's seen worse, I can assure you. Is that your duffel bag?" She started toward the lumpy canvas bag lying on the unmade bed.

Miles stepped toward her, intercepting her. She had to look up into his eyes now, and from where she stood, he looked peeved.

"I'll get it. Bad enough they want me to leave here in a wheelchair." Abruptly his frown faded into a look of grave concern, at least equal to the ones Sam had given her the past two evenings during chores. But Miles studied her so intently that she felt herself blushing. "How's your face?"

"Stiff. Sore." She shrugged off her self-consciousness about the Technicolor bruising on one side of her face. It had defied her meager attempts to camouflage the worst of it with makeup. Now she wished she'd tried harder. This was infinitely worse than a bad hair day. "I'm using a lot of ice. How are you feeling?"

"Better." His gruff answer wasn't very convincing. She knew from experience that better was a very relative concept.

Sasha wished she could use the healing power of touch to reach Miles's pain, but she didn't dare touch him the way she would touch a patient. Long, soothing strokes. Gentle, focused pressures. Familiar, reassuring touches. Loving touches. The kind of comforting touches she sometimes ached for, body and soul.

Oh, no, touching Miles like that would be highly inappropriate. Being touched like that by Miles would be even worse. The awkwardness of the situation weighed on her. Not for the first time, she wondered if her impulse to help had gotten her into deep water. Or hot water.

"Let's go," Miles said gruffly.

He grabbed the strap of the duffel bag and tried to maneuver it despite using the cane. The bag must have hit him in a sore spot—one other than between his ears, Sasha thought—because he cursed and dropped it. Sasha stepped around Miles and hefted the duffel bag. It was heavy, but not as heavy as a bale of hay or the front end of a trailer stuck in the mud. Miles glared at her.

She paused. "Didn't you say something about a wheelchair?"

"Yeah, but I won't repeat it in mixed company." She smiled. His glare faded. "Let's go. I paid my bills and signed about twenty forms saying they aren't responsible for anything they did or didn't do to me, for me, or with me. Makes me wonder what the hell I even came here for."

As he spoke he moved toward the open door. She followed him out, reluctantly realizing that her own aches were making Miles's duffel bag feel heavier by the second. It took long minutes to reach the exit, with the silence between them stretching until Sasha felt as if her nerves would snap.

She wondered—not for the first time—if she was doing Miles a disservice. He wasn't a mistreated horse. He was an intelligent, proud and vulnerable man, and he was in distress beyond her expertise. What if, despite her good intentions, she made things worse for him? She'd invited him to the farm hoping that the peace and quiet would help him heal spiritually as well as physically. But even a few days' stay might be too long for him to be away from the things that could trigger his recovery.

Timing in any healing process was vitally important. What if she was interfering at precisely the wrong time for Miles to ever regain his memory? She would have to make sure neither of them got too comfortable with their arrangement. She'd never forgive herself if her well-intentioned interference set back his recovery.

Sasha followed him through the automatic exit doors. The late-afternoon sun sent shafts of light between the clouds. The cool air snuck into her open jacket, making her shiver after the heat of the hospital. Miles, wearing only a light shirt and jacket, didn't seem to feel the cooler air. Instead, he paused, looked up at the sky and took in a deep breath. Probably too glad to be free to care about the temperature, she guessed.

"What are you driving?" Miles's gruff voice broke into her thoughts.

"The white pickup truck with the shell, over there."

He started across the driveway, moving quickly despite the exhausting trip from his room to the exit. It gave her some insight into how strong, and how determined, Miles was.

"Will you be able to get in? I'd forgotten how high that first step is."

"I will get into your truck, even if you have to haul me in with a winch," he said from between clenched teeth.

"Stubborn fool," she muttered. Miles grunted.

Sasha sighed but smiled. She also favored determination over resignation. That was one of the things that had drawn her to Desperado—and to Miles. "Let me stow your bag inside, and I'll see if I can help you without resorting to the winch."

Once she'd tossed his duffel bag into the back seat, she studied him and the situation, trying desperately not to notice that Miles seemed more attractive every time she saw him. It was an attraction she understood well, even though it was inexplicable. It was an animal magnetism. A powerful appeal that had nothing to do with common sense or reason or how many things they had or didn't have in common, and everything to do with chemistry. Sasha had never had trouble resisting animal magnetism in the past, but then, she'd never before met Miles Kent.

Miles gazed down at her, one eyebrow lifting. "The way I see it," Miles drawled, "you can either get in front of me and push, or get behind me and pull."

Either way, she understood she'd have to put her hands on him. She felt heat rise in her cheeks at the same time that her dependable resistance slipped dangerously. "I think I'll be more effective behind you. Give me a second to climb in from the other side."

Grateful for the chance to get away from his intense scrutiny, Sasha dashed around the truck and climbed into the driver's seat. Miles already had the passenger door open and had slid the cane into the back with his duffel bag. He stood with his back toward her, leaning against the seat. Sasha knelt on the edge of the passenger seat behind his broad shoulders and took a deep breath.

"Okay, I'm ready," she said.

"So am I," he answered, and she wondered if they were talking about the same thing.

Miles gritted his teeth against the pain in his ribs and left arm and tried to hoist himself backward into the passenger seat of Sasha's truck. Too late, he realized the damn thing was higher than he'd thought. At the moment that he was slipping back to the ground, without the damn cane for support, and his bad leg unwilling to hold him so he could use his good leg to push him up from the running board, he felt Sasha's arms slide under his from behind.

Her scent, her warmth closed around him as she locked her arms across his chest. He felt the pressure of her shoulder, the softness of her breasts against his back and the kiss of her breath on his neck. Through the layers of their clothes he felt her strength as she held him from sliding down.

"On three," she said, her voice low and a little shaky.

Miles got some satisfaction that the situation was having some effect on Sasha, too. It took some of the bitterness out of having to accept her help just to get his butt into the truck.

"One, two," she counted.

On three, he pushed upward against the running board and Sasha pulled backward, her grip somehow avoiding the sore ribs that protested the sudden movement. His hand slipped from the doorframe with a painful thump on his chest. He just barely swallowed his moan. A second later he felt himself falling backward into the truck.

Sasha made a soft little sound of surprise as he crushed her backward, but her arms stayed locked around him. He didn't know whether to laugh or groan. There he was, in pain, rolling around in the front seat of a truck with a beautiful woman, and he couldn't do a damn thing about the woman or the pain.

"Sorry," he muttered when he caught his breath. "You okay?"

"I'm fine. It's just like assisting at a foaling, suddenly finding a hundred and seventy-five pounds or so in my lap." He felt her shift slightly under his back. "Fortunately, you aren't nearly as wet as a foal, and you're a lot less helpless."

He felt himself smile a little, relax a little. "I take it that's a hint for me to move."

"If you can."

He could, but some devilish impulse made him hesitate. Leaning against Sasha like this was pretty damn pleasant, even if it made him look like a wimp. He'd stayed awake a long time last night, thinking about kissing her. That first kiss had been sweet, oddly innocent. He wasn't sure how he was going to stay under the same roof with her and not want more, and it would be a rotten violation of her hospitality for him to try for more. Miles was pretty certain he'd spent a lot of his life wanting what he couldn't have. That was probably the engine that drove him. The question was, did he have enough conscience not to take Sasha just because he wanted her?

Holding back a groan, he eased himself upright. Immediately the cool, damp air replaced the warmth of Sasha against his back. While he was gathering himself for the next move, she slid out her side and appeared at his knees. He could see the worry in those big doe eyes of hers, and cursed himself for a fool. While he'd been thinking about kissing her, she'd been thinking of him as a helpless, two-legged patient.

"Would you like a hand swinging your legs inside?" Sasha asked.

She was hugging herself in that dark green parka, as if the cold was seeping through her jacket. Personally, he felt as if he had a furnace going full blast inside him, thanks to that impromptu tumble with her. He didn't want to accept her help, especially since her offer made him wonder what her hands would feel like on his knees, on his thighs.

"I can do it," he told her, more gruffly than he'd intended.

He succeeded, but it was a while into the drive before he could manage to speak. He flashed on a barely remembered impression of being in the passenger seat of a big car, too small to see out the window or above the dashboard. He felt the helplessness, and the fear, that belonged to that brief memory and shifted in his seat, trying to push it aside. "How far are we going?"

Sasha glanced at him quickly, smiled, then turned her eyes back to the narrow country road. "About ten more minutes."

She was a good driver, he noticed. At ease with her truck and the road. Every few seconds she'd flick her gaze up to her rearview mirror, then back to the road. What was going on in her head? he wondered. Regrets, no doubt. He had a few of his own.

Finally Sasha flipped on her right-turn signal and slowed to turn onto a narrow dirt-and-gravel road. He could feel the ruts grabbing at the truck's tires, but Sasha seemed perfectly at ease wrestling with the steering wheel. She slowed the truck almost to a crawl and made a left turn onto a long, straight gravel lane lined with tall cedars. As they drove toward the parking area, Miles looked around and whistled under his breath.

The photos hadn't done this place justice, he thought. The old stone farmhouse sat perched at the top of a small hill, with enough trees around it to protect it from the weather without blocking the spectacular view of farms and forests for miles around. The hills rolled gently for as far as he could see, marked off in rectangles of brown, gold and pale green, with the shapes of houses and barns dotted here and there. The roads ran straight as a grid.

In Sasha's yard the deciduous trees were loaded with swollen buds, and there were green shoots poking up through the brown pastures. The tips of the evergreens all had tender green shoots of new growth. A pair of cardinals swooped in front of the truck, then headed for the bird feeders hanging from the trees nearest the house. On both sides of the porch steps the garden beds were full of purple, white and yellow flowers. Even with the mud and the mist and the clouds blocking the sun, Miles saw the peaceful, timeless beauty of the farm. It was, he decided, a perfect reflection of the woman beside him.

Sasha switched off the ignition and pulled out the key. Then she turned her bruised but beautiful face toward him. Her dark eyes looked so earnest. Whatever was on her mind, he knew he was about to find out.

"Miles, I want you to understand that you're a welcome guest here, but I also want you to know you're free to leave at any time, without worrying that you'll be hurting my feelings or insulting my hospitality. I know you have a lot of healing inside to do, and I'm not sure if this is the best place to do it. Okay?"

He could read between the lines easily enough. *Don't overstay your welcome.* He nodded. "Okay."

Her smile lit her dark eyes softly. A man really could get lost in those eyes, he thought. But only one who was welcome there.

"Then welcome to Lilac Hill Farm. Ready to get down?"

"Ready enough."

"Want me to get in front or behind?" she asked.

Lord, didn't the woman have a clue how suggestive that sounded? He grinned at the impulse to show her. "Isn't that supposed to be my line?" he asked quietly, holding still and wondering how she'd react.

He could see the unbruised side of her face blush. "Don't tempt me to let you starve in the truck," she muttered. He was still chuckling perversely when she jerked open his door and scowled at him. Then she reached into the truck and caught his calves in her hands and he stopped laughing. He felt the heat of her touch through his jeans, heat that radiated upward to parts of him he'd lain awake nights imagining her touching. She looked up into his eyes and drew a shaky breath, sending his pulse into overdrive.

"Steady," she whispered, and he wondered to which one of them she was talking.

With Sasha's hands guiding his legs, Miles eased himself around to face out of the truck. The pain in his ribs faded to nothing compared to the ache of having Sasha's hands on his thighs and knowing she didn't see him as a man who could be turned on by her touch. She saw him as a patient, a problem to solve.

Sasha brought his cane out of the back seat and leaned it against the side of the truck. She stood in front of him, looking at him but not quite meeting his eyes.

"Now what?" he asked, although that was obvious. They had to get him down to the ground somehow. He was more curious about what she was thinking than about what she intended to do.

"Put your arms around me and lean on me while you get out," she said, getting way ahead of him without warning. "I'll use the roof to brace myself."

He should have told her to just pass him the cane. He hated this dependency, but she was right, he had to accept her help or he'd be there all night. He reached out and slid his good arm around the back of her neck, feeling the strength in her shoulders as she braced her hands on the top of the door opening. Slowly he eased himself toward her, toward the long step down to the ground. Sasha shifted her feet, widening her stance. He worked his way closer, feeling drugged by the earthy scent of her skin mixing with the spring air. When he was almost off the edge of the seat he sought the ground with his feet, bringing their bodies together. Her jacket was open, and now he felt the soft mounds of her breasts, the resilience of her flat belly, the sharp curves of her pelvic bones, the long, tense muscles of her thighs against him.

He stood without moving, his feet planted between hers. His sprained ankle and wrenched knee added their complaints to those of his ribs, but it was as if the pain belonged to someone else. All he really felt was Sasha, so close she was under his skin. She was trembling. He felt the tension in her arms as she gripped the truck roof over his head. She was open to him. If she gave him the slightest hint, he'd have her mouth under his.

He felt her stiffen and suddenly knew, deep in his gut, that she wouldn't wrap her arms around him and give in to the chemistry between them. Not then. Maybe never. Certainly not while she thought he needed her help. It wouldn't fit her image as the Good Samaritan. And he'd be damned before he'd accept that kind of charity. The thought gave him the strength to tamp down the desire that raged in his veins.

"Thanks, Doc," he said, releasing her.

She let go of the truck and moved away fast. Miles reached for his cane and cursed to himself. So much for chemistry, he thought. She couldn't put enough distance between them. Still, angry as her rejection made him, he had to concede it was probably better for both of them this way. He didn't have anything to offer her, and he sure as hell didn't want to need anything from her.

Sasha backed away from Miles, embarrassed by that sizzling moment between them. Well, at least, it sizzled from her perspective. Miles hadn't seemed as affected by their impromptu embrace, since he'd just stood there like a fence post. He must think she was desperate, luring him to her isolated farm, telling him he was free to go whenever he wanted to, then rubbing up against him like a mare in season.

"Come inside, where you can get comfortable," Sasha suggested to cover her discomfort. "It smells like rain."

"That's not all it smells like," Miles muttered.

Sasha smiled. "It's a farm. You'll get used to the odors quickly enough."

"I doubt that. Hey, what are you doing with the bag?"

Sasha picked up Miles's duffel bag, ignoring his scowl. "Go on up to the house. I'm right behind."

But not close enough, she discovered a few seconds later. Miles had made his way up most of the stairs with the support of his cane. Just as he reached the top step, one of the cats ran between his feet. Miles would have crashed back down the stairs, except that he dropped the cane, twisted around and with his right arm grabbed the column supporting the porch roof. Sasha heard his grunt as his body hit the column. She dropped the duffel bag onto the wet gravel and dashed up the stairs to support him. He shook her hand off his elbow.

"What the hell was that?" he barked.

"Just a cat. Are you all right?"

"Never better, thanks. This is part of my physiotherapy program."

She rolled her eyes and turned her attention to selecting the right key from her key ring.

"Hey, Doc, I think you should see this," Miles said. To her relief, the humor seemed to be back in his voice.

She looked down to where he was pointing. In front of the door, looking immensely pleased with herself, sat Pretty Polly, one of the barn cats. Under one of the tabby's white-booted front paws wiggled a small, very agitated green-and-yellow garden snake. Sasha groaned.

Miles chuckled. Polly looked up at him and twitched her ears. Sasha sighed.

"You're in trouble now. Polly's a shameless flirt as well as a fearless hunter. Now that you've admired her, she'll probably bring you more gifts." At his skeptical expression, Sasha smiled. "Once she brought a whole litter of live bunnies into the house, one at a time. Sam's daughter, Maggie, and Peter's son, Jimmy, spent hours catching them to set free. Polly never forgave them."

He snorted, obviously unfamiliar with the emotional range of felines. He'd learn. "I expected a guard dog, not a guard cat," he commented, grinning.

"I usually do have a dog, but I haven't found one to replace Topsy, so the cats take turns playing sentinel," she told him, then basked briefly in his warm, amused gaze.

Sasha knelt in front of the loudly purring cat. "Good girl, Polly!" she said, then reached out and stroked the mink-soft fur. "Thank you very much. It's a lovely snake, but I don't think it's going to eat the grain the way the mice do, so I'd like to let it go. Is that all right?"

"I don't believe this," Miles muttered. "You're negotiating with a cat. I've been kidnapped by a fruitcake!"

Sasha smothered a laugh, unwilling to hurt Polly's feelings. After scratching around the tabby's ears and white chin for a moment, she gently took the unhappy little snake out from under the cat's sharp claws. Snakes were definitely not her favorite critters, but she was a vet, after all, so she smothered her reflex to cringe. She went down the steps holding the snake firmly but gently. It wriggled frantically, not knowing that it was safe.

She knelt next to the porch. "Okay, Mr. Snake," she said, "head for the hills."

After turning the snake loose in the garden beside the house, Sasha picked up the cane Miles had dropped and held it out to him. Then she hoisted the duffel bag again and went back up the steps to unlock her front door. Walking ahead of Miles, she made her way to the kitchen, flipping on lights as she went.

"You're really something, Doc."

His voice came from directly behind her, startling her. Even leaning on his cane, he seemed to fill the space around him. It surprised her—it *kept* surprising her—how nervous he made her. He was just a man. Just a handsome, grumpy, sexy, unattached male who was going to be living in her house for an undetermined length of time. Absolutely *nothing* to be nervous about, just because it was the first time they'd been alone without the possibility of interruption since she'd found him in his wrecked car.

Sasha turned around slowly, fighting her sudden breathlessness. He tipped her chin up with one warm finger. Reluctantly she met his eyes.

"Mr. Snake?" he murmured.

She shrugged, feeling a little foolish. "I guess it could have been Ms. Snake. The poor thing seemed more concerned with escape than political correctness."

Miles chuckled softly. "Are you talking about the snake or yourself?"

"Political correctness seldom interests me," she hedged. "Right now, it's way down on the list of things I have to do. Let me show you to your room."

He released her chin. "Lead on."

She grabbed his duffel bag and started toward the stairs. "I'm sorry I don't have a guest room on the first floor. There are four spare rooms upstairs that are always ready for company, but I can make up the chesterfield in the living room if the stairs are too much for your bad leg."

"Thanks, but I can use the exercise," he told her with a half grin.

She found herself smiling back even though her sore face protested. Then she turned away and led Miles up the stairs.

"This is really nice," he said behind her. "It must be old."

"The house itself is about a hundred and twenty years old, but it's been modernized several times. No more outdoor plumbing and gaslights, although we've kept most of the old fixtures."

"Almost like a museum, with all these antiques and family portraits."

"I guess it is, in a way. A lot of good memories live here." Sasha stopped just past the door to her own room, the first and largest, which used to be her grandparents' room. "Take your pick," she told him, gesturing down the hallway. "Although you may prefer the farthest one. Sometimes I get emergency calls in the middle of the night, but you won't hear the phone down there." *And I won't be tempted to tuck you in.*

"Is this one yours?" Miles asked, nodding back toward her door.

"Yes," she managed to say in a fairly steady voice. Ordinarily she loved showing guests the antiques and heirloom linens, the framed needlepoint pictures and carefully collected silver and crystal vanity items that filled her private space. But the idea of inviting Miles into her overtly feminine bedroom sent dizzying waves of heat to her head. What would he think of the normally practical country vet if he saw she slept in eyelet laces and down quilts? She didn't think she could deal with the sight of him moving around her room, perhaps touching her things with those utterly masculine hands—perhaps touching *her*.

Sasha started to move past Miles, intending to carry his duffel bag to his chosen room. He reached out and gently took the carry strap out of her hand. Hesitantly she looked up to find Miles studying her. "I'll take the far room," he murmured. "That way, both of us will sleep."

That's what *he* thinks, she told herself as she returned to the kitchen.

Chapter Seven

Wonderful, rich aromas lured him out of a deep sleep. The clock by his bed told him he'd been asleep for over two hours. His body felt as if he'd been sleeping for a hundred years—achy, clumsy, heavy. His head felt as if his brain had been replaced with cotton. Silently cursing his awkwardness, he limped his way down the long flight of stairs with their softly worn, faded carpet runner. When he finally reached the first floor, he followed the sounds of dishes and glasses being set down. Sasha was moving around the kitchen, setting the old wooden table with one hand and holding an ice pack against the bruised side of her face with the other. She smiled over her shoulder, making him feel even more guilty. Sasha was in no condition to be waiting on him.

"Why didn't you tell me you needed help? We could have ordered pizza. Sit down."

She shrugged, but at least she sat on one of the caned ladder-back chairs, still holding the ice pack to her face. "I didn't need help."

He snorted. "Right. That's why you have an ice pack on your cheek."

"No. I'm using an ice pack because my face hurts. But I don't cook with my face, so I managed very well." He was about to say something rude to express his disbelief, but she smiled again, and he felt his anger melting. "Thank you, Miles. I guess I'm too used to living on my own to think of asking for help."

Her answer touched him in an odd way. "Well, think of it now," he said, more gruffly than he intended. "I'm not here for a free ride. Don't treat me like an invalid."

"Sorry. I hope you like chicken paprika."

Her comment caught him off guard. "I don't know," he admitted slowly. "I probably do, because it smells great."

He could see his own confusion reflected in those dark eyes and it ripped at him. He had to turn away before he broke down and made a fool of himself. There was a glass in the sink. He rinsed it and set it in the dish drainer as an excuse to keep his back to her.

"Oh, Miles!" she said softly. "I guess I don't really understand what you're going through. Is it that bad? That you've forgotten your likes and dislikes?"

"Seems like it," he conceded, reluctant to admit to even that small weakness. "Food isn't so hard to figure out. I don't mind tasting things, except for hospital food. If I thought I liked hospital food, I'd probably throw myself off a bridge." Her laugh took away some of the sting of confessing. "What can I do next?"

"Everything's ready. It just needs to be served."

"I can do that," he told her when she came toward the stove with a long-handled spoon. Gently but firmly he took the spoon from her fingers.

He managed to scoop the food from the pots of chicken and rice without spilling. Sasha carried their plates to the table. She took a bowl of salad out of the refrigerator and a basket of rolls out of the oven. Then they sat down across the table from each other. He couldn't remember if he'd ever shared kitchen duties with a woman, couldn't recall inti-

mate meals for two, but he didn't need memories to know
this was special. It felt comfortable. Too bad it couldn't last.

"Bon appétit," she said.

The first bite melted in his mouth, leaving the spicy sauce
dancing on his tongue. He suspected that kissing Sasha, *really* kissing her, would be like that. The thought was so en-
ticing, so forbidden—he'd forbidden it himself—that he
almost welcomed the sound of voices in the front of the
house. He recognized them immediately. Peter Simmons,
the shrink, and Sam.

The way that people simply walked in made Miles edgy.
It was an invasion of privacy that felt familiar, yet he
couldn't place why. Surely, if he'd come from the kind of big
family where everyone tumbled over everyone else, the police or Eleanor Dobbs would have mentioned parents or
siblings. No one had said anything about anyone missing
him, looking for him. The obvious conclusion—that he had
no one—settled on him like a dark cloud.

"Hi, guys!" Sasha called out. "Who's hungry? There's
plenty left."

The two men walked in grinning and shaking their heads.
"We just came from dinner," Peter said, his gaze shifting
from Sasha to Miles as if he were trying to read their minds.
Miles forced himself to meet that probing look evenly. "Just
wanted to make sure you could handle all the chores and
didn't need anything for the pain. Your face still looks pretty
awful, Sash."

"Thank you so much," she retorted, but her smile told
him she wasn't offended by Peter's comment. "Everything's done, except for the last hay feeding. That's not a big
deal."

"Okay," Sam said. "I'll do it. Won't hurt the horses to
get their hay a little early."

"You're going to the barn right now?" Sasha asked. Sam
nodded. She stood. "I'll go, too. It'll go faster, and Desperado won't freak when he sees a man." She grabbed a slice
of cucumber out of the salad bowl. "Miles, don't feel you
have to wait for me. Your dinner will get cold. I won't be

long." She popped the cucumber slice into her mouth and followed Sam out of the kitchen.

The last thing he was going to do was wolf his dinner down while Sasha was out there battling with that crazed beast. He started to rise, to go after her, but Peter stepped to the table and turned one of the chairs around so he could straddle it, facing Miles. There was no way to mistake the other man's intentions.

"How's it going?"

Miles smiled grimly. "You working overtime?"

Peter shrugged. "I don't exactly punch a time clock. I've been reading up on memory deficit."

"And?"

"And I thought you might like to know there's someone you can talk to, if you have any questions."

"*If* I have any questions?" He kept his rage under control, but just barely. "My life is one big question. You have any answers?"

"I wish I did." Peter met his eyes with no apology, and Miles knew what was coming. "I'd like to know what kind of man Sasha has taken into her home."

"So would I, Simmons. So would I."

Sam flicked on the barn lights, then planted himself in Sasha's path. "You trying people medicine on that crazy horse, or horse medicine on that man in your kitchen?"

"Tactful as always, Sam." She shooed him out of her way and headed down the aisle to the hay stall. All the horses nickered and pawed, impatient for their meal.

Sam stayed right on her heels. "You can't heal every hurt critter, man or horse."

"I can try."

"How's the man going to get his memory back when he's with you? You aren't part of his history. You came out of his darkness, his accident, not his light. If he tries to stay with you, he's going to lose the light from his past. He'll never know who he is."

Sasha tore off a flake of hay from the open bale, scattering loose hay with the force of her movements. "Give me a break, Sam! I'm not some nut case from a Stephen King novel, keeping the guy here against his will. He felt disoriented, and he's still bashed up from the accident, so I offered him a place to rest before he has to tackle his problem. We both know he's leaving soon."

She thrust several flakes of hay at Sam, then stomped up the aisle to distribute the rest. His heavy sigh followed her, audible over the thumping and neighing of the horses.

"I don't want to see you get hurt," he said when they met at the end of the aisle.

Sasha felt some of her anger melt under the wistful expression in Sam's black eyes. "You know me," she said lightly. "I'm too busy to get involved. I won't get hurt."

Sam gave her a crooked grin. "Maybe it's Miles I should be warning."

"Maybe you should just remember I'm over thirty and have been taking very good care of myself for years."

"Maybe," he conceded. "What about Desperado? You still have to throw his hay over the fence?"

She grabbed the flakes meant for the trumpeting stallion outside and grinned at Sam. "Yeah, but he lets me get closer to the fence before he goes ballistic."

Sam grinned back. "Careful. That could be a sucker move to soften you up. Maybe someone told him ladies like a little danger."

That made her laugh, despite the soreness of her face. "Not this lady."

When Sasha walked back into the kitchen she found Peter and Miles sitting at the table, discussing the possibility of the Toronto Blue Jays winning another World Series. Amazing, she mused, how a man's entire identity can be wiped out without damaging his baseball knowledge.

"Sam's waiting in the car," she told Peter. "He said he promised to get back and read a story to Maggie before bed."

"I'm gone," Peter answered, standing. "How's Desperado?"

Sasha sighed. "As well as can be expected for a basket case. Very defensive. He could use a couple of hours on your couch."

Peter chuckled and shook his head. "No, thanks. I don't keep a shovel in the office. Give him some space. And call if you need me," he said, giving her a gentle pat on the arm. "For anything," he added quietly as he walked past her.

Alone again with Miles, Sasha felt the large room close in on her. It was too silent. She could hear her own breathing, her own pulse. He was too real, too attractive, too dangerous. After Sam's pointed comments, she was feeling too vulnerable.

Miles got to his feet. "I put our plates in the oven."

To her chagrin, his thoughtfulness brought tears to her eyes. "Thanks," she managed to say hoarsely. "I'll get them." That gave her an excuse to turn away from him, an opportunity to compose herself.

They ate without speaking for a while. Music, Sasha thought. She should have turned on the stereo. Anything would be better than this echoing silence that crackled with speculation and temptation. The silence focused her thoughts on Miles, and on Sam's warnings not to get involved, not to let herself get hurt.

Distance. Objectivity. They were her professional armor, keeping her from feeling too personally every loss of a patient, every departure of a fostered animal. But sometimes she feared she'd lost the ability to care deeply. She wanted to fall in love with someone so deeply that she *could* get hurt, but with the right man, she wouldn't get hurt. And anyone with the brains of a fruit fly would know Miles couldn't possibly be the right man for her.

The sound of him clearing his throat made her look up. He met her eyes with a steady, assessing gaze that made her realize he'd probably been following his own train of thought while they'd been eating in silence. What does a man think about when he's lost his memories, lost his identity? How does he put his life together again? What happens when the past comes crashing back? Or does it work that way? So many questions, so few answers. No wonder he seemed angry so often. She probably would be, too.

"I guess we can safely assume I like chicken paprika," he said, giving her a wry grin when she glanced at his empty plate. She managed a small answering smile despite the soreness of her face. "Sasha, we need to talk."

"About?"

"Us." He set his plate away from him and leaned forward over the edge of the table. "I just want to make sure you know you don't have to lie awake nights expecting me to pounce."

"Thank you," she said as neutrally as she could, wondering what kind of surgical procedures Peter had threatened if Miles did attempt to seduce her. "I really hadn't thought about it," she fibbed.

He nodded. "Just so we understand each other." He stood. "I'll wash, you can dry."

Sasha took a towel out of the drawer, pondering their conversation. Miles had no identity, but he had scruples. Or a healthy respect for her foster brothers. Either way, she was safe in her bed, or anywhere else. So why, when she should feel relieved, did she feel like breaking a plate over his head?

Miles finished washing before Sasha finished drying, and sat at the kitchen table watching her put the clean dishes away. Exhaustion had caught up with him so suddenly it was a miracle he hadn't fallen asleep over the sink. His head felt heavy, and all his aches were nagging at him, but there was one more thing he needed to do before he could go back to the bed waiting for him upstairs.

Sasha folded the dish towel over the rail and turned to study him. Her expression was as objective as any of the doctors who had peered at him in the hospital, and despite his promise not to act like a sex-starved maniac, that rankled.

"Would you like an ice pack? There are always several in the freezer, ready to go." Her smile lit her eyes. Even with those bruises, her beauty gave him another, deeper kind of ache no ice pack or aspirin could cure. "I'm my own best customer."

"No, thanks. All I need is a good night's sleep. Every time I drifted off in the hospital, someone would come in to mess with me, or there'd be an announcement on the loudspeakers."

"Well, the ice packs are there if you need them. There should be ibuprofen in your bathroom. If there's anything else you need, feel free to hunt around. I'm going upstairs to wind down with a bath and good book. It's only Sunday, and I'm beat already."

He studied her beautiful, battered face, resisting the urge to stroke her unbruised cheek. Her skin looked as soft as a rose petal. "Are you feeling all right? No concussion from that devil you call a horse?"

"No, I'm fine. Sore, but nothing I can't deal with. You can meet Desperado tomorrow if you want."

"I can hardly wait."

"Good." She gave him a quick smile. "Sleep well. I won't wake you when I get up."

He shook his head. "No, I'll get up with you." The words hung in the air between them.

Sasha's cheeks turned pink. Turning away, she murmured, "Well, good night."

"One more thing, Sasha?" She turned, and the innocent expectation in her eyes convinced him that he'd made the right decision. "I'll be leaving tomorrow afternoon, whenever I can get a flight out." She blinked, then stared at him, obviously waiting for an explanation. "I don't want to make any more work for you, and I have to get back to my life and figure out why I ran away from home." He tried to make the words come out light, but the sadness in her eyes told him he'd failed.

"I've been thinking a lot about this, Miles. It's a golden opportunity to decide who you want to be, instead of worrying about who you were. You can create a new identity. The future is wide open. Why not leave the past behind and start over?''

His anger rose swiftly, blinding him to the sweetness he'd been taking for granted. ''Cut the Pollyanna crap, Doc! It's not like turning off a switch. My past is still with me, even if I can't remember it. I can pretend to start over all I want, but what about when that past catches up with me? Who will I be then, Doc?''

He watched her swallow, wanting to press his mouth to her slender throat despite his anger. ''You'll be what we all are, Miles. A combination of past and present.''

''That's the point, Sasha. I have to know what that past is, before I can decide about the future.''

''You have to do whatever you think is right, Miles,'' she answered evenly, gently, as if he hadn't been bellowing at her.

''You think I'm wrong,'' he challenged, needing to work out this pent-up belligerence toward fate. ''You think I should stay and let you treat me like that godforsaken beast you think you can make nice to. I'm not a horse, Doc. I'm a man, and that makes me a lot more dangerous. Isn't that what your friend Sam told you? That I'll use you, then leave you.''

She fussed with the already neatly folded dish towel, then shrugged. ''I'm not a teenager with a crush, Miles. I'm an adult offering aid and comfort to another adult. Sex has nothing to do with it.''

He had her in his arms and pressed against his body so quickly that he felt as surprised as she looked. He felt her stiffen, then relax and lean into him, pliant and yielding. Her head tipped back, her eyes meeting his. Her pulse surged wildly at the base of her throat. His breath fought its way past his own galloping heart. When she slowly ran the tip of her tongue across her lower lip, he felt the blood race to his loins. As he grew harder, Sasha's eyes widened, but she didn't try to escape his hold.

The knowledge that he could have her, that she felt the same desire he did, rocked him to the core of his soul. It took every ounce of his self-control and whatever was left of his self-respect to release her before he gave in to the temptation to take her mouth. She stood before him, her breathing as rapid and shallow as his.

"Smarten up, Sasha!" he growled, clenching his hands to keep from reaching for her again. "If you give me half a chance, damn it, I *will* use you and leave you. I'm trying to get out of your life before it comes to that."

Very slowly she nodded. "I'll get you my travel agent's phone number for the morning," she said, her voice nearly a whisper. "She also can get you a flat-rate taxi to the airport, since I'll be out on calls all day."

His anger dropped away. All he felt was exhaustion and regret. "Thanks. See you in the morning."

She smiled, but there was a sad light in her eyes.

"Good night, Miles. Sleep well."

Sasha knew she couldn't follow Miles up the stairs as if nothing had happened between them. She wasn't sure *what* had just happened, but something very powerful had nearly gotten out of control. Her nerves still tingled with the imprint of Miles's body on hers. Her pulse still fluttered. Her hands still shook.

Bemused and confused, she grabbed her jacket and went outside to clear her head. The night air was cool and damp, but even with her jacket open, she felt overheated.

Never had a man touched her like that. Not physically, although it was true no one else had ever grabbed her like a pirate seizing the spoils of a battle, but emotionally. Miles touched her deep inside. No other man had made her tremble like that. No other man had made her hunger for passion, for a bonding that reached beyond sex. Like a ready mare, she'd become instantly receptive at the first wild step of the ageless mating dance.

With a shiver Sasha realized she'd walked most of the way to Desperado's paddock. His white coat shone like a reverse shadow in the security lights of the stable yard. Head up, he sniffed the air, then blew and snorted. A moment later, as Sasha reached the fence, he began a nervous jig, turning first one way, then the other.

Sasha dug a piece of horse crunch out of her jacket pocket and crooned gently to the uneasy stallion. To her amazement and delight, he stopped his frantic pacing and slowly made his way toward her. With his muzzle extended suspiciously, Desperado halted several feet from the fence. She held the piece of crunch out on the flat of her palm.

"Here you go, sweetheart," she coaxed. "It's for you. All you have to do is take it nicely. There's a good boy."

The horse sighed deeply and began to inch toward her extended hand. Sasha stood motionless and continued to croon at him, waiting patiently for him to lip the treat off her hand. When Desperado was within easy reach, he paused, then came even closer. At the very moment that she expected him to take the piece of crunch as a token of his acceptance of her presence, his neck snaked toward her and his teeth snapped. With a gasp, Sasha pulled her hand back a split second before those teeth would have closed on her hand.

"Didn't you ever hear the advice not to bite the hand that feeds?" she muttered.

Miles shut the door to his bedroom and called himself every kind of jerk for snarling at Sasha. She was only trying to help him find a way out of this maze with no landmarks. Hell, she had her own problems. He knew she had to be sore from the stallion's attack. If he really was this selfish bastard, he didn't think getting his memory back was going to do anyone any favors.

"M'row?" came from somewhere in the room. He looked around, taking in the simple, sturdy furnishings, the tasteful prints in wooden frames, the cheerful curtains and upholstery. No cat in sight.

Then the bed skirt moved, and a black-and-gold cat slunk out from under the double bed. It yawned, stretched and licked its chops, then parked its butt on the faded Oriental carpet and blinked up at him. Its long tail curled around its feet, the tip slowly rising and falling in a regular rhythm.

"Okay, pal," he muttered, feeling foolish for talking to the damn animal. "Here's the door."

He stood by the open door, but the cat continued to stare at him as if he'd missed some subtle but important point. Finally the cat simply shrugged off their staring contest by lifting a forepaw and delicately licking at it, then scrubbing its face. Bemused at being outmaneuvered, he shut the door and moved toward the bathroom.

When he came back out, the damn cat was curled in the middle of the rumpled bed, looking very much at home. Suddenly too tired to argue with anyone or anything, Miles pulled back the down quilt and sat on the edge of the bed. The cat made room for him to lie down, then curled up against his hip, purring loudly. The last thing he remembered thinking, before he closed his eyes, was that he'd never get to sleep with the cat making that much noise.

When Miles awoke, his watch said it was past midafternoon on Monday. Stiff and woolly brained, he managed to get downstairs to the kitchen, where he found a note from Sasha and a pot of hot coffee. Attached to her note, which simply said, "Good luck," was the business card of a travel agent. Holding the card in his hand, he turned to look at the phone on the wall. It seemed very far away.

The black-and-gold cat leaped onto the counter beside him. He pivoted quickly, too quickly. The kitchen tilted and darkness pressed in on his eyes. Gripping the edge of the counter, Miles fought to control his breathing and clear his vision. He finally straightened and found the damn cat watching him.

"M'row?"

"I know, I know," he muttered. "Even you wouldn't drag me in." He considered the coffeepot. Immediately his stomach rose in protest. No way he could face coffee, even though he was desperate for a jolt of caffeine to wake him up. The cat yawned widely. Miles grunted in agreement. He put the travel agent's card down on the counter. "Later."

Slowly he made his way back upstairs. His entire body felt heavy, as if he were dragging a ball and chain. Darkness threatened to close in on him with every movement. Dimly he wondered why he felt so much worse now than he had the previous night. Then his stomach rolled in a clear warning. Calling on his last reserves of strength, he reached the bathroom before he was violently sick.

The next time Miles awoke, he was shaking with cold. The room was dark. No light came through his closed blinds. He clenched his teeth and hunched under the thick quilt. A flash of memory drifted through his fevered brain: a little boy, sick like this. Himself in thin pajamas. Crying quietly in the dark, curled in fetal position on a cold concrete floor. Angry voices coming through the ceiling from the rooms upstairs.

He closed his eyes to erase the images. When he awoke again, the sun was shining overhead, and according to his digital watch, it was Wednesday. Vaguely he recalled Sasha speaking to him, touching his shoulder, offering cool water. Had he been dreaming? Where had two days gone? In disbelief and exhaustion he closed his eyes again.

The faint ringing of a phone in the distance penetrated his dreams. Opening his eyes, Miles glanced at the lit numbers on the clock radio on the bedside table. Two twenty-five Thursday morning. He'd fallen asleep again. The black-and-gold cat lay curled against his side. His head no longer throbbed with every pulse, and his stomach had settled, but he felt as if his limbs were floating. He struggled to get up, then decided it wasn't worth the effort. As soon as he moved, the cat started to purr.

He was almost asleep when he heard Sasha close her bedroom door. A stair creaked. A moment later he heard the front door shut, and then the muffled roar of her truck starting in the quiet of night. The thought that she'd been tending him, as well as her patients, sent a wave of guilt washing over him. She must be exhausted. The best way to repay her would be to leave soon.

"M'row?"

"Must be an emergency call."

"M'row," the cat agreed, then yawned widely. Miles yawned, too, then let himself drift back to sleep. This time he felt as if he were sinking into Sasha's embrace, the way he had in the front seat of her truck. This time his dreams left him smiling.

The first thing Sasha noticed at seven in the morning when she tiptoed into the house was the rich aroma of freshly brewed coffee. She peered into the kitchen and found Miles standing at the counter, the morning paper spread in front of him. For a moment she leaned against the doorframe and simply savored the sight of a beautiful male animal in her kitchen.

And even from the back, Miles was a beautiful male animal. Tall, broad shouldered, lean hipped, long legged. His faded jeans rode low on his hips, and his torso was bare except for the shadows of his healing bruises. The muscles of his back, shoulders and arms bunched and flowed into each other as he turned over a page of the newspaper. If he were a horse, she'd definitely recommend him as a stud.

The sudden *clunk* of the toaster startled her. Miles turned and gave her a long, assessing look that made her wonder if he could read her thoughts. Lord, she hoped not!

"Coffee's ready. Want toast or cereal?" he said in that gruff voice that could set up walls between him and the world, or sound so intimate that it gave her shivers. At the moment, with him offering her breakfast, she was fighting shivers and wishing for walls.

"Toast, thanks. How are you feeling?"

"Better. I think a flu hit me. I couldn't wake up."

She nodded. "That's what my doctor thought, too. She said to let you sleep, and let nature take its course."

He gave her a sheepish smile. "Thanks."

"No problem," she told him. There was no way she was going to tell Miles that she'd also been in his room as often as possible, offering him sips of water and clear chicken soup, sponging him off and changing his sweat-soaked bedding around his weakened body. Instead, she said, "I'm a mess. Give me a couple of minutes to clean up."

Sasha hurried upstairs to change into clean jeans and shirt and wash her face and hands. Her shower would have to wait until the end of the workday. There was too much to do and not enough time to do it all, as usual. Still, she looked forward to sitting with Miles before she had to start her rounds.

Thank goodness he was over the flu, although, of course, that meant he'd be leaving soon. Tugging a clean sweatshirt over her head, she reminded herself once again that the best way for Miles to regain his memory was to go home to things that were familiar. She could nurse him through a stomach flu, but she couldn't cure his amnesia. And even if she could, his life was on Secret Island, in Florida, and hers was here, on Lilac Hill Farm, in Ontario. They didn't even live in the same country.

Any fantasies to the contrary would only make her miss him more than she already did—and he hadn't left yet.

She found Miles sitting at the kitchen table, coffee mug in his left hand, frowning at the newspaper open over his untouched toast. A pad and pen sat to the right of his plate, the pad covered with scribbles. On the counter another mug stood beside the coffeemaker, and two slices of bread sat waiting in the toaster. She crossed the room to pour her coffee and push the lever on the toaster. He glanced up when she pulled the chair out opposite him.

She smiled, much too aware that shirtless, from the front, Miles was a disturbing sight this early in the morning. His shoulder muscles flowed into his chest muscles, which were covered with silky dark hairs. His abdomen, as she'd noticed in the hospital, rippled with taut muscles. With the bruises and cuts on his face almost healed, he was ruggedly, breathtakingly handsome. Much too distracting. It was just as well, she told herself firmly, that he was leaving before she got in over her head.

"Thank you for breakfast," she said as she sat, "but you really didn't have to get up so early."

"Yeah, I really did, with that damn cat line dancing on my face." He brought his mug to his lips. She watched his Adam's apple move when he swallowed, watched his tongue slide across his lips. She pictured her own lips touching his lips and tongue, imagined kissing his neck and the hollow of his throat, and felt her pulse race. "Besides, I owe you for taking care of me while I was sick."

So he'd been aware of her! Her face burned as she wondered how much he recalled. It was much less complicated treating horses. Much less . . . intimate. She decided to ignore his reference to his illness. "The cat is Princess," she managed to say reasonably evenly. "She's like the five-hundred-pound gorilla. She sleeps wherever she wants. All the other cats give her plenty of room, although she loves people." The toaster clunked and ejected her toast. She took a plate and carried her breakfast back to the table.

"So I noticed. Once I got used to the purring, it was nice to have company."

Miles spread jam on his toast, then held the jar across the table for her. His gaze met hers and held. She took the jam but had to force her attention back to her own toast. Was it lack of sleep, or was everything from the cat to the jam involved in a conspiracy to make this setup look more intimate than either she or Miles wanted?

"I heard you go out pretty late last night. Emergency?"

She swallowed her bite of toast and, despite her exhaustion, smiled at the memory of the past few hours. "Not exactly. More a case of new-mother panic, except the one in a panic was the owner, not the new mother."

"Everyone okay?"

She beamed. "Everyone splendid, after the owner came out of a dead faint." His eyebrows shot up. She chuckled.

"I haven't lost an owner yet. We have a beautiful filly, and a doting mom."

He smiled. "So what's on your agenda for today?"

"The usual. Barn calls all day." She took a breath, then plunged in. "So. Have you decided when you're leaving?"

Chapter Eight

Sasha held her breath, not wanting to hear his answer, yet knowing it was better to make the break quickly and cleanly, rather than to drag it out. It was right for Miles to go now, when there was nothing more between them than simple physical attraction. Real feelings didn't grow this fast, so what she felt was only infatuation, and that would fade as soon as Miles left and she got back to work. Out of sight and all that. But still, Sasha held her breath, not wanting to hear the words.

"Probably this afternoon, or early evening, depending on what's available. I'll call the travel agent after breakfast."

It was what she had expected to hear, but the words still hit her like a low punch. The breath she'd been holding escaped. "Oh." She got up and carried her dishes to the sink, to prevent him from seeing her sudden distress. "Well, I've got to get to work." Her forced cheer sounded lame.

In the past she'd said goodbye to animals under her care and men she'd dated with the calm acceptance that parting company was in everyone's best interests. But Miles was different from other men. He made *her* feel different. For the first time, letting go was going to hurt, and Sasha didn't know how to pretend otherwise. She braced herself for his farewell.

He crossed the kitchen to stand beside her. She felt acutely aware of his bare torso, the scent of his skin, the heat of his body. His eyes met and held hers, and she knew that if he touched her, her fragile self-control would break.

He cleared his throat. "I'm out of clean shirts. Okay to use your washer and dryer before I go?"

Her nerves were stretched so tightly, Sasha almost giggled at his mundane question. "Of course. They're in the basement, through the door next to the pantry."

Miles glanced behind himself, to the door she'd pointed out, then turned back to her. A strange expression crossed his face.

"Well, I guess this is goodbye," she said, determined not to make a fool of herself. "Good luck, Miles. I'm sorry I couldn't help you more."

His smile didn't quite reach his golden eyes. "You saved my life. What more did you expect to do?" Before she could think of a reply, he reached up and settled his hands on her shoulders. His touch made her skin tingle, right through her clothes. She couldn't remember another man's touch having anything like this wild effect on her nerve endings. Breathlessly, she felt him draw her closer.

Miles looked down into Sasha's eyes and saw himself reflected in those dark mirrors. He wondered if his hunger showed in his own eyes, the way desire showed in hers. It would take very little effort to seduce her now. He knew, without knowing how, that he had used and cast off other women for his own convenience. Some instinct deep within told him that Sasha was different from the other, nameless, faceless women he had known in his murky past. She didn't deserve to be hurt by him.

"I don't think I like long goodbyes." He bent his head until his lips just brushed hers. Her earthy scent stole into his senses like wine, tempting him to deepen that token kiss and drink in her sweetness. "I wish things could be different, but I don't have anything to offer a woman like you."

"I never asked for anything, Miles."

Her dismissal cut like a razor. "You didn't have to." He pressed a kiss to her forehead, then released her before she could feel him trembling like a randy teenager. "Goodbye, Doc."

He got out of the kitchen as quickly as his still-sore knee would let him move. The front door closed even before he was halfway up the stairs. Miles told himself it was the best—the *only*—course of action, but that didn't make it any easier.

Princess raced upstairs ahead of him, tail straight up. She was waiting for him when he reached the bedroom where he'd been sleeping. She watched him gather his meager laundry into a bundle, then raced downstairs again to wait for him in the kitchen. He opened the door Sasha had said led to the basement laundry room. The bare wood-plank stairs disappeared into pitch blackness. Miles stuck his hand into the opening, searching for a light switch.

Without warning, the darkness clutched at him, trying to suck him down into a vortex of swirling, oppressive images and sounds. He swayed, fighting the power that pulled at him. A band tightened around his head, making circles of light and color dance in his eyes. Something closed around his chest, stopping the air he struggled to breathe. Sweat broke out over his face, his body, but he shivered from a cold deep inside.

His knees buckled. He started to fall into the yawning blackness of the basement. Groaning, he caught at the doorframe and crumpled to the floor at the top of the stairs. Nausea threatened as he gripped the pillowcase full of laundry and stared down the stairs into the abyss waiting for him.

"Miles?" Sasha's cry broke into the swirling darkness. "Oh, my God! Miles! What's wrong? Miles? Are you still sick? My God! You could have fallen down the stairs!" He felt Sasha kneel beside him and slip her arm across his shoulders. Her breast pressed against his arm, warm, soft. Her hand gripped his other arm. "Let me help you—"

"No! I can get up myself!"

She eased away, still on the floor but not touching him anymore. "Okay. Fine. What happened?" she asked, her voice less urgent, but he still could hear her tension.

"Nothing."

"Nothing? I find you groaning on the floor at the top of the stairs and you say *nothing* happened? Miles, I'm not stupid. You're in a cold sweat, your pulse is racing and you're shaking like a leaf. You could be having a relapse of the flu. *Please* tell me what happened so I can help you."

If he pretended it was the flu, she'd try to persuade him to stay. If he told her the truth, she would try to wrap him in her pity. "I don't need your help!"

"Fine." She stood. "I just came back to get some insurance forms I need to fill out. Sorry I intruded."

He knew he should reach out and stop her, but she was out the door before he could get to his feet. It was a hell of a way to say goodbye. Cursing his insensitivity, his stubbornness, he forced himself to feel along the inside stairwell wall for the light switch. He found it without having to look down into the black tunnel leading into the basement, and flipped it up. The lights flickered on, bright. No more abyss. No more shadows. Nothing to turn a grown man into a cowering wimp with legs like rubber.

He took a step forward and the stairs seemed to rear up at him. Suddenly he *knew*. He saw it all like a movie in slow motion. Shapes. Faces. No—one particular face. Ugly. Twisted. Mean. He saw the dark reaching for him, heard the screaming. High-pitched screams. *No! Please don't hurt me! Please don't do it!* They couldn't be his screams.

But they were.

Sasha knew it was folly, but she drove home at half past eleven that morning, as bound by compulsion as a moth hovering around a flame. On the flimsy pretext that she had to check on the horses before she picked up Sam's daughter for their weekly lunch date, she parked in the yard. Hands shaking, pulse racing, she sat in the truck for a few minutes, taking calming deep breaths. She wanted to do or say something to make up for that awful scene at the basement door. That was no way to say goodbye, but then, was there any good way to say goodbye? No, seeing Miles again would only be awkward. Mentioning the incident would only embarrass them both. Better not to, she decided. Giving in to cowardice, she climbed down and strode toward the paddocks instead of the house.

Houdini and his buddies were dozing in the spring sunshine that beat down on them. Several of them lifted their heads to gaze at her, but only Houdini approached the fence to greet her. She spent a while scratching around his ears and speaking softly to him before giving him a pat and sending him back to sunbathe. Then she made her way around the back to Desperado's paddock.

The stallion was cropping grass near the fence line when she approached the gate. He snorted and blew before trotting toward her. With his ears forward, he looked eager, alert, unthreatening. It was the first time he had come to her without wearing his ears pinned back in hostility. She smiled at his progress and held out her hand, offering a piece of the crunch she always kept in her pockets.

Her heart pounded, but she kept her hand steady. Desperado sniffed suspiciously at her palm. Then, after several false starts, he reached his head out and delicately lipped the treat off her hand. Her heart soared at the tiny triumph.

"Good boy," she crooned to him. His ears flicked back and forth. "There's more crunch for you if you'll be a good fellow and let me come in. All I want to do is rub your neck and give you another piece of lovely crunch."

She felt his eyes on her shaking hands as she unlocked the gate to his paddock. He must have suddenly realized her intentions, because as she slipped the latch, he snorted, pawed, then lifted his front legs off the ground in restless leaps. Speaking softly, moving in slow motion, she pushed the gate in a few inches at a time, mindful of those potentially lethal hooves dancing in front of her. To her relief, Desperado suddenly stopped his nervous movements and extended his nose toward her. Murmuring praise, she eased a piece of crunch out of her pocket and held it out.

Desperado blew at her hand, then picked the crunch cube off her palm with barely a tickle from his muzzle. Then he lifted his head, pinned his ears and wheeled away. Sasha squeezed out of the gate seconds before he landed an explosive backward kick aimed at her. Adrenaline rushed hot and cold through her veins as she secured the gate with shaking hands. The stallion snorted, then took off bucking across the paddock, sending clods of dirt and grass flying.

"This round is yours," she muttered, "but I'll be back. You *will* learn to accept me."

At the back of the house, Miles frowned as he took the shirt he'd hand washed off the old-fashioned clothesline. Was that a car door? He walked around to the front of the house, but the parking area was as empty as it had been since Sasha drove away. As empty as his memory. As empty as his life.

With an angry grunt he went back into the house to get ready to leave. After washing his shirt in the sink, he'd spent most of the morning talking on the phone to Eleanor. Now he needed to pack his few things into his duffel bag, and erase all traces of his presence. It was the least he could do for Sasha, now that he knew more about the kind of man he really was.

Upstairs, Princess sat on the bed and watched him button his shirt. The fabric smelled like sunshine. Suddenly he saw a woman hanging clothes on an outdoor line very much like the one behind Sasha's house. She was talking to him and crying. What was she saying? Something about having to send him away because she was sick. He could see himself clinging to one of the sheets hanging from the line—how old was he? six? seven?—just breathing in the scent of sunshine and clean fabric and trying not to cry, too.

Ma Danby, the kids called her. She and her husband had been foster parents. Good ones. Miles smiled at the memories that shifted through his brain now, hazy but warm. Good food, clean bedding, laughter and hugs. And then Ma had gotten too sick to take care of any more kids. Miles had been the last to go.

Shaking off the image of himself clinging to his foster mother as a witch of a social worker tried to drag him away, Miles went downstairs for a last cup of coffee. His taxi to the airport was due in an hour.

When he walked into the kitchen he found himself face-to-face with Sam Hunter. The other man stood leaning against the counter, a mug of coffee in one hand. The sense of having his territory invaded was irrational—it was Sasha's home, not his—but Miles felt compelled to stake his own claim. He walked across the room to take a mug out of the cupboard next to Hunter's head. Without a word he poured the last of the coffee into his mug, then crossed to the table and sat down as if he were in his own kitchen.

Hunter took a sip of his coffee, then gave him a slow half smile. "You're pretty comfortable here," he commented dryly.

Miles sipped his own coffee before answering, "So?"

"So, I'm suggesting you don't get any more comfortable. I don't want you taking advantage of Sasha. You look like the kind of man who takes what he wants and doesn't worry about the consequences. I don't want her getting hurt."

"She's capable of making her own decisions."

"She's too generous for her own good. Everyone else comes first with her."

"So you're her self-appointed guardian."

Hunter shrugged, then raised his mug to drink.

"I've got an airport taxi coming in an hour." The relaxation in the other man's stance was subtle, but Miles noticed it. A cold certainty settled in his gut. "You're in love with her."

"Only on my masochistic days." Hunter flashed him a lopsided grin. Miles suspected that Sam Hunter had a lot of masochistic days. He could feel the emptiness the other man covered with quiet humor. "We have too much history, including my wife. Annie was Sasha's best friend."

"What happened?"

"Annie died three years ago. Allergic reaction to a hornet sting. Sasha kept Maggie and me going. She wants me to be her friend, so that's what I am."

"But you don't want her to get involved with anyone else."

Hunter crossed the room, pulled a chair out from the table and sat facing Miles. "Sasha doesn't get involved. There's always guys hanging around her. Like bees to honey. None of them ever shake her out of that serene groove she's in."

The other man's smile was wry. "Sasha is a healer. She can't fall in love with a man who needs to be healed. A man has to be very strong to make a place for himself in her life. He has to have something to give her, equal to what she can give him. A man with no past has no future to give."

"Is that what you say, or what Sasha says?"

Sam shrugged. "She says she won't settle for less than fireworks, and so far she hasn't met a man who can compete with her work."

Miles set down his mug and leaned back in his chair. He knew with sudden certainty that all he had was his work. Without it, he was nothing. The knowledge twisted inside him.

"Work can be a jealous lover."

"And a cold companion." Hunter stood. "Good luck." He extended his hand across the table. Miles clasped it and they shook hands, adversaries who had declared a draw.

"Take care of her," he said as Hunter reached for the back door.

"Easier said than done," Sam reminded him with a grin.

Alone again with his thoughts, Miles finished his coffee, then went upstairs to bring his duffel bag down to the porch. His taxi was due in a half hour.

After dropping Maggie back at her sitter's house, Sasha was grateful that her afternoon rounds were mainly routine. All she wanted to do was slink off alone somewhere like a wounded animal and lick her wounds. The way she and Miles had parted left her feeling ill. She should have understood his pride and his anger, and not pressed him to bare his soul to her. She'd chickened out of her one chance to say goodbye properly. Now he was gone, and she felt as if some vital part of her had gone with him.

As if reflecting her dismal mood, the clouds burst into a steady, heavy rain right after lunch. Shortly before two, as she was giving her full attention to a puncture wound a rambunctious yearling colt had given himself in his chest, her pager beeped. When she finished with the colt, she discovered that it was her own number she was supposed to call. Puzzled, she phoned from the truck. On the third ring, Miles answered and her heart leaped into a wild dance.

"I thought you'd be gone by now," she blurted.

"So did I."

His amused tone grated on her already taut nerves. She was definitely not in the mood for teasing. If he'd changed his mind about leaving, she didn't think she could take saying goodbye again later, when she'd had even more time to fall for him.

"Then why—?"

"Can you pick up some dog food on your way home?" he interrupted.

That made her frown. "Dog food? Miles, I don't have a dog."

"You do now. Someone left it tied to the front porch. It was there when I went out for the airport taxi."

"And you canceled your flight?"

There was a long pause before he answered, "No. I postponed it. The dog was whining, and looked pretty miserable. It's been raining pretty hard."

Sasha sagged against the wall beside the phone. "How big is it?"

"Big. Looks like a golden retriever, but it's dirty and matted. I kept it on the porch. I didn't think you'd want it in the house."

"Thanks. Can you give it some cool water? There are bowls—"

"In the barn. Did that."

She sighed in relief. "I'll stop at the feed store on my way home. I'm sorry you changed your plans for the dog."

"I know. Totally out of character." She wasn't sure, but she thought she heard him chuckle. "You must have brainwashed me. Sasha, I'm no expert on dogs, but this one doesn't look healthy."

"Okay. I can postpone my last appointments and get home early. Page me again if it seems to be in distress."

"No problem."

Sasha disconnected, then phoned her remaining clients to ask them if she could put off her appointments until the next day. With her stomach knotted from worry, she was grateful that all but one client could rearrange their schedules. She made the last call, then drove to the feed store to buy dog chow. The drive home was slower than usual because the rain had made the roads slick.

Finally home, Sasha grabbed the sack of dog food and her medical toolbox and ran through the now-driving rain to the porch. A quick look around revealed no dog, no Miles. Only a greasy, frayed rope tied to one porch column. With her stomach clenched again, Sasha pushed open the front door.

"Miles?"

"We're in the kitchen." His low voice held a trace of amusement. Intrigued, she went inside and stopped short in the doorway, her jaw dropping. Miles looked up from the floor where he sat. Their eyes met, and the smile he gave her warmed away the chill of the rain. "Hi. I think we just became godparents."

The bedraggled golden retriever, which lay on a horse blanket in the corner of the kitchen, looked up at Sasha and gave a doggy grin and a weak wave of a matted tail. Sasha set down her things and crossed the floor to kneel beside Miles. Nestled next to the grungy dog, blindly drawing life from its mother's milk, lay a wet golden puppy.

"Oh, Miles!" she breathed, sinking down onto the floor.

His arm came around her back and she leaned into him. He felt solid and warm against her side, and smelled wonderfully male. Sasha tipped her face up to look into his eyes. He gazed back steadily. Slowly she drew closer to him as he drew closer to meet her. She let her eyes drift closed and savored the first tentative touching of lips.

She heard his breath catch, felt her pulse surge. As if in a trance, she let her lips part under his. Miles took what she offered, so gently that she couldn't help but offer more. When his arm tightened around her, she opened her lips to his hot, wet tongue. One touch. One searing touch, and desire scorched her from deep within. The soft sounds she heard came from her own throat. Sounds of longing. Sounds of need and want.

The high-pitched yelp of the mother dog made Sasha jump. Miles lifted his head, his reluctance clear in his hooded eyes. Sasha drew a deep breath, trying to steady herself. Slowly, but inevitably, she turned her attention to the mother dog.

Two hours later the dog lay panting on her blanket, a totally satisfied, dopey look in her eyes, as six pups finally fell asleep curled against her.

"There was a note with the dog," Miles told Sasha when she came downstairs later. She wore ivory-colored leggings and a cinnamon-colored overblouse that made her look fresh and elegant. For the first time, her long, thick hair hung loose, shiny and soft from washing. Miles's fingers curled with the need to reach out and touch her. He was glad he'd postponed his flight until late the next day. It was heartlessly greedy, but he wanted every second he could get with Sasha.

She moved to the pan where a steak lay marinating in teriyaki sauce. "Oh? Where is it?"

"Right here. When she started to have that first pup, I stuck the note in my pocket so I could get her inside." He unfolded the stiff piece of yellow paper and held it out for her. Sasha read it, then handed it back. Tears glistened in her dark eyes when she looked up at him. "Yeah. The cops need to know about this."

He watched her throat move as she swallowed, wanting to pull her into his arms to comfort her, but she stood just out of reach, as if she needed to deal with this alone.

She nodded. "I have Dave McLeod's card. I'll call him. Can you throw the steak on the grill? The rice will be ready just about when the steak is done. I'll make a salad when I finish calling."

Miles watched Sasha walk out of the kitchen, heading for her office, clearly troubled. He turned the gas up on the indoor grill under the exhaust hood. Then, while the lava rocks heated, he reread the note that had been awkwardly printed in heavy pencil.

Plees keep ar dog Copper. Ar moms boyfrend sais he will kill her becaws she ait his shoos. We beleev him becaws he killd ar boy dog and he hits us wen ar mom is at werk. Dont try to giv copper bak or we will get in trubble.

P.S. She is a good dog.

Something deep inside resonated at the thought of this "boyfriend" hitting children when their mother was working. Something about that scenario stirred uncomfortable feelings. Much as he wanted to know who he was, the growing realization that he'd probably been a battered, bullied child made Miles feel raw and vulnerable. And angry. Deeply angry. How did the real Miles Kent deal with these kinds of emotions? Did he lash out irrationally, the way he felt like doing now? Did he keep everything buried, letting the feelings poison him?

Sasha came back into the kitchen just as Miles was turning the steak. She took a bowl of lettuce from the big refrigerator, then tossed him a fat red tomato. He caught it and started slicing it on the cutting board beside the sink. Sasha tore up half a head of lettuce before she spoke. Miles could feel her tension as if it were his own as she ripped lettuce into a wooden salad bowl.

"Dave will be over in about an hour," she said finally.

He grunted, irrationally irritated at her calling the young cop by name. It shouldn't matter to him what she called the guy, Miles reminded himself. Just this morning he'd flat-out told Sasha that there could be nothing between them. Tomorrow he'd be gone. He had no right to be jealous. Nevertheless, he was.

Sasha lifted the steak onto a grooved carving board and carried it to the table. Then she looked up at him. "How are you feeling? No more flu symptoms?"

"That wasn't the flu this morning," he admitted. He pulled her chair out for her, but she didn't sit down. "I had a flash of a memory that hit me hard." He watched her face for signs of pity, but she only looked interested. Probably because he was leaving, she felt she didn't have to work at healing him.

"Was it something you could make sense of? Something connected to your other memories?"

"Not really. Just random flashes. Too little, too slow. It makes me feel raw, like I've got no skin." The admission spilled out before he actually realized the truth of his words. Then he felt even more vulnerable. He didn't understand why he'd confessed his weakness to Sasha, except to guess that he felt safe, knowing he was leaving tomorrow. After he left, he wouldn't have to deal with her pity when he wanted so much more.

"Things will come back to you, Miles. I suspect it would be worse if you remembered everything all at once. Too overwhelming, especially if there really is something horrible that triggered this—what did Peter call it? Memory deficit?"

He shrugged. "It will be worse if I never remember."

Across the room again, Sasha took two wineglasses from the cupboard and brought them to the table. "I know you think I'm wrong, but if things in your past were so awful, perhaps the best thing to do is start over now."

"That's not what your friend Sam Hunter says."

Sasha sat down and lifted an eyebrow. "Oh? When did you speak to Sam?"

"He came over this afternoon, while you were with Maggie. He wanted to make sure I kept my distance."

She sighed. "I wish Sam would stop playing big brother."

To his surprise, Miles felt compelled to defend Sam. "He cares about you. And he's right. Without a past, there's no future."

"That's a matter of opinion. Some people would give anything to be able to start over with a clean slate," she said softly.

"I'm not some people. Until I get my memory back, I'm not *anyone,* damn it!"

Sasha didn't say a word. With a surgeon's skill she sliced the steak diagonally, then helped herself to several perfectly medium-rare slices. Miles began to feel like an idiot. Sasha passed the salad bowl across to him, her bruised face beautiful in its serenity. By the time she'd given him the bowl of rice, he was squirming with guilt over losing his temper. And feeling guilty, according to Eleanor Dobbs, wasn't something he did on a regular basis. At least, in his business dealings he'd been pretty ruthless and single-minded.

"Thanks for staying with Copper, Miles. I appreciate you changing your plans for her."

He set down the rice bowl and looked into her soft, dark eyes. "Sasha?" He had to clear his throat to speak again. "Some of the things I've remembered about myself... Don't be so grateful. I'm a selfish bastard. I don't do favors for free. Everything has a price, and from what I've learned about myself, I always collect."

Chapter Nine

The questions in Sasha's eyes warned Miles he would have
to explain his last remark. He owed her honesty, but the
truths he'd been learning about himself would turn her
against him. Before he could come up with some delaying
tactic, the doorbell startled a muffled *woof* out of the dog
in the corner. Princess, the cat, flew from the chair where
she'd sat watching the puppies. Sasha got up from the table. "That will be Dave," she said as she hurried out of the
kitchen.

Miles frowned at the sudden stab of jealousy. He didn't
need any kind of memory restoration to tell him that Sasha's
quick dab at her lips with her napkin and the way she
brushed at her hair with her fingers were the things a woman
did when she was interested in a man. Well, that was none
of his business, but *McLeod?* He was too young, too cocky,
too...*here.*

McLeod's laughter made his ears itch. When Sasha led the
guy into the kitchen, they were both chuckling. McLeod

offered his hand to Miles with a long, assessing look that Miles returned.

"I thought you'd be back in Florida."

"I'm not."

He held McLeod's gaze, daring the other man to challenge him. The silence stretched.

"Come see the puppies," Sasha said, as eager as a little girl. "The mother doesn't have an ear tattoo, but these all look like golden retriever pups, so I'm guessing whoever had her was breeding unregistered purebreds." Her tone hardened as she went on. "They sell for a fraction of papered pups, but you have no guarantees about their health or dispositions. A lot of them end up being destroyed, or suffering, because of serious breeding faults."

McLeod squatted beside the makeshift nest, frowning. He put out a hand to let the mother dog sniff. She wagged her tail with much more enthusiasm than Miles thought the guy deserved.

"Well, even if we can't prove this creep killed another dog, there's the charge of beating the kids. The letter might be the wedge we need to get in and lay some other charges that might stick. Looks to me like the tip of an ugly iceberg. Losers like this don't normally limit themselves. We go into a situation like this, something like cruelty to animals, we uncover all kinds of stuff. Drugs. Battering. Illegal weapons. Smuggling. It's like hitting the jackpot."

McLeod stroked the mother dog's head. One of the pups squeaked in its sleep. He grinned. Sasha beamed. Miles felt his mouth draw into a hard, thin line. McLeod got to his feet, towering over Sasha in a way that thoroughly irritated Miles.

Sasha sighed. "How about some coffee and a puppy? Coffee now, puppy in seven weeks." She tipped her head and looked up at the cop in a way that reminded Miles that she was one powerfully attractive woman. Not that he needed reminding. And neither did McLeod, he'd bet.

"Coffee, with sugar, thanks. Hold the puppy," McLeod said with a laugh. "We always had goldens when I was a kid, but I'm not home enough for a dog. I'll check around with the married guys who have families."

"Great. I can keep the mother, and maybe one pup, but not all six." She brought the coffeepot to the table and topped up Miles's mug, then poured a fresh mug for McLeod. Her simple gesture of putting him first lightened Miles's mood irrationally, as if he were a moonstruck adolescent.

"Let's see that note," McLeod said after a swallow of coffee. Miles handed it to him and watched the other man's face as he read. McLeod's expression went from grim to murderous. "I'd like to nail this bastard," he growled. Miles agreed totally with McLeod. "And the mother... How can she leave her kids with a monster who beats them and kills their dog?"

A vision flitted through Miles's brain of a woman smiling gaily, blowing a kiss from the doorway. The door closing. A man coming toward... *him*. An ugly, twisted face coming closer and closer. A hand lifting, then descending....

Miles blinked away the image.

"I'll take this in and start working on it first thing tomorrow," McLeod told Sasha. "The Children's Aid Society will be interested."

"I don't doubt that," she agreed, almost fiercely. "If there's anything else I can do, let me know."

"Yeah, well..." McLeod got up from the table. "Thanks for the coffee, Doc. I'm out of here." He sent Miles a look that said he'd rather stay. Then he put his hand on Sasha's shoulder in a way that looked way too familiar to Miles.

Why did he care? He was leaving tomorrow.

McLeod turned his head toward Sasha and lifted his free hand to cup her chin. Something ugly with sharp claws ripped at Miles's heart. Sasha smiled up at the young cop. Miles clenched his fists at his sides.

"Stay away from that devil, eh?" McLeod released her chin and glanced at Miles, making it clear he wasn't talking about the stallion.

"We're working on a truce," she said with a saucy grin, apparently missing the double meaning. "He let me feed him."

"Be careful he doesn't bite the hand that feeds him," McLeod warned her.

Miles anticipated her answer, but the soft words still hit him too hard. "He already has," Sasha said, meeting his eyes.

Sasha hung up the dish towel and turned to Miles. What was going on in that thick skull? she wondered. He hadn't said a word since Dave had left. The silence that vibrated between them made her edgy. She wasn't used to feeling edgy. She didn't like it.

"I'm going to take Copper outside for a few minutes," she told Miles. "Don't worry if the pups start to cry."

He grunted, which she took for agreement. Copper responded quickly to Sasha's invitation, stopping only briefly at her water bowl. The dog followed her outside and sniffed around while Sasha checked on the horses and made sure all the security lights were working. In the barn she located some plywood that would be suitable for a box to keep the pups from wandering once their eyes opened and their little legs grew stronger. She wished that taking care of the kids who'd left Copper with her could be as simple.

Back in the kitchen, Sasha found Miles sound asleep on the floor beside the puppies' nest. Copper grinned at her, then picked her way past Miles to join her babies. Miles didn't stir. For just a moment, before she had to wake him and send him upstairs to bed, Sasha allowed herself the luxury of simply gazing at him.

The bruises had faded, and sleep had softened the hard lines of his face. His hair fell across his brow, appealingly shaggy and boyish. But she knew how deceptive that was. There was nothing boyish about Miles when he was awake. He was all man. Now that he wasn't scowling at poor Constable McLeod, Miles's mouth looked soft, in a very masculine way. And he knew how to use his mouth very effectively, she recalled with a delicious little shiver.

From out of nowhere Princess flew across the room. She landed with a surprised *meow* on Miles's unprotected belly, then streaked off and away with an indignant yowl. Miles sat up with a muffled bellow, followed by a groan. He glared around the room until he met her eyes. Sasha clapped her hand over her mouth too late to smother her snicker. His glare threatened thermonuclear meltdown.

"I didn't do it! Honest!" she said, then gave in to her laughter. He raked his hand through his tousled hair and sighed. Sasha managed to get herself under control. "I think Princess was trying to tell you it's bedtime. When is your flight tomorrow?"

"I'm not going tomorrow," he told her, his voice sexily rough.

She felt as if the floor had shifted under her, and sank down beside him before her knees gave way. "You're not?"

"No. I want to find out what happens with those kids."

"Oh." She considered that. "Why? I thought you were a selfish bastard."

His grin looked rather wolfish. "I am."

"So you have some ulterior motive for being concerned about the kids?"

"Probably."

She felt herself smiling into his half-closed eyes. "Am I going to find out what that motive is?"

His grin widened. "Possibly."

When he teased like this, he seemed to be a different man. A very likable man. "How enlightening. I can't tell you how glad I am that we're having this conversation." Then she took a chance. "What if it takes a long time to find the kids?"

He caught a strand of her hair in one hand and wound it around his fingers, slowly, gently drawing her closer. She trembled with the effort to resist letting herself sink onto his broad chest. His warmth drew her, the fullness of his lips tempted her. His hand hovered inches above her breast, its phantom caress making her yearn for real contact. Why, she asked the Fates, did she have to feel this way about the wrong man?

"I won't overstay my welcome," he said. "Assuming I am welcome."

"You are," she breathed.

"Aren't you afraid I'll bite again?"

His challenge caught her by surprise. "No. I'm not afraid of being bitten." *I'm afraid it will never happen again,* she wanted to add. But that would be taking too much of a chance.

"You should be." Perhaps he meant the words as a warning, but they sounded like a promise to her. His fingers in her hair drew her a little closer. She felt his breath kiss her cheek and let her eyes drift shut. Her head tipped back, her lips parted.

"Don't you ever listen to your friends' advice?" he murmured, his breath warm in her ear.

"Only when it suits me," she whispered.

He released her and stood so abruptly that she nearly tumbled to the floor. "Go to bed, Sasha," he growled. "Alone."

According to the clock radio, it was 6:02 a.m. Miles stretched and rolled out of bed, feeling rested and ready to go. Fifteen minutes later, showered and shaved, he dressed in his jeans and only clean shirt, which Princess had been using for a mattress. Then he stalled.

He still wasn't sure why he'd decided to stay. The kids? Yes, but that wasn't all. Sasha? Definitely. But why? From clues Eleanor had dropped, he suspected he had seldom done anything truly altruistic in his real life. But here he was caring what happened to a couple of kids he didn't know. And restraining the constant, clawing urge to make love to Sasha, because he didn't want to hurt her when he left.

So which was he, a selfish bastard or a human being? Would the real Miles Kent stand up?

With a hollow laugh, Miles stood. Princess wound herself around his ankles, trilling softly in her throat. When he opened the bedroom door she raced down the stairs, then waited for him and entered the kitchen at his heels.

Sasha stood at the kitchen counter, washing down her usual handful of vitamins with orange juice. She looked the way he'd seen her every day. Faded jeans, T-shirt, thick socks showing over the tops of scuffed work boots, and dark hair in one long, thick braid down her back. Practical. Countrified. Unglamorous. And so appealing that his throat closed with the sudden ache that rose from somewhere deep inside him.

"'Morning," he said quietly, not wanting to startle her. She turned and smiled, but there was an uncertainty in her expression he hadn't seen before. It cut like a knife that he'd done that to her. Even that damn stallion Desperado hadn't destroyed her faith or trust in spite of the bruises he'd given her. "I think we can safely say I'm a morning person."

Her smile widened, chasing the uncertainty out of her dark eyes. "Good morning, then. Coffee's almost ready."

"How are the pups?"

"Have a look. You can pick them up if you want. Copper won't mind. She's so proud of them."

He crouched beside the nest of blankets holding the mother dog and her squirming, squeaking babies. "They look like little pigs."

Sasha laughed. "They are little pigs. Poor Copper is going to need megadoses of vitamins to keep up with them. Go ahead, pick one up. They feel great, all soft and warm."

It wasn't an image of puppies that flashed into his mind at the words *soft* and *warm,* but of Sasha in his arms. Giving himself a mental shake, he slid his hand under the tummy of one of the fat little pups and lifted it gently. The thing squealed as if it were being murdered, but Copper just looked calmly at him and grinned. Sasha was right. The pup was soft and warm, and touchingly dependent the way it rooted blindly against his fingers.

"I wonder how those kids are," he said. "Think the cops can trace them from that note?"

Sasha shook her head. "I don't know. I hope so, and soon. It's heartbreaking to think Copper's pups are getting more love and TLC than they are." With a little catch in her voice, she added, "It's not fair."

"Sometimes life isn't. We have to play the hand we're dealt and hope for luck if we can't get fairness."

Sasha turned from the coffee she was pouring. "Sounds pretty cynical."

He shrugged. "What I've remembered so far doesn't make me believe I'm any kind of optimist."

The pup chose that moment to cry piteously. Carefully he tucked it against his chest and stroked it with his fingertips. To his surprise, he found himself murmuring nonsense sounds in an effort to soothe the little guy. Must be some universal human reaction to babies, to forget your dignity and start cooing. Still, there was something sweet about...

A warm, wet patch spread over his shirtfront. He set the pup down against Copper's side and stood. Gingerly he plucked the wet, now-cooling fabric away from his skin.

"Uh, Sasha? These things aren't wearing diapers."

"No, of course not!" She chuckled. "Their mother takes care of... Oh, no!" She covered her mouth with her hand, but her eyes widened and finally a laugh burst out. "Oh, Miles! Oh, dear!" And she laughed again, not even trying to tone it down.

"It's not that funny," he said, but he couldn't help grinning. "This was my only clean shirt."

"Oh, no! Oh, Miles, I'm sorry. I can lend you a T-shirt."

The thought of having something on his body that Sasha had worn on hers sent blood rushing to his loins. Dumbly, he nodded.

"Come on. And the least I can do is wash your stuff with mine."

He followed her upstairs and stood outside her door until she came out with a large white T-shirt with a horse head on the front. In the bathroom, he tore off his wet shirt and washed his chest, then slid the shirt over his head. It smelled of sunshine and Sasha. Back in the kitchen, he found her still smothering the occasional giggle. There was something warming about sharing a laugh—even at his own expense—with her.

"So what's happening today?" he asked, sitting at the place she'd set for him. His mug stood beside a plate holding a carrot muffin. The first bite melted in his mouth.

"Rounds. It's a light day, so far. If I don't get any emergency calls, I have a long list of odd jobs to tackle."

He watched her pop a bit of muffin into her mouth and chew it. Still faintly bruised, she was so beautiful. Her soft lips were mobile, temptingly mobile. He could still feel the way they'd responded under his kisses. Her throat moved when she swallowed, and he imagined pressing his lips to that tender, vulnerable spot.

"What about you?"

"I was thinking of renting a car. And I was wondering if I could use your computer?"

"Sure."

"Do you have a modem?" She shook her head. "Do you mind if I get one so I can download files from my computers in Florida?"

"No problem. I've got two phone lines. You can use the private one. If you can wait until late morning, I can swing by and pick you up. That should give you enough time to arrange for a car."

He marveled at the way giving came so easily to her. "I owe you." It was an understatement.

She smiled. "Okay. You can help me feed after breakfast. And maybe I can shunt some of my odd jobs off onto you."

"My pleasure," he assured her, but a few minutes later he wasn't so sure.

The barn smelled pretty strong, Miles noticed immediately. It was an earthy, animal kind of smell, not unpleasant exactly, but completely unfamiliar. Some brief flash of memory told him he'd smelled worse at some point in his life. It was like a good-news, bad-news joke. The good news was he might be getting his memory back. The bad news was that when he did, he might want to forget all over again.

Shrugging off the thought, he followed Sasha inside. Her entrance was greeted by all sorts of animal noises, mostly friendly sounds from the horses, and some insistent meowing from the cats that appeared from all over. He watched her moving around the barn with long-legged, athletic grace. God, she was beautiful!

Had he ever known a woman like her? Was she his type of woman? He suspected not, in either case, but who cared! He just wanted to appreciate her. Somehow she managed to look totally feminine in worn jeans, work boots and a sweatshirt the color of the daffodils he'd noticed in the front garden. Feminine, desirable and positively out of his reach, unless he was more of a slime than even he suspected.

"Come on, Miles. Meet the gang," she called. It still startled him to hear her call his name, but every time she did, it felt more familiar. Miles stepped inside, dodging the train of cats following her down the wide, clean concrete aisle. Pretty Polly ran up to greet him. He bent to stroke her. Princess streaked in, swatted at the other cat, then flew out of the barn. Sasha glanced back and smiled broadly. He grinned back.

"I'll give these guys their grain and turn them out when they're done," Sasha called to him. "Desperado is around back in a special paddock. We'll get to him next."

She was already in a small storage room, scooping grains into plastic buckets lined up on a shelf. With an economy of motion that was a pleasure to watch, she added scoops of powders from a variety of containers on another shelf to each of the buckets. Then she piled the buckets into each other and started to lift the tipsy tower.

"Give me those," he said, stepping toward her.

Without a word Sasha lifted half the stack of buckets and passed them to him. He grasped them in his right arm and used his left hand to steady them. It occurred to him that having a flu that forced him to sleep for four days had been a blessing in disguise. He felt strong, and had hardly any aches left.

Sasha led him down the aisle of the barn, tipping a bucket of food into each stall and pausing briefly to speak to each horse. These were her pensioners, her beggars. If anything, they looked worse than their pictures, but by now he knew better than to say that out loud.

When Sasha's buckets were empty, they traded burdens. The last stall had a wooden name plaque hanging from the barred door. A magician's top hat and magic wand decorated the top left corner, above the carved name Houdini. He looked inside and saw a long, sad face looking back. This horse, too, was homelier in person than in his photo, but there was something appealing about him.

Sasha took the empty buckets back to the storage room. Miles watched her check the cat-food feeders and the water bowls, shaking his head at the way the cats swarmed around her. Brazen things. They rubbed against her and patted at her braid. A couple licked her cheek or hand. One climbed up her jeans leg, begging for attention. She snuggled or scratched or stroked each one, crooning in that low, soft voice he remembered from the night he wrecked his car. If it wasn't the most ridiculous thing, he'd think he was jealous of the damn cats.

"Where are those black horses you showed me pictures of?" he asked as she led him toward the back door of the barn.

"They're boarding with a trainer. I don't have the time to finish them, but they're worth too much to sell untrained. I want to make sure they'll go to people who recognize their potential and will show them." She opened the back door and waved him through.

He turned to wait for her to step outside. "They're for sale?"

"To the right buyers." She started walking around the corner of the barn, toward an eight-foot-high fence with a gate. "I barely have the time and energy to care for these old guys. The hunters need hours of training and showing that

I can't give them. I haven't ridden competitively since my undergrad days.''

Sasha stopped at the gate. Miles halted beside her and looked through the wooden bars of the fence.

"I thought you were so proud of those hunters. How can you get rid of them?''

She looked at him, a sadness in her gentle eyes that made him want to take back what he'd just said. "I am proud of them. I want to see them do very well on the hunter show circuit, but I can't do it with them. The worst thing I could do is let them go to waste by keeping them here, doing nothing with their talent. My grandfather bred them to compete with the cream of the crop. The best thing I can do for them is find new owners who will appreciate them.''

"Seems kind of cold-blooded.''

"Sometimes I have to be, to do what's best.''

For some reason he couldn't pin down, her reversal of attitude made him uneasy. He could hear himself espousing that kind of bottom-line talk. Eleanor had told him enough about his business activities to know sentiment had no place in his financial equations. But Sasha was so soft, so compassionate. Until now, he wouldn't have believed she would give up any creature she'd taken in. But she was already looking for new homes for Copper's pups, and buyers for her grandfather's hunters.

The sudden appearance of a black-spotted white horse interrupted his thoughts. Dirt flew from thundering hooves as the horse galloped toward the fence where they stood. If he hadn't known better, Miles would have said this was a fire-breathing dragon. The beast was puffing and blowing and screaming, and his breath hung in the cool morning air like smoke. The ground actually shook with the pounding of the stallion's hooves. Miles stole a quick glance at Sasha. She was watching the raging beast with a rapt look in her dark eyes that made him wonder about her sanity.

"Easy, boy," Sasha crooned. "Here's your breakfast. I'm coming in. You have to come and get it." She unhooked the gate and slowly stepped inside with the last of the feed buckets.

"Are you nuts?" he said between clenched teeth. "Forget the oats, Sasha. He's going to have you for breakfast. If I ever knew first aid, I can't remember, so don't expect me to put you back together."

"Hush. And move a little away from the fence. He doesn't trust men."

"Right. And I don't trust homicidal horses." He stepped back, measuring the distance he'd have to leap to drag Sasha's body out of the enclosure. "Have you looked in a mirror lately?"

"Chill out, Miles. This is just a little macho display. He's hungry. This is the way to his heart."

Sure enough, the beast stopped tearing up the grass and came toward Sasha, still puffing smoke from red-rimmed nostrils. Desperado made raw grunting noises as he walked closer, his neck snaked low toward the bucket. Sasha stood steady, crooning to the big monster. Miles held his breath. The filthy horse stuck his head into the bucket and started eating with the daintiness of a bulldozer. Sasha gripped the bucket, nearly being knocked off her feet by the burrowing of the horse's head.

"See?" she said over her shoulder.

That split second of inattention was all the opportunity the horse needed. The beast moved so fast Miles didn't see what it did. All he saw was Sasha falling backward toward the fence, the bucket flying out of her hands, scattering grain. To his relief, the horse moved away from her and she dropped to a crouch before she hit the boards. Miles measured the distance between himself and Sasha, and decided to drag her out of the enclosure—to hell with the stallion's dislike of men.

Miles squeezed through the open gate, hoping the horse wouldn't notice until he could get Sasha out. Desperado snorted and danced closer to Sasha's crouching form. There wasn't enough space under the lowest fence board for her to roll to safety. The only way out was back through the gate, and the horse knew it. He rolled his eyes at Miles and danced around Sasha. Miles felt as if his heart had lodged in his throat.

And Sasha, damn the woman, was still talking nicey-nice to the crazy creature!

"Back off!" Miles growled, stepping farther through the gate. The horse stopped short and stood stiff legged, staring at him. Miles widened his own stance and glared back. "You ungrateful monster," he added, keeping his voice low but meaningful. "If you twinkle those toes anywhere near that woman, you're going to end up in cans faster than you can say 'pass the gravy.' You got that?"

The stallion snorted, but he didn't move. Miles decided that was agreement and stepped toward Sasha, keeping his eyes on the horse all the while. When he was next to Sasha, he held out his hand to her.

"Come on," he urged, "before Slick here changes his mind."

She grasped his hand. He drew her slowly upright, then eased her behind himself. "Okay, we're out of here."

The instant they squeezed out of the gate Desperado neighed, then charged off across his paddock. He came to a halt, gazed at them, then thrust his head down and started cropping grass. Heart still galloping, Miles turned his attention to Sasha. She was gazing up at him, her dark eyes slightly dazed.

He put his hand on her shoulder, feeling the strength under her trembling. "Don't ever do that again!" he snarled.

With a soft smile in her dark eyes, Sasha tipped her head until her cheek touched the back of his hand. Awareness slashed through him, but he stood still, refusing to give in to the urge to cup her face in his hand and hold her there for his kiss. Instead, he withdrew his hand and turned away from her.

"Thank you, Miles," she said, her low voice a little huskier than usual.

"Hell, one rescue deserves another. Are you okay?"

"Yes. Just a little shaky. And filthy. I better clean up before I head out."

He nodded and walked beside her toward the house, flexing his hand to erase the feel of her silken cheek against his skin. Once inside, Miles paced the living room while Sasha was upstairs. When she came down the stairs in clean jeans and shirt with her wet hair shiny in a neat braid, he had to fight the urge to march her right back upstairs and make love to her until the fear in his belly subsided.

Instead, he said, "I'll drive for you this morning. I told Peter and Sam I'd look after you."

To his amazement, she simply said, "Okay."

For the next couple of hours he watched Sasha deal with her clients and their horses, and wished he was entitled to the pride that welled up inside him. Her ability was obvious, even to him, but there was more to her than that. She treated every client equally well, from the obviously wealthy to the barely scraping by, from the knowledgeable to the ignorant. The horses loved her. Even the ones she wasn't actually treating demanded that she spend a moment patting them.

It didn't take him very long to discover he was intensely jealous of the attention those four-legged beasts were getting. He began imagining her sensitive, gentle hands stroking his body, and her low, soothing voice crooning love words in his ear. He marveled at the elegance of her movements, at the sexiness of her competence. And he came to the conclusion that he wanted more from Sasha than her compassion. If he was going to impose himself on her, he owed it to her to find out the truth about himself. If he had to hire an expert to investigate his own life, he would. Immediately.

Chapter Ten

Sasha dropped Miles in Newmarket at a car rental office, did her banking and made a quick run through the grocery store, then drove home to feed the horses and herself lunch. The knock on her front door came as she was taking cold cuts out of the fridge. In her nest, Copper woofed softly, then waved her tail and grinned her goofy doggy grin. Hands full of sandwich ingredients, Sasha called, "Come in. I'm in the kitchen."

Footsteps came down the wooden hallway, then paused in the kitchen doorway. "You're way too trusting, Doc," Dave McLeod's voice announced. "I could be some lowlife here to steal your drugs, or worse."

Sasha turned and smiled into Dave's unsmiling face. "True, but I doubt you'd knock if that was the case. I'm making lunch. Hungry?"

He grinned. "Always. I wouldn't say yes, except I'm on a break anyway."

"Oh?" She turned back to assembling smoked turkey and lettuce sandwiches.

He crossed the floor and knelt by Copper and her pups. "Yeah. I, uh, happened to be in the neighborhood, and I, uh, thought I'd come by and tell you we don't have anything yet on those kids. But, uh, the Children's Aid Society is on it, too."

"Good. I know you haven't got much to go on, but I can't stop thinking about those kids trying to save Copper's life when they're being treated so badly."

"There's a lot of that going around. Some days I can't find any faith in my fellow man." Dave stood, then crossed to the sink to wash his hands. Sasha passed him a towel on her way to the table with their plates. "Thanks. Then I meet someone like you and figure there's hope for the human race after all."

Sasha laughed. "Why? Because I gave you a towel?"

Dave's face reddened. "No. Because you're about the nicest person I've ever met."

"Well, thank you," she said, smiling and gesturing for him to sit down.

"I mean it, Sasha. I, uh..." He ducked his head and bit into his sandwich. After he'd swallowed, he looked into her eyes. "Sasha, would you go out with me Saturday? I thought we could have dinner, then go to a movie or something?" His face reddened again, even more than before.

Sasha felt her heart sink. She'd really walked wide-eyed into that one, she thought. Poor Dave. He was sweet, but he wasn't the hazel-eyed grouch she was in love with.

"I'm sorry, Dave, but..." But *what?* she thought. She wasn't actually dating Miles. He'd kissed her a couple of times, but he'd hardly declared himself interested. If anything, he'd made it clear that his interest in her couldn't dissuade him from leaving.

The closing of the front door saved her from having to reply. Now all she had to do was stop Dave from drawing the gun his hand rested on as he stood on the alert. In the tense silence Miles appeared, his smile fading as he looked from Sasha to Dave, then down to their half-eaten lunches.

"What is he doing here?" Miles demanded.

"I could say the same thing," Dave replied.

"I live here, which is something you can't say," Miles growled.

"Gentlemen?" Sasha said. They glared at each other and ignored her. "Okay, guys. Listen up." They continued to glare, ignoring her. "Fine. Suit yourselves," she muttered.

Picking up her plate and her can of diet cola, Sasha went outside to the porch. Sitting on the top step, she munched on her sandwich and waited for the showdown in the kitchen to resolve itself. She'd seen too many similar encounters in the animal kingdom to take their rivalry seriously. It was testosterone. That was all. If they didn't have a woman to fight over, men could always find a suitable substitute, like a football or a corner of ground or a flag or the last beer in the fridge.

She was just finishing her cola when she heard Dave's even footsteps behind her. He walked past her and down the stairs.

"Sorry if I put you on the spot," he said when he reached the bottom step. "I didn't realize you guys were, you know. Anyway, thanks for the sandwich. I'll let you know when we find those kids."

"Thanks," she managed to say. What on earth had Miles told Dave about them? Her cheeks burned when she realized Dave hadn't been implying she and Miles were just dating.

The moment Dave's white OPP cruiser slid down the driveway, Sasha got to her feet and marched into the kitchen. Miles, making himself a thick turkey sandwich, looked up, his face a mask of innocence.

"What did you say to Dave?" she asked, trying not to put him on the defensive.

"I told him to find his own woman," he said with equal mildness.

Sasha clenched her hands. Her face flamed. "Excuse me? I don't suppose it occurred to either of you cavemen that I happen to be my *own* woman."

Miles lifted one eyebrow. "Yeah, it occurred to me. That's why I didn't think you'd want a lovesick puppy hanging around."

"I see. And you didn't think I could handle Dave myself?"

Miles set down the knife he was wielding and crossed the floor until he was towering over her. His familiar scowl was back in place, but she was beginning to understand that most—if not all—of his anger was directed at himself.

"That isn't the point."

"What is the point, then?"

"The point is..." Red patches appeared on Miles's cheeks, highlighting the angles of his face. "The point is, *I* don't want him hanging around you."

Her heart leaped. Her pulse raced. She could barely find the breath to ask, "Why?"

He glowered at her. "Because, damn it! That's why."

Somehow she managed to repress her smile. "Oh. Well, that makes perfect sense." Then she did smile. "Now that we've cleared that up, I've got to get back to work." She turned to suit action to words.

"Sasha, wait."

She turned back and gazed up at his handsome, troubled face. The tension of waiting for Miles to admit he might have feelings for her stretched her nerves taut.

"Sasha, I hope you like shrimp."

Her tension suddenly turned the consistency of overcooked spaghetti. "Yes, Miles. I love shrimp."

He nodded. "Good. Because I bought a ton of 'em for dinner."

After that encounter she wasn't surprised to find Desperado willing to let her touch his neck through the fence. Men had no business calling women unpredictable. This silly beast grunted when she scratched at his withers, then groaned in pleasure, without threatening once to inflict further damage on her. His improved attitude pleased and excited her, but she still didn't trust either Miles or Desperado not to hurt her accidentally.

* * *

That afternoon while waiting for Sasha to return from her rounds, Miles found the courier packet of photos, which Eleanor had sent the day he'd left the hospital, in a back corner of his duffel bag. Would the contents trigger any memories? A feeling he didn't want to name, didn't want to give power to, crippled him and sent butterflies rioting in his gut. By the time he made his way down the stairs to the kitchen, he was sweating.

Sasha sat with two puppies in her lap, crooning to them in her low, soothing voice. He hadn't heard her come in, but his pulse surged at the sight of her. Copper lay on her side, the other puppies nursing and wiggling against her, a look of pure adoration for Sasha in the dog's dark eyes. Smart dog. He paused in the doorway, just to watch Sasha. She was like some earth-mother goddess.

She'd make a wonderful mother.

Wife and mother.

For one long, bittersweet moment he let that thought play through his mind, putting himself in the picture. Husband and father. Had he ever wanted a wife and children? Had he ever wanted to be a husband and father?

A swift flash of memory slashed at him. A woman screaming, "I never asked to be your mother!" Was that his mother? Or was seeing Sasha with Copper's pups making him think of those poor kids who'd left the dog?

He knew what he wanted to believe, but he suspected he'd be fooling himself.

Taking a deep breath, Miles walked into the kitchen. Sasha looked up, a sweet, dreamy look in her dark eyes. She raised the two fat pups to her face and nuzzled them, then set them back in their nest with the others. Copper sniffed at them, then lay back and grinned.

"How are you going to let any of them go?" he teased.

She sat at the table and sighed. "I know. It looks like I'll end up with all six plus Copper. But I really will find homes for them all. Except Copper and the runt."

"Why the runt?"

"Because no one else will want it."

He sat opposite her. "Can't say much for your logic. You mean you only adopt creatures no one else wants?"

One shoulder lifted, pulling her T-shirt a little snugger across her breasts. "My primary criterion in adoption. The less desirable the critter, the more welcome it is here."

"Is that why you invited me to stay with you?"

She flashed him a playful smile. "No, actually. You were the exception that proves the rule."

He gave her a smile he hoped didn't look as wolfish as it felt. "Meaning I'm desirable *and* welcome?"

"Let's just say you aren't a runt. Are those your photos? I've never met anyone who lived on a private island. Doesn't it get lonely?"

"I wouldn't know," he said flatly, opening the packet.

"Oh, Miles! I'm so sorry. That was so thoughtless."

He looked up from the first of the envelopes of photos and forced a smile. "Hey, it's okay. Just don't say you forgot I've got amnesia."

Sasha groaned, then chuckled, as he'd hoped she would.

He took out the photos, aware of Sasha's gaze on his face as he looked at the top one. A woman somewhere in her fifties smiled at him self-consciously from a very fancy wheelchair. Silvery hair. Round face. Glasses. A nice-looking person, but no one he knew. The label on the back of the photo said it was Eleanor Dobbs. He passed it to Sasha.

Another photo of Eleanor, this time at a sleek white desk, phone at her ear, waving the photographer away with a laugh. Over her shoulders he saw a desktop computer. What he could see of the desk surface was neatly organized into piles of papers and files. He looked again at his administrative assistant, wishing he could remember her. The last time he'd talked to her, she'd been so optimistic. He hated to have to tell her that her son's efforts had been wasted.

The next few photos had been taken from various angles in the same office. Lots of state-of-the-art equipment, what Eleanor claimed he called "bells and whistles," but nothing that looked familiar. Even the phrase didn't sound familiar.

He passed them all to Sasha. She whistled. "Sharp stuff, Miles. Looks like you're set to communicate with most of the known world."

He shrugged self-consciously. "Apparently I do. The world at my fingertips. A hermit's paradise."

The next photos were from his island. Secret Island, the label on the envelope said. He laid out the photos so he could share them with Sasha. Lush trees and shrubs. White sand beaches. A modern house tucked into the greenery in the center of the island. Several motorboats of different sizes tied at a small dock. An impressive sailboat anchored a little distance away.

"Miles, it's gorgeous!" Sasha gasped. "*This* is paradise."

He met her sparkling eyes and ached for even a shred of memory, something he could offer her, something that would make him worthy of the sweetness she offered. Nothing.

"Paradise or prison," he muttered.

And then he saw the last photo, one that had gotten stuck under the previous one. A shot of sand at the edge of the beach, the sunlight glinting off the wavelet washing up over a pile of seashells. Suddenly he could smell the sea, smell the salt tang of the breeze, feel the heat of the sun on his shoulders. Then he saw himself walking, barefoot in cool sand. The sun coming up over the mainland, blinding him with crimson-and-gold rays. And seashells. Smooth and cool in his fingers.

"Miles, what is it?" Sasha's soft question broke into his vision. "You have such a strange look on your face."

He put the photo in her hand. "I used to get up early every morning and walk the beach while the sun came up. I'd pick up shells sometimes and try to identify them. Look up where they came from. They come from all over the world, washed up on my beach. Some are so scrubbed that you can't see any color, any markings. But some are full of color." He looked into her eyes and smiled. "I think I like the idea that the shellfish carry their homes with them. Wherever they go, they're always home."

"That's such a beautiful thought," she said, making him feel a little foolish, as if he'd suddenly gotten up and spouted sonnets. On the other hand, the look in those doe eyes of hers made the idea of waxing poetic a pretty appealing notion. "It's a nice memory."

He shrugged. "Another piece of the puzzle, but I can't figure out where it fits."

She reached across the table and put her hand on his wrist. Her fingers felt warm, firm, comforting, yet disturbing. "At least you found another piece of the puzzle, Miles. Don't push yourself too hard. Let the pieces pile up and eventually they'll fall into place."

He smiled to cover the fact that he was equally afraid that his memory would return, or that it wouldn't.

Sasha brought a cold bottle of white wine up from the basement refrigerator. When she closed the door behind her, Miles turned from the pot of spiced shrimp he'd been stirring and smiled his approval at the bottle in her hand. It was a perfect opening to ask him again what had driven him to his knees yesterday morning, but she decided not to take it. She knew Miles well enough to know that if he wanted to talk about it, he would bring it up himself.

Besides, she thought as she took two wine flutes from the cupboard, she was always rushing in to offer help to wounded beasts. If Miles was strong enough to deal with his problems by himself, she should respect that. No, she should *welcome* that. Just once, she'd like to have a relationship with someone who didn't need her to be the strong one.

She glanced quickly at him, then, while he was occupied with the stove, she dared a longer look. He wore jeans that hugged his muscular legs and framed his *very* well-shaped glutes. His navy cotton sweater outlined his broad shoulders and, with the sleeves pushed up, revealed tightly corded forearms. Ah, yes, interesting *and* attractive.

"Is it my imagination, or is spring over?" Miles asked, startling her by taking the wine bottle from her hand. She felt her cheeks burn at the possibility that he'd caught her checking out his physique. He sliced off the wrapper at the bottle top and wielded her corkscrew expertly. "It was downright hot this afternoon, but it feels cold again now."

Sasha grinned playfully, relieved that he hadn't noticed her lecherous perusal. "Not your imagination. Welcome to spring in southern Ontario. Variety is the key. Some people think the weather bureau makes their predictions by spinning one of those big carnival wheels. I prefer to ask the horses."

The cork slipped out of the bottle with a soft pop. She held out the glasses. Miles poured, then set the bottle into the Lucite wine cooler.

"You ask the horses? Like, ask Mr. Ed?" His brows rose.

She laughed. "Not exactly. I watch their coats. In spring I don't send my winter jackets to the cleaners or pack away my long johns until the horses start shedding. And when the mustangs start growing their winter coats in August, I order extra firewood. Last year I knew in September that we were going to have a wicked winter, but the weather guys didn't announce it officially until December first."

"So it stays cold until what, June?"

"Not usually. Spring stutters and belches like an old engine, trying to warm up. Some January days can get into the low teens—that's Celsius. Forties in Fahrenheit. This year March was milder than usual, and April has been cold. Did you know that in April of '77, the Blue Jays played their first ever home game in a snowstorm?" She smiled at his incredulous expression.

He shook his head. "I wonder if I ever saw snow before. The image doesn't feel familiar." He met her eyes and shrugged. "Then again, I don't feel familiar, so I guess I wouldn't know," he said, an edge to his voice. She started to say something placating, but he cut her off, saying, "Hey, let's drink to spring and hope Mother Nature takes the hint." He raised his glass toward hers, his hazel eyes now sparkling with good humor.

Sasha smiled and touched her glass to his. "To spring."

The wine tasted crisp and light, but it was the warmth in Miles's answering smile that made her light-headed. To hide her reaction, Sasha lowered her lashes and sipped again.

"I'd say I can't remember ever enjoying a conversation about the weather as much as this one," Miles murmured, "but that line probably wouldn't impress you, since you know I can't remember much."

She coughed on her wine. He flashed her a purely wicked grin. Sasha decided two could play.

"Miles, do me a favor?" She smiled sweetly. "Just for tonight, could you forget you have amnesia?"

His laugh rang out, the first truly lighthearted laugh she'd heard from him. She was so pleased with the success of her little witticism that she didn't notice Miles reaching his free hand toward her until she felt his fingers comb through the hair near her face. Wide-eyed, she looked into his face. He was still smiling, the lines around his mouth and eyes deepening appealingly. If he leaned toward her, she knew she wouldn't be able to resist the temptation to accept his kiss, to kiss him in return.

"I'm glad you let your hair loose tonight," he murmured. "I've been wondering what it would feel like out of that braid." He dropped his hand, but his gaze still held hers.

Breathless, she asked, "Are the shrimp ready?"

"And waiting."

"I'll get the veggies."

Sasha stepped away from Miles. When she set her glass down on the counter, she discovered her hand wasn't quite steady. Taking a deep, steadying breath, she turned and reached into the refrigerator for the platter of cut, raw vegetables she'd prepared before showering. A few feet away Miles was rinsing the cooked shrimp over the sink, whistling softly along with the Bruce Springsteen song playing on the stereo. It struck Sasha that they'd settled into a very easy domesticity, without drawing up contracts or setting down ground rules. None of the men she'd dated had fit so casually, so easily into her life. One more irony, she mused, that Miles was the one man who had the least reason of all of them to share anything with her.

"Hey, Doc? Are you tuned out or is something wrong? I called you three times," Miles said from inches behind her. She started and he caught her shoulders in his big hands. "Sorry. I thought you heard me. Are you okay?"

How could she be *okay* when he was touching her like that, making her aware of his strength and his tenderness, and of the impossibility of this situation? "Uh, yeah. Just daydreaming."

"I was thinking it might be a good night to start a fire," he murmured, still holding her so close to his body that she could feel his heat whispering along her back. "That okay with you?"

He had to be aware of the suggestive, seductive message under that innocent-sounding suggestion. He had to know the reason for her silence was *her* awareness of the other possible meaning for his words. Thank goodness he couldn't read her mind, or he'd discover that she was sorely tempted to throw him to the floor and start that fire right there in the kitchen!

She felt him lift her hair from her neck, felt the tickle of his breath on her skin. Dear Lord, he *had* read her mind! He was going to kiss her neck, and that would be like touching a match to dry kindling. It would be like spontaneous combustion! It would be...the stupidest thing she could do, and absolutely heavenly.

"Sasha? Light that fire," he murmured huskily, a breath away from her neck. "I'll bring in the food and wine. We can have a picnic."

He released her abruptly. By the time she had turned to gape at him, he was across the kitchen, loading plates and cutlery onto a tray. With a shake of her head she walked out of the kitchen and into the living room.

The second that Sasha disappeared into the hallway, Miles let his breath out slowly. He was trying. God knew, he was trying. He was trying to match her casual mood. Trying to keep their relationship strictly friendly. Trying—a little desperately, by now—to recall what his other relationships with women had been like. Dredging through the black hole of his memory for any clue as to how he usually was with a woman who interested him.

Interested him? Hah! A pretty lukewarm phrase to describe how he felt about Sasha. He *wanted* her. Wanted her in his arms, in his bed, in his life. Unfortunately, he was sleeping in a bed that belonged to her, and his life, at the moment, felt as if it belonged to someone else. That left having her in his arms. He'd settle for that, no sweat.

Miles poured the cooled spiced shrimp into a big serving bowl. Princess leaped onto a chair to watch. She responded to his stern warning look with a wink and a swipe of her chops with her tongue. Feeling more than a little foolish, he broke off a piece of shrimp and offered it to her, enjoying her enthusiastic purring.

"The fire's going," Sasha said from the doorway. When he met her eyes, she smiled. "No mystery why she's named Princess."

He smiled back, drinking in the beauty of the woman across the room. Even in jeans and a big, soft sweater the color of honey, she made him ache. Had he ever felt like this about another woman? He wanted to be able to say she was *the most, the best,* but he had no memories of other women to compare her to. For him she was *the only.* It scared the daylights out of him and made him feel exhilarated at the same time. Like driving too fast around a blind corner.

"We better eat before there's nothing left for us," he answered, amazed that his voice worked at all.

Sasha had pulled two huge cushions onto the floor in front of the hearth. The fire was starting to catch at the logs in the grate. Together they set the food platters down. Sasha sank onto her cushion gracefully. He grunted when his knee protested, then found a comfortable position. Sasha picked up a carrot stick and bit into it. He watched the way her lips closed on the vegetable and felt the blood rush to his loins. Oh, man, was he in trouble!

"Do you have plans for tomorrow?" she asked, reaching for a shrimp.

"I need to hook up with Eleanor's computer and download as many files as I can, but the computers can do a lot of that without me. Why?" He popped a shrimp into his mouth.

"Pony Club starts at ten."

"Is that an invitation or a warning?"

"Take your pick."

"Okay. I'll call it an invitation. I can probably work in some of those odd jobs around the place while you're doing whatever you do with the kids."

She nodded, then washed her shrimp down with a sip of wine. The silence stretched between them for a while, until she said, "Have you remembered anything else that might help you figure out why you were driving up here?"

"Not specifically." He didn't want to talk about the flashes of nightmares that had turned him into cowardly mush at the basement door.

"What I find interesting is the way you can simply do some things, like work with your computer or drive, or talk about baseball stats. But you can't remember facts about yourself."

"Yeah. It's weird. I sat down at your computer and knew exactly what to do. Same with the car. But the only reason I know my name is Miles Kent is that I've got a photo ID and the cops say my fingerprints match. But I don't really *know* that's who I am. When someone says 'Miles,' I know they mean me, but I don't *feel* like that's who I am."

He shrugged, uncomfortable with having revealed so much of his confusion. Sasha was watching him with such understanding in her soft eyes that he found himself asking, "Does that make sense?"

"Yes, it does. Peter said he believes whatever your mind wants to forget probably doesn't have anything to do with computers or baseball."

He grinned. "How could anything about baseball be bad enough to forget?"

She snorted. "Bless that Y chromosome! What would you guys do without it?"

"Sing soprano?"

Her laugh started as a low chuckle, then rose to a peal of musical giggles. He savored the luxury of simply watching her sparkling dark eyes and her soft, expressive mouth. When her laughter faded she shook her head and reached for another shrimp.

The Springsteen CD ended, and a Bonnie Raitt one started. Sasha's eyes reflected the change in mood, looking softer, the last traces of her laughter gone. She met his eyes, held his gaze for a long moment, then looked away. No wariness, but no invitation, either. What was she thinking? That he was an interesting puzzle, as Peter Simmons considered him? A special rescue project, as Sam suspected she felt? Or a man who had nothing to offer yet selfishly wanted her anyway, which he knew was the closest to the truth.

"Miles?" She spoke without looking at him.

"Hmm?"

"I wish you'd talk to me about what happened at the basement door. It scared me, because I realized I couldn't do anything."

"You don't have to do anything, Sasha," he told her gruffly. "I don't want anyone doing things for me."

"Why?" She turned her dark eyes on him, as if trying to see into his thoughts.

"I'm not your problem to solve."

"No, you aren't." The touch of her fingers on the back of his hand zinged through his nerves like a shock. "You aren't a problem. You're a friend. Someone I like and care about. Someone who *has* a problem I'd like to help solve, except I don't know how. I don't know what you need."

He turned his hand over to capture her fingers. To his relief, she didn't pull away. "Do you really want to know what I need?" he asked softly. Her slender throat moved, then she nodded. "I need to hold you and kiss you." He circled his thumb over the soft skin of her hand. "I need to hear you whisper my name in the dark. I need to make love to you."

Chapter Eleven

"Oh," she said, her voice a husky whisper.

Sasha's tongue slid along her lips. Miles gave in to the instinct to mirror her action, and smiled inwardly when her eyes darkened.

Using her free hand, Sasha raised her wineglass to her lips. Miles watched the delicate bones of her throat move as she sipped and swallowed. As she lowered the glass, he took it and set it out of the way, then pressed his thumb gently into the yielding flesh between her thumb and forefinger. Sasha's smile wavered. Miles heard her breath catch. His heart hammered, but his head was sounding a warning he knew he had to listen to.

"But I'm not sure that's the best thing for either of us right now." He released her hand. "That last shrimp is yours."

She drew a shaky-sounding breath, then let it out on a soft sigh. "Split it."

Her long, slender fingers broke the shrimp in half. After popping one piece into her own mouth, she held out the other piece to him. Miles looked at the delicate morsel in her slender fingers and, leaning toward her, captured the piece of shrimp with his mouth, lingering a second longer than necessary to savor the feel of her fingers against his lips.

"Miles," she whispered. The ragged sound snagged at his breath. He waited for her to speak again, to pull her fingers away. She didn't move.

Firelight flickered on her ivory skin, gilding it, casting shadows that couldn't hide the way her eyes darkened. He moved slowly toward her, hardly daring to breathe. The subtle flowery musk of her skin mingled with the scent of the fire. He paused, giving her a chance to decide. Her eyes widened, then drifted shut, long lashes casting shadows on her pale skin.

Trembling, he closed the distance between them. Her lips accepted his. In some way he couldn't explain and didn't understand in words, Sasha had a key role in helping him reclaim his lost memory, his alienated self. He didn't dare risk losing her by taking her now, when everything between them was so tentative.

"Sasha?" he whispered against her lips.

She made a soft sound. Her lips touched his, sending his pulse into overdrive. For the moment, needs overcame caution. Miles pressed closer, seeking and offering. Sasha's lips parted under his. She tasted of wine and spice and a sweetness of her own. Her mouth was warm, smooth, moist. When Miles slid his tongue over the inside of her lower lip, Sasha caught her breath. When the tip of her tongue met his, Miles caught his breath.

He was hard and aching with need, yet they'd only kissed twice. Their hands were still braced on the floor. Now Sasha increased the pressure of her mouth on his, offering him a glimpse of her response. Miles closed his eyes and gave himself up to the sensual torture of sweet kisses. His tongue slid deeper, filling his senses with the taste of her. She drew him into her mouth with a sweet boldness that sent lightning bolts to his groin.

Miles felt as if he'd never kissed a woman, but he didn't doubt he knew how. Was he always so quick to arouse? Or was it just Sasha who made him hunger like this? Part of him raged that it didn't matter what he was like before, but part of him argued that he needed to know what he was offering this special woman.

Sasha's fingertips touched his jaw, as light as a butterfly's wings. Miles groaned and reached for her. His hand found her hip, and he felt a jolt run through her. It was enough to shake some sense into his hormone-fogged brain. Reluctantly he took his hand off her hip, yet the heat of that brief contact tingled on his palm.

"Too much, too soon," Miles murmured. "I don't want either of us to hate me in the morning."

He moved back enough to look into her eyes. For a moment he saw the regret in their dark depths. Then he saw an entirely different face, a face in his mind. A blonde, with turquoise eyes. A model-perfect, beautiful face spoiled by rage. *I hate you, Miles Kent! I hate you because you let me love you and you can't love anyone!* she was saying, this face without a name. A memory. A memory merging with the present.

"What is it, Miles? Did you just remember something?"

Either he was as transparent as water, or she was incredibly perceptive. "Yeah, but not enough to talk about."

"I'm here whenever you want to talk, Miles. All I want to do is help you to help yourself."

He nodded at her words. "I'm going outside for a while. I'll throw the horses their last hay."

Liar! Sasha accused herself as she gathered the remains of their firelight picnic. What simpering nonsense! *I want to help you help yourself.* She wanted to throw caution and logic and good sense out the window, and give herself up to the raging need she'd seen in Miles's eyes. She could still taste the primal hunger of his kisses, restrained as they were. No other man had wanted her like that, or had made her want him like that.

The man must have a will of iron, and some powerful reasons for stopping. If he hadn't, he wouldn't be in the barn and she wouldn't be on her way to the kitchen. They'd be naked in front of that fire, making love on the floor.

The next morning, by the time Sasha had finished her early chores, Miles had made coffee and was sitting in front of the computer, looking as if his mind were a million miles away. She gulped her breakfast, then went outside to work with Desperado. Unlike yesterday, he refused to come near her. Then Houdini and one of the mustangs got into a dustup and took down a fence board. Muttering about their childish behavior, Sasha stomped into the workshop to get a hammer and nails. Then she stomped out to the paddock to repair the fence before Donna and Marie and the Pony Club kids arrived.

She had intended to call Miles from his work herself, but Donna climbed out of her car, with four kids bounding after her, saying, "I hope it's okay for the kids to see the puppies." A moment later the six of them, followed almost immediately by Marie and four more youngsters, were trooping into the house. They made more noise shushing each other than they made talking.

Miles appeared in the kitchen doorway. Sasha looked up from handing one of the pups to Caitlin Dunne and felt her heart leap at the sight of him. He looked a little rumpled, as if he'd been running his fingers through his hair, and a little dazed at the activity in the corner of the kitchen. She smiled at him, then felt Marie tugging on her shirt. Donna quietly cleared her throat. Sasha grinned at her friends' not-so-subtle hints.

After introducing everyone and promising a contest to name the puppies, Sasha shooed the kids outside.

"Do you still want to join us?" she asked Miles. "It could be pretty chaotic for a man who lives like a hermit."

He grinned sheepishly. "I think I can stand it for a couple of hours. If not, Desperado and I can cut out and go fishing."

He followed her outside and placed himself behind the little group of kids. During her talk about leg bandages and protective boots, she was conscious of Miles's eyes on her and of Donna and Marie casting surreptitious glances between them. It was a miracle she could concentrate at all. Finally she and her friends sent the kids to bring out the horses and practice some of their new grooming skills.

Sometime later, Sasha looked up from supervising the small hands carefully wrapping the scarred lower leg of one of the aging mustangs. Where was Miles? she wondered. A few minutes ago he'd been patiently helping Caitlin balance on a stool while she practiced braiding Houdini's unruly mane. Now she couldn't see those strong legs braced behind the girl.

"Higher, Mr. Miles," a little voice commanded. "I can't reach my brush up to his poll."

Sasha hid a smile. That was Ashley Reilly. Small for her seven years, she always had trouble grooming much above any horse's shoulders. She was one of those girls born with all her feminine wiles already highly developed. Fortunately, she had also been born with a stubborn streak and a large dose of perfectionism. Ashley wheedled help, but she never allowed anyone to do her work for her.

"Better now?" Miles asked, and Sasha could hear the suppressed smile in his low voice.

"Much, thank you. I'm not supposed to leave any dust up here between his ears. He really likes the way the brush feels. See?"

Sasha peeked just in time to see Drummer Boy nod in pleasure at the grooming he was getting, then butt his bony head square into Miles's chest. His breath came out in a *whoosh*. Sasha cringed in sympathy for his healing ribs. Then the old gelding snorted, covering Miles's shirt with moisture. Ashley's giggles rang through the yard. Sasha bit her lip to hide a smile, then approached the trio.

"You okay?" she asked Miles. "There's a stepladder Ashley usually uses, if you need to set her down."

Donna and Marie, making no pretense of not watching, started to laugh.

"I've been had, huh?" A sexy half grin curved his beautiful mouth. His eyes sparkled like sunshine.

"Looks like it," she agreed. "Also looks like you have a way with kids."

He gave her a long, searching look.

"Houdini! You come back here, you big dummy! We aren't finished!" Caitlin Dunne's voice shrilled, startling Sasha.

She turned to see Houdini, who had probably gotten bored, walking nonchalantly across the yard with Thomas Wilton hanging on to the tail he'd been learning to braid.

Miles snickered. "Looks like the old boy lives up to his name."

Sasha dashed off to catch the escaping horse. Eventually everyone completed their lessons and had their efforts checked by Sasha, Marie or Donna. Then the horses were returned to their stalls, and the kids clamored to see the puppies again. This time, Miles stationed himself beside Copper's nest and sternly hushed the rowdiest of the group. One by one, he let them sit beside him and hold a puppy—on a towel.

Miles caught Sasha's eye over the head of one of the children. The thought that this was like a family—*their* family—struck Sasha like lightning. Quickly, so that Miles couldn't see sudden longing in her eyes, she turned away.

The phone rang. Still shaken by her insight, Sasha climbed over humans and dogs to answer it.

"You up for a friendly game of poker tonight?" Sam's voice asked by way of greeting.

She smiled. "Could be. Let me ask the assembled multitude."

"I was afraid of that."

"Too bad. Hang on a sec." She put her hand over the phone and relayed Sam's invitation to Miles, Donna and Marie. Miles gave her a slow nod. Donna and Marie called out that they were also interested. She told Sam, then asked, "What time?"

"Eight. Bring food." The dial tone followed.

Herding the kids outside, Donna and Marie told Sasha they'd meet her at Sam's with suitable snack food. Miles stood beside her on the porch as the two cars drove out of the yard.

"Nice kids," he said quietly. "Lucky, too. I don't think the kids who brought Copper here are in anything like the Pony Club."

"No, I doubt they are. I wish they'd come back to see her, so we could find out who they are, and do something. They could be placed in a foster home and—"

"That doesn't always work," he interrupted. "Not all foster homes are like your parents'."

His bitterness sounded personal. She looked up at him, trying to read the thoughts in his golden eyes. "Did you remember something while you were working with the kids?"

"Maybe," he said. "I don't know for sure yet." He turned away, then met her eyes again. "I hired an investigator."

"To look into your background?" He nodded. "I think that's a brilliant idea. Has he found anything yet?"

"No. I just brought him on-line."

Even though the spring sunshine was quite warm, Sasha felt a chill. She wanted the best for him, and that was the full recovery of his memory. But she couldn't help the selfish little feeling that once Miles regained his memory or learned the reason he'd driven from Florida to Canada, he'd leave.

"Whatever he finds out," Miles said, as if reading her mind, "whatever I remember, I'm not leaving until we find those kids and make sure they're safe."

At eight that evening Miles parked his rental car in front of Sam's house. The lights from another car followed them. From the rearview mirror he recognized Donna and Marie in Donna's Jeep. Aware of Sasha's gaze, he gave her a quick smile. She didn't smile back. *Now what?* he thought.

"Are you sure you want to do this?" she asked.

"Is there a reason I shouldn't?"

"Sam hasn't exactly been your good buddy. I don't want you to feel uncomfortable for my sake."

"Since the accident I'm not exactly comfortable anywhere, Sasha, so it might as well be for your sake as anything else." Behind them, the Jeep doors shut. "Let's go."

Donna and Marie caught up with them. Miles liked Sasha's friends. They were down-to-earth, like her. After an afternoon sleuthing through his computerized address book, he knew that none of the high-profile, fast-track women he'd dated could ever be described as remotely down-to-earth. Now he couldn't imagine why he had collected fashion models, actresses, recording artists. His tastes had apparently changed, for the better. Too bad he was the same S.O.B. who had "liked them and left them."

Miles let the three women get ahead of him while he took in first impressions of Sam's place. The house was wood shingled, but the design was similar to Sasha's, right up to the wide front porch. There was a barn, but no sign—or smell—of horses. A swing set, a wagon and some other things he couldn't make out in the falling darkness stood in the yard to one side of the house. On the other side there was a wooden doghouse painted the same white and green as the house. Standing braced for action was a dog that looked a lot like a grizzly bear.

"Hi, Mo-Jo," Sasha said. The on-guard stance suddenly became puppylike wiggles as the dog rushed to greet her. "That's my boy, isn't it? Who's the best boy?" she crooned, bending to cuddle the beast. Then she turned back and smiled, making his breath catch. "This is Mo-Jo. He's an Akita. Very fierce guard dog."

"So I see," he said, stopping to let Mo-Jo sniff his hand.

"Well, he's off duty now, but he was bred to fight bears, so he's one tough baby-sitter, aren't you?"

The front door opened and Sam's daughter, Maggie, flew off the porch and into Sasha's arms. The dog wagged his tail so hard that the rest of him wagged with it. Miles found himself watching and grinning.

"Aunt Sasha! I can ride my new bike all by myself. Daddy took the training wheels off!"

Something inside Miles seemed to swell, to shift, at the way the little girl said *daddy*. He pushed it aside.

After a big hug and lots of giggles, Maggie stepped back to peer up at him. Then she looked at Sasha, a frown puckering her little face. "Daddy says Mr. Miles lives with you now. Does that mean he's my uncle?"

Miles felt his jaw start to drop. Ahead of them, Donna and Marie were watching. Sasha looked at him, her smile turning a little stunned. Miles thought fast. He bent and offered his hand to Maggie, who put her tiny hand into it, and looked up at him with wide, dark eyes.

"Miss Maggie, I'm Aunt Sasha's friend, not your uncle," he told her very seriously, "but if you'd like to call me Uncle Miles, I'd be honored."

Maggie frowned, smiled and nodded. "Okay." She took her hand from his and said, "Are you here to drop a bundle?"

Ignoring Sasha's muffled snicker, Miles brushed his fingertips over the top of Maggie's sleek head and grinned down at her. "I'm going to try not to."

"It's okay if you do. We only play for nickels and dimes, and the pot goes to the horses, anyhow. Hurry up! Daddy made popcorn and he said I could stay up to have some." And suddenly she was racing up the stairs, dashing through the front door and yelling to Sam that everyone was there.

Sasha paused on the bottom step. When Miles caught up with her, she smiled. "She's like a puppy when she's excited."

Miles grinned back. "Cute kid," he said, but what he was really thinking was how lucky Sam was to have her. The unexpected thought stunned him.

The door swung open again and Sam scowled at them. "Come on, you two. You're holding up the game." The other man's obvious disapproval fueled Miles's annoyance.

Deliberately he took Sasha's hand in his and led her up the stairs. At the door he stopped and let Sasha pass through first, making sure Sam saw his finger brush her shoulder as she passed.

Sam's living room was full of contradictions. Some of his furniture looked like the contents of a yard sale, but the cabinets and side tables were beautiful examples of woodworking by a master craftsman. Chips and popcorn had been set out in old-fashioned-looking crockery bowls, but the stereo system in the oak wall unit was state-of-the-art.

Peter came out of his chair to shake his hand, his eyes assessing behind his glasses. He introduced his wife, Marla, a small, warm-eyed woman Miles liked on sight. Sam introduced Ray, a carpenter and also a Native Canadian Miles figured to be in his early to mid-thirties. Ray shook Miles's hand with guarded friendliness, making Miles wonder what Sam might have said about him and Sasha.

"Hey, Miles?" Sam said. "You remember how to play poker?"

Sasha started to sputter at him, but Miles only grinned. "We'll see, won't we?"

"Did Sasha tell you where the pot goes?" Marla asked him, her sweet voice cutting through the chuckling and teasing of the others. He shook his head. Marla smiled. "It goes to help Sasha's old pensioners, because she won't accept a direct offer from us."

He looked at Sasha. She shrugged, but her cheeks turned pink.

"Okay. Let's get started," Sam ordered. "We can draw cards to split into two tables."

To Miles's relief, he and Sasha drew the same table, but so did Sam and Peter, which made Miles wonder if Sam was a creative card shuffler. They played a few hands, and Miles watched carefully, feeling suddenly and totally at home with the cards in his hand. The mood stayed tense until Peter won on a terrific bluff. Then even Sam lightened up and raised his next bet with a cocky grin. Peter and Sasha saw and raised his bet. Miles studied his cards, then looked down at his depleted store of coins. He slid the correct amount into the pile in the middle of the table, then glanced at the faces opposite him. As he'd suspected, the other three looked as if they felt pretty sorry for his bad luck and lack of skill.

Sasha drew two cards, but the face she made gave away her poor hand. Peter folded with a groan of disgust. Sam snapped his cards one at a time down on the table, then stood and reached for the coins piled in the middle.

"Hold it," Miles told him. Sasha looked at him, her eyes wide. He smiled at her, then fanned his cards. Ace. King. Queen. Jack. Ten.

The muscle in Sam's jaw clenched, but he sat down. The battle line had been drawn a little closer, Miles thought, but the stakes were more than a few coins. This was about Sasha, and Miles intended to win.

He did. Often enough that Sasha finally laughed and threw down her cards. "We've been had! We've got a shark in our pool!"

Peter snorted and threw his cards down, too. "Hell, Kent's been losing on purpose, sizing us up. Good thing none of us bet the family farm."

Miles heard the laughter from both tables, but suddenly he was seeing another poker game, at another time and place. Another piece of the puzzle fell into place.

He felt Sasha touch his arm. She was leaning so close that the scent of her perfume chased away the remembered stink of stale cigarettes and spilled beer. "Miles, what is it? Are you all right? You look as if you've seen a ghost."

"In a way. I just remembered how I started."

"Started what?"

"In business. I was about twenty-two, flat broke. I won a guy's business in a poker game." He felt everyone's eyes on him now, but it was Sasha's stricken look that troubled him more than being the object of their curiosity.

"You won a man's business in a poker game? And you *kept* it?"

He heard the censure in her voice and nodded. "Yeah. He was a lousy player, but he couldn't stay away from the game.

It was one of those copy shops. He'd run out of cash and it was all he had left that was worth anything. The other guys in the game refused to let him put up his wife and kids as collateral."

"Oh, my God!" Sasha gasped. Her face had gone white. He wondered if he should do something for her.

"How could you take his business when he had a wife and kids depending on him?" Sam demanded.

Miles smiled grimly. It was coming back faster now. "Easy. His wife and kids were two steps away from starving, so I hired her. Neither of us had any business experience, but we got the business going again. She divorced him, and I sold out to her and her new husband." He looked at Sasha. The color was back in her face, but her eyes were still wide. "I guess I got a kick out of saving a sinking ship."

"Fascinating," Peter murmured, staring at him. "The way such a casual comment can trigger the retrieval of a memory of profound significance." He leaned over the table. "Did it all come back in a rush, or bit by bit, almost as you were telling us? Was it a verbal memory, or visual? Could you see yourself playing poker with this fellow, then see yourself working in the shop?"

"Peter! For pity's sake!" Sasha scolded.

Under cover of the table, Miles touched her thigh. He heard her breath catch, felt the warm, firm muscle under his fingers tighten. "It's okay, Sasha." He turned to Peter. "I got a sudden picture of the guy looking at his cards and offering his copy shop instead of cash. The rest came back like frames of a movie played too slow. Images I suddenly understood as I saw each one."

"I still think the best place to get your memory back is your own home," Sam muttered. "Coffee's on in the kitchen. Help yourselves."

Sasha felt the sudden tension in Miles's touch on her leg. She wanted to kick Sam, but he'd already gotten up, out of range. Miles probably wouldn't appreciate another one of her impassioned defenses, anyway, she thought. All she could do was offer her support, silently, through her presence. With his hand on her thigh, sending a tingling awareness along her nerve ends, that seemed to be enough.

Everyone else got up and filed into Sam's kitchen, but Sasha needed another moment to assimilate what had just happened. She wanted to apologize for her brief loss of faith in him, but the longer he kept his hand on her thigh, the harder it was for her to think coherently. As if reading her mind, he took his hand away, and Sasha felt a chill replace his touch.

How had she ever thought she could heal this man without getting her feelings any more involved than if he were a horse? She'd always been strong enough to let go before, but she'd never cared so deeply before, about a creature or a man. Would she have enough strength left over for herself when Miles finally left?

She would have to, she promised herself, but it felt like a very hollow promise.

In the morning Miles found Sasha in the kitchen, bending over the open freezer. He stood in the doorway, silently admiring the way her faded jeans molded to her trim little bottom. Then Copper trotted over to sit at his feet, giving him away. He scratched the grinning dog's ears.

Sasha turned to face him, her smile bright, almost too bright. He'd bet anything that something was bothering her. But what? The evening at Sam's had ended peacefully enough, and she'd seemed genuinely pleased that he'd remembered something important about himself. And when he'd kissed her lightly, standing on the upstairs landing, she had kissed him back sweetly, without any reserve. So now what?

"I'm just making coffee before feeding the critters," she told him. "I hope I didn't wake you."

"Nah. Princess got the jump on you." He grinned and stepped into the room, Copper at his side. "Got the jump on me, too. Literally." Sasha laughed softly and shook her head. "That's okay. She's good company."

"You might want to consider getting a couple of cats when you go home." She reached into the cupboard for mugs. "Or a golden puppy?"

A little of the morning's brightness faded as her words sank in. He'd been thinking hard about *being* at the place he called home, but he hadn't been thinking about actually *going* home. Clearly, Sasha expected him to leave, regardless of his vow to make sure Copper's kids were safe. Hell, he probably should go, before he did something unforgivably stupid and selfish, like seducing her. He decided to push the whole subject out of his mind for now.

"How are the pups doing?"

"They're doing great," she said, wiping her hands on the hips of her jeans. "Which I doubt we can say about the poor kids who left her. They must be good kids at heart. Look at what they went through to save their dog. But violence is learned. How are they going to grow up still being good, with this creep killing animals and beating them and their mother?"

A chill settled in his heart at her passionate words. He knew she was right. The faster those kids were found and taken away from their mother, the better. But other kids weren't that lucky. How did they grow up to be good people? Or did they? Knowing more about himself every day, but still not enough, he wasn't so sure how to define good anymore.

"The kids may get themselves rescued, now that they've taken care of Copper. They seemed pretty resourceful and gutsy," Miles said, hoping to reassure her. And himself.

Sasha nodded. "I sure hope so." She handed him a glass of orange juice. "Miles, do you have any idea if you know how to use tools?"

The change of subject caught him by surprise. He swallowed his mouthful of juice. "Like what?"

"Hammer? Drill? Screwdriver? Pliers? Tractor?"

"I don't know."

"Want to find out after breakfast?"

He'd do anything to see that teasing light in her eyes more often. "Sure."

An hour later, after they'd fed the horses and themselves, Miles followed Sasha back outside to the barn. Opposite the row of stalls for the old horses, two stalls had been combined into one well-equipped workshop. He looked around at the hand and power tools, at the battered but sturdy workbench with the vise mounted on one end, at the sawhorses in a corner, at the extra lighting hanging from the rafters, and whistled.

"Most of the older tools belonged to my grandfather," Sasha said. She picked up a chisel, then replaced it on the Peg-Board rack. "Sam drops by from time to time with some new gadget he thinks I need, but really, it's so he doesn't have to lug all his stuff from home whenever he comes by to fix something." She smiled. "So, does any of this look familiar?"

He reached for the pistol grip of a power drill. The instant his fingers wrapped around it, he saw himself using it, long ago and far away. He could hear the whine of a power saw. Smell wood freshly cut. Feel the way the wood yielded to a nail pounded in just right. He grinned.

"I worked construction a few summers," he told her, marveling at the way his memory could simply slip back into place like that, or elude him like a mosquito at night. "I also worked with the crew, on the house on Secret Island."

"I thought you knew how to work with your hands," she murmured.

He held his hands out in front of him, studying their familiar, yet oddly unfamiliar, shape and surfaces. "Why'd you think that?"

"Your hands are very strong, a little rough for someone who works at a desk or does meetings, and very competent looking." Her eyes met his boldly, but her cheeks turned bright. He felt his own cheeks heat up at her unexpected compliment. And at the realization that she'd been thinking about his hands.

"So," he began, then had to clear his throat. "What needs work?"

"There's the list, on the white board behind you. Take your pick." He turned and studied the neat lines of script covering the message board. Only the top three items had been checked off. He looked back at Sasha to find her frowning. "Don't feel you have to do it all. Some of them have been waiting long enough that I can almost get along without taking care of them."

Feeling equal to the tasks of Hercules, Miles grinned. "Good thing I'll be around for a while."

Chapter Twelve

Sasha turned away before Miles could see the hope she suspected must show in her eyes like a neon sign. There was no point in fooling herself. She knew his primary reason for staying was to make sure Copper's kids were going to be all right. So much for his self-proclaimed selfishness.

After leaving Miles whistling under his breath and examining the tools, Sasha approached Desperado in his paddock. This time, unlike so many of their other encounters, he seemed to remember that he had already trusted her. He allowed her into the paddock, ate out of her hand and stood quietly while she handled his feet. Figuring she'd gotten that far and was still alive to tell the tale, she decided to try grooming him properly. He needed to look his best when potential buyers came to inspect him.

She couldn't tie him, since he still wouldn't allow her to put a halter on him, so she simply stayed with him as he wandered around cropping grass or dozing in the bright sunshine. Moving quietly, crooning softly, Sasha curried the mud-crusted coat until her arms ached. When she decided to quit, Desperado nuzzled her bare arm with his nose, making her laugh when he tickled her. He even trotted along the fence line when she went back to the barn, nickering as if inviting her to play some more.

"That beast's a real smooth talker, isn't he?" Miles asked from the shadows, his voice low and husky. Her heart leaped and began to beat in overtime.

"He's a silver-tongued devil, all right," she agreed, her own voice coming out unusually husky, "and he's finally figured out what's good for him."

"Looks like it," Miles murmured, leaving her to wonder if Miles was having second thoughts about staying—or about going.

"Interested in learning to play telegraph with the computer?" Miles asked after lunch. "I want to download some financial reports from one of the bulletin boards."

"Sure." Sasha bit into a crisp, slightly tart apple, then met his golden eyes. He'd been watching her mouth. She wanted to reach for him right then, and kiss him silly until he got the message that she wanted him to make love to her. The very thought brought heat to her cheeks. It had never been her style to pursue a man she liked. Then again, she'd never before felt she *had* to.

She definitely needed to get her mind off kissing and back on something safe and dull, like computers. "Is it hard?"

Miles cleared his throat. "Is what hard?"

"To learn?" She took another bite of apple.

"Oh. No, it's not, uh, difficult." His hesitation made her realize the double entendre of her simple question. Immediately her cheeks burned. "Come on," he invited, turning, giving her a moment to compose herself as she followed him into her office.

Sasha stopped short in front of her desk. "Good grief! You've been busy. There must be a ream of faxes here."

"Close. Eleanor faxed my mail, and I've gotten some faxes from business associates."

"Anything from the investigator?"

Miles sighed. "Not yet. But I'm hoping he'll turn up something that rings a bell. Okay, sit here and type what I tell you."

"I thought you were going to show me," Sasha said as she sat in the new gray tweed typing chair she'd never seen before. Miles must have gotten it when he bought the other gizmos for the computer. It was much more comfortable than the antique leather armchair she used.

"Hands-on works better," he assured her in that intimate, low voice of his, and her cheeks went hot again. She resisted the temptation to tell him she'd been thinking exactly that only a moment ago.

Trying to ignore the scent, the sound, the feel of him so close behind her, Sasha typed as Miles instructed her. She felt all thumbs, but he was patient. It didn't take long before her computer was dialing some distant number. The machine made an awful screeching noise, then flashed "CONNECT" on the screen. Within a few minutes she was much more comfortable about following Miles's directions around the bulletin board's menu. When the little blue box on the screen announced that her first file transfer was completed, she gave a little yelp of pleasure.

"This is fun. Now what?"

"Now we download another file." Sasha could tell Miles was smiling by his voice, and didn't dare look up at him. That would be too intimate, too tempting.

Miles talked her through the steps again. When the computer took over, she considered the files he was requesting from the bulletin board. "These are Canadian businesses you're getting financial reports on."

"Yeah. I started reading some of the Canadian business papers just to keep busy. It seems that a lot of good, small businesses are having trouble finding Canadian investors to keep them going. They're looking for U.S. angels with money to invest. I saw a couple of companies that interested me, so I'm checking them out before I approach anyone."

"Oh." The little box flashed that this transfer was now completed. "This is amazing! What else can this thing do?" Without thinking of the possible consequences, she tipped her head to look up at him.

Miles smiled, apparently enjoying her enthusiasm over his technological toy, but her heart did a quick flip over the look in his golden eyes. "You can type messages back and forth to another computer," he told her, bringing her back to reality. His touch on her shoulder was light as a feather, but she felt it over every inch of her body. "Want to try?"

Her pulse surged. "Try what?"

He gave her a half smile. "Calling Eleanor. Her computer stays on all the time. It will beep to let her know she has a call coming in."

Still trembling inside from that light touch, Sasha fumbled her first attempt to type Eleanor's phone number. Finally the screen flashed "RING," twice, then "CONNECT," and the words "Hello, Miles," marched across the screen.

Sasha typed back, "Hi, Eleanor, it's Sasha Reiss."

"Well, hi, Doc! It's about time!" Eleanor typed back. "How is Miles really doing?"

Miles leaned over her and his big body seemed to engulf her. He typed, "Miles is fine, damn it," his fingers flying over the keys. "I'm going to upload some files. I want you to set up the usual feasibility studies."

"Gotcha. Be nice to Sasha. She must be a saint to put up with you."

Miles typed, "Were you always this disrespectful?"

"While the cat's away, etc.," Eleanor typed back. Sasha laughed at Miles's disgruntled expression. "Anything else, or can I get back to my TV program?"

"Over and out." Miles pressed a couple of other keys and the screen flashed the box again.

"That was fun, but you better take over the important stuff," Sasha said. "I'd hate to do something wrong." The truth was, she didn't know how long she could maintain her sense of propriety with Miles practically surrounding her as he stood behind her.

"That's okay. It gets routine after a while."

"Mind if I hang around and work on this week's bills?"

"It's your office, remember?" he said with a grin she couldn't resist answering with one of her own.

Just then her fax machine gave its earsplitting screech and began cranking out pages. Miles reached for the cover page. Sasha watched a frown form on his handsome face as he read it, then picked up the other two pages that came out of the machine, his frown deepening as he read.

Impulsively she put her hand on his arm. "Miles, what is it?"

He looked at her hand, then at her face, his expression clearing a little. "A message from my investigator."

"Bad news?"

"Not really any news. He's confirming my birth certificate, a couple of dead ends, and what he's going to do next."

"What is he looking for?"

"Who my parents were—or are, if they're still alive. Brothers or sisters. Schools. People I knew. I've gotten a couple of flashes about being with other kids, but nothing specific enough to identify people or location. If I have siblings, who are they? Where are they? Could they be in my address book and I don't know because I can't remember? Or am I the kind of man who burns his bridges? I hate not knowing."

"What if you don't like what you learn?"

Miles shrugged, then covered Sasha's hand with his, pressing it to his arm. The simple gesture touched her deeply. "I already don't like some of what I've remembered. I need to know how bad I really was."

"Why? If you were truly a ruthless, cold, selfish person, what good does knowing do you? Right now I see you as a decent, honorable man, a compassionate and generous man. Would a cold, ruthless man put his life on hold until a couple of abused kids he doesn't even know can be rescued? I don't think so, Miles.''

The bleak expression in his eyes nearly broke her heart. "I don't know what good it will do me to know if I was a bastard, but I believe I have to know before I can decide what to do with the rest of my life." Sasha opened her mouth to protest, but he pressed his forefinger to her lips, silencing her. "We aren't ever going to agree on this, so let's agree to disagree. Okay?"

The smile Miles gave her could have tempted an angel to sin, and Sasha was far from angelic. She was so close that she could see the black flecks in his golden eyes. She could feel the heat of his body. Her voice refused to work. Instead, she nodded her agreement.

"Don't look at me like that, Sasha," he ordered gruffly, "or I'll forget all about that decency and honor you think I have."

Her pulse raced at his tempting warning. She almost closed the distance between his mouth and hers. The only thing that held her back was the realization that this was the first time she'd wanted to give her heart to a man, and the first time she'd felt the need to guard her heart at the same time.

"Right," she whispered, pulling back. She stood and cleared her throat. "I'm going to clean up. I'll do my bills later, when you don't need the computer."

As soon as Miles was certain Sasha had gone upstairs, he opened the file containing his personal calendar and address book. He had already listed several women's names recurring over the past five years. He'd tracked the times he'd spent with each of them and discovered that no relationship had lasted longer than six months.

Then he looked up each name in the address-book files. That software had been designed for storing important details about each person listed. He had filed away facts such as birthdays, employment, preferred types of entertainment, favorite restaurants, favorite flowers, even habitual perfumes. As he scanned through the data, he confirmed his earlier memory. Every one of the women he'd dated had a profession that kept her traveling, making commitment difficult. Several were fashion models, a couple were actresses and a couple more were singers and recording artists. Once again he combed through his entire personal address book, but didn't find a single woman listed who had a normal office career that kept her in one place.

More than a little disgusted with this revealing discovery, Miles got up and poured himself a few fingers of the single malt Scotch whiskey he'd bought at the duty-free store and which had miraculously survived the car wreck. The smoky-smooth liquid slid down his throat and landed in the pit of his stomach with a cold fire. Then he went back to the desk and looked up the number of the last woman whose name appeared regularly in his calendar.

With a sinking feeling in his gut, he picked up the phone and dialed. He was about to face his past head-on, and his gut told him he wasn't going to like it.

Sasha came out of the kitchen to find Miles lighting a fire in the living room fireplace. He crouched on the hearth, with the light of the flames flickering across the planes and angles of his face. His jeans showed the power of his leg muscles, bunched and ready to spring. With his black T-shirt stretched over his broad back and wide shoulders, he looked primal, dangerous and very, very sexy.

Perching on the arm of the chesterfield, she asked, "Do you think you were a Boy Scout?" The question earned a dismissive snort. "Well, you do know how to light a fire," she added, unable to resist the little double entendre.

The long look Miles gave her then sent shivers of awareness over her skin. "Maybe I was an arsonist," he countered.

She smiled into his eyes, hoping that his earlier dark mood had lifted. "Maybe you still are."

He stood abruptly. Towering over her, he scowled. "I'm going to get a book."

"That sounds like a good idea," she answered his retreating back, determined to be cheerfully persistent about breaking through this new layer of wall between them.

Sasha fetched the novel she'd been reading from her office, pausing to look briefly at her calendar for the next week. When she returned to the living room, Miles was already sitting on the chesterfield, as far into the corner as possible for such a big man. A Tom Clancy novel lay open on his knee. He barely looked up when she sat at the other end of the chesterfield, but she could feel his tension as if she were touching him. After a few minutes of trying to concentrate on her book, Sasha couldn't stand it anymore.

"Miles, is something bothering you? Something new? I heard you make a couple of phone calls before, and you've been in a strange mood since before dinner."

He spoke without looking away from his book. "Nothing new is bothering me, Sasha."

"But you seemed so optimistic before, when we were playing with the computer. I mean, you were looking into business deals and joking with Eleanor and—"

"Drop it, Sasha."

"Sometimes the only way to heal something is to keep probing until it's clean."

His book hit the floor with an impressive smack. From the kitchen Copper woofed a soft warning at the noise. Miles shifted sideways on the cushion and glared. She faced him and gazed back, keeping her expression neutral.

"Will you stop thinking of me as a damn injured horse?" Miles barked.

"I don't think of you as any kind of horse, Miles. Believe me, I know you're a man."

"Fine. So cut me some slack. I'm dealing with this on my own."

Common sense told her to respect his request, but Sasha's instincts as a healer, and as a woman, prompted her to persist. She figured she could handle the consequences. "Dealing with what?"

Miles gave her a look that could have withered concrete. "Amnesia, damn it! Remember?"

Sasha ignored the sarcasm and shook her head. "You've been dealing pretty well with your memory loss. This is something new, something since this afternoon. I'm getting good at reading your moods, you know. I'm sure you think bottling it up is the strong, manly thing to do." She put her hand on his forearm, absorbing a little sensory shock at the feel of warm skin and silky hairs. His muscles bunched under her touch. A muscle in his jaw clenched. Her pulse pounded in her throat. "But honestly, Miles, it really will help to talk about whatever is troubling you."

"Damn it, Sasha! You're worse than a mosquito in a tent!" he growled. He moved quickly, and now it was his large, hard hand wrapped around her upper arm. "You want to know what happened this afternoon? Okay! This afternoon I phoned two of my most recent lovers. I didn't like what I heard."

Sasha had suspected that he'd learned something disturbing during his phone calls, but hearing him say the word *lovers* struck her hard. The man she'd come to think of as a hermit had had lovers. She shouldn't be surprised, but she was. Or maybe she was shaken by the notion that Miles had cared about these women, had had intimate relationships with them. He hadn't been so closed off from people as she'd believed. Obviously, he was capable of deep feelings. Had he been hurt by one or more of these women from his past?

Sasha searched his hard face for some clue. All she saw was anger, but she knew he used anger to protect himself from other feelings. Most men did. She'd simply have to convince him it was safe to confide in her. "What did they do that upset you, Miles?"

To her surprise, he laughed. It wasn't a laugh of amusement, however, but a bitter laugh of disbelief. "*They* didn't do anything to upset me." His fingers tightened on her arm, not enough to hurt but enough to pull her off-balance a little. "Except tell me the truth about myself."

"And what is that?"

"You don't want to know."

The man had a head like a brick. "I just asked, didn't I?"

"No wonder you keep getting kicked by horses. You ask for it." She opened her mouth to prompt him, but he went on in a grim tone. "I used them, Sasha. I took their company. Their love. Their dreams. And then I dumped them, just when they were sure I was about to propose marriage."

Sasha shifted so she was kneeling beside him on the sofa, looking him in the eye. He still held her arm. "That's their story, Miles. Isn't it possible that you just didn't feel the same way about them and decided to end the relationships?"

"It's *possible* that little green men from outer space are taking over the phone company, but it isn't likely. The facts are in the computer. Every woman I've dated has a career that makes a traditional permanent relationship difficult, if not impossible. What does that tell you?"

Sasha considered what he'd said, then drew her conclusion. "It tells me that you're attracted to independent, dynamic women, but haven't fallen in love yet."

Miles made a noise that sounded like teeth gnashing. "It tells me I'm only interested in women I can't have a normal relationship with. As soon as they get close, I shut them out."

"Like you're trying to do to me?" Sasha whispered.

Miles swore and gave her arm a shake. Caught by surprise, she lost her balance and tumbled toward him, landing against his broad chest, his arms around her, her breasts plastered to him, her face pressed to his. Trying to regain her balance, Sasha wiggled around until she ended up straddling his thighs. Under her, Miles seemed to freeze. She couldn't even feel him breathing. But his heart was pounding so hard that his pulse seemed to beat within her.

Finally Miles groaned. "Sasha, what are you doing to me?"

She turned her head so that her lips could just brush his tense jawline. "I'm trying to get you to consider alternative points of view." She pressed a kiss to his cheek. "I'm trying to convince you that the man I see here doesn't act like the selfish S.O.B. he claims to be, so maybe there's another explanation."

"Like what?"

Very slowly she let herself sink down into his lap. Even through their jeans, Sasha felt his heat. She felt him stir to arousal under her. And she felt herself quicken and ache for him.

"Like, maybe you shut people out before they can hurt you, because someone or a number of someones in your past hurt you very much."

Sasha drew back enough to look into his face. In the flickering firelight she could see the anger struggling with the indecision and something else she couldn't read. And then one of his hands slid up to cup the back of her head and she drifted forward until his mouth met hers.

Miles's kiss felt tentative at first, as if he expected her to break away. She couldn't have even if she'd wanted to. Her bones were turning to liquid and she flowed into his arms, letting him part her lips for his hot, probing tongue. Breathlessly, Sasha clung to him, absorbing the taste of his anger, his hunger, his desperation. With a soft little sound of her own need, she settled deeper into his lap.

And then Miles drew his mouth from hers. "Sasha, I'm trying to be decent and honorable, but you're not making it very easy for me," he murmured.

Sasha smiled wickedly, dreamily. "I believe I'm making it hard for you," she teased, her voice husky.

"Oh, God, are you ever," he breathed. Then he grasped her hips in his strong hands and lifted her up above his lap. "I don't want to have sex with you because we're in the same house and we both feel sorry for me. I owe you more than that, Sasha. So..."

Still shaken by the depths of her own responses, Sasha rested her forehead on Miles's and tried to get her breathing under control.

"You're wrong about the reasons, Miles, but I'm not going to beg you to make love to me." Slowly she eased herself off him. His hands supported her, but they didn't push her away. She decided that was a small victory.

Miles slid his hands down her arms to clasp her fingers, then released her. There was a lifetime of sadness in his eyes. "I don't want you to get hurt, Sasha."

"Well, that makes two of us." She smiled a little lamely. "There's some wise advice trainers give riders. Don't rush your fences. I'm going upstairs to read. When the time is right, we'll both know."

"The time may never be right for us," Miles warned as she walked away.

At the doorway into the hall Sasha turned and met his eyes. Time wasn't the problem, she knew, but they'd already agreed to disagree about his relationship with his past. With a sigh she turned away and went upstairs to her room.

The next morning Sasha was gone before Miles got downstairs. He filled the hours working at the computer. Shortly after noon he heard her truck stop in the yard. Copper woofed and trotted out to meet her. Miles followed the dog onto the porch, looking around as he waited for her. It was another sunny day. The breeze smelled sweet, and the sky was full of fluffy white clouds and birds. A new wave of spring flowers had started to bloom, and the lilac bushes were heavy with dark purple buds Sasha had promised would be opening by the end of the week. It felt good to be here, watching spring unfold. Miles wondered if he felt as much at home on Secret Island.

"Hi!" Sasha called. "I picked up some chicken salad and rolls for lunch. Interested?"

His stomach growled at the mention of food. "Is the sky blue?"

"For now," she answered with a chuckle. "As soon as Copper is ready to come back inside, I'm digging in." She lifted a full paper bag. "This is strictly self-serve."

By the time Miles walked into the kitchen, the pups were squealing in protest at their mother's desertion. They didn't have a clue how lucky they were, Miles thought. Their mother was devoted to them, and wouldn't leave them for more than a few minutes at a time. Not like the adults who were neglecting and abusing the kids who had brought Copper to Sasha's.

Miles crouched beside the box he'd made for the puppies from scrap plywood. They still looked like fat little golden piglets. Carefully he touched several of them, savoring their warmth, their silky coats. They responded by making mewling sounds and rooting blindly toward his hand, making him smile. Cute little devils. It might be nice to have one of Copper's pups, and maybe a couple of the barn kittens, when he returned to Secret Island. But then, there were probably plenty of abandoned dogs and cats back there, too.

The kitchen door swung open on that grim thought. Copper trotted to the box, stopping to grin and nudge him for a bit of attention. Scratching the dog behind her ears, Miles looked up at Sasha and felt his insides do a slow somersault. Dear God, she was beautiful!

It wasn't the way her faded jeans hugged her trim figure, or the way her vest opened over a T-shirt that clung to her ribs and outlined her small, round breasts. It wasn't the slight flush on her high cheekbones or the sparkle in her dark eyes. It wasn't even the tempting way her smile parted her soft lips.

It was her energy, her sweetness, her intelligence and unselfconscious sensuality. It was her insistence on thinking the best of him, despite facts to the contrary. It was her determination to heal him with love he didn't deserve and couldn't return. It was everything about Sasha that made her so damn beautiful, that made him feel as if he were staring into the sun, awed and blinded.

"What a gorgeous day," she said brightly, shrugging out of her vest. "I think we're going to have an early summer.

There's carrot salad in the fridge, to go with the sandwiches."

Apparently unaware of her ability to reduce him to mush, Sasha scrubbed her hands at the sink, then reached up to take plates and glasses out of the cupboard. She was acting as if nothing had happened between them last night. Tamping down the temptation to make up for his noble intentions of yesterday, resisting the urge to slide between her and the counter and pull her slender body against him, Miles gave Copper a final pat and got up to wash his hands.

"How was your morning? Did you get much work done?" Sasha asked when Miles joined her at the table.

"Yeah. Oh, the manure man came by and hauled away a truckload. He left a basket of mushrooms. Real beauties. I put them in the fridge."

"Oh, good. Do you like mushroom soup?"

"Probably. But why would the manure man bring mushrooms?"

Sasha chuckled. "Guess!" She laughed at the face he made. "Relax. It's sterilized first. That's why I always wash my mushrooms, no matter what the cooking experts say about just brushing them off."

"That's a relief," Miles told her with a quick grin. It seemed as natural as breathing to anticipate she'd need the mustard at that precise moment, and to pass it to her without a word. "How was your morning?"

"Busy enough," Sasha answered before biting into her sandwich. "There's a runny nose bug going around some of the stables, and an increase in lameness and pulled tendons. It's spring, so everyone is training for competition or out riding on uneven terrain. Or the horses go out in the fields feeling so good that they run themselves sore."

"Any more babies?" Miles bit into his sandwich, then had to force himself to choke it down while the image of Sasha holding his baby flashed into his mind.

"A couple arrived without much fanfare," she answered, drawing him back to the present. "Experienced mares, experienced owners. I usually just have to check the foals, make sure they're progressing well and don't have any problems that require early attention." A soft light came into her dark eyes. "I love those little ones. Seeing them with their mothers always chokes me up. It's such a strong, special bond."

Once again, Miles pushed away the image of Sasha holding his baby. "What about the fathers?"

She shook her head. "It's unusual for stallions to be buddies with other horses, especially younger males. They see them as rivals, with good reason, and can be pretty brutal. Some studs can be pretty rough with their mares, too. In a well-balanced broodmare band, you'll see 'aunting,' where the mares look out for foals that aren't their own. The stallions see their jobs as protecting their mares and getting them pregnant." She grinned. "Not very politically correct."

At the moment, neither were Miles's thoughts. He was thinking the impossible.

Chapter Thirteen

"Time for me to get back to work," Sasha said. Then she tipped her head as if listening to something in the distance. "Sounds like a fax coming in."

"Probably," Miles agreed, reluctant to end the time with her. "I'll walk you out to the truck. I can use some fresh air before I go back to the computer."

The smile Sasha gave him could have enticed him to walk barefoot on broken glass, let alone to her truck. Miles held the door for Sasha, stepping back to let her walk out of the house. As she passed, he caught another breath of her scent and marveled that he'd managed not to grab her the entire time she'd been home for lunch. Her hair and skin smelled of horse and fresh air, flowers and woman. His hand, when he let go of the door, shook with suppressed desire.

Now he followed her to the truck, torturing himself with the sight of her slim hips swaying just a little in her well-worn jeans. She was dressed for work, but Miles liked the way she had tied the tails of her chambray work shirt around her waist, over the plain black T-shirt. Even in men's clothes, she was completely feminine. It was a powerful combination.

Sasha opened the driver's door of the truck, then turned around. Her dark gaze held Miles's as her hand rose to touch his face like the brush of a butterfly. Miles wanted to reach up and hold her hand to his heart. He wanted her touch to heal him. But he couldn't take without giving, and he didn't have anything to offer besides heartache. So he stood still, forcing himself not to respond, until Sasha lowered her hand and climbed into the truck.

"See you tonight," she said, her voice a little husky.

Miles waved once, then strolled around the grounds for a while, with Pretty Polly at his heels. He really did need to clear his head. He'd spent a sleepless night pondering Sasha's words from last night, and he was beginning to think she might be right about some things. Not about the way he'd treated the women in his still unremembered past, because judging by the blistering things Lina and Natalia had said, he'd been a cold, heartless bastard. But Sasha might have been on the right track about the reasons he'd deliberately sought women who were so independent that they were virtually unattainable.

Of course, so was Sasha. She thought she wanted to make love to him, but he knew she was searching for another way to try to heal him. Her compassion made her too easy to exploit, and if Miles was ever going to set his past behind him, he was going to have to stop using women who thought they could be the one to break down the walls around his heart.

Miles was also going to have to find out why he'd built those walls. Why didn't he let anyone get close to him? Why couldn't he let himself get close to anyone? The answers were locked in the vault of his memory, but having the answers was no guarantee that he'd be able to put the past behind him.

As he bent to pluck some of the many tulips and daffodils blooming around the side of the house, Pretty Polly rubbed against his ankles. Miles smiled and stroked the silky fur, earning a loud, trilling purr. If only it could be that easy, he thought, he'd let himself fall in love with Sasha in a heartbeat.

Sasha phoned at five. "Grab something to eat when you get hungry," she told Miles. "I've got a difficult foaling going on, so I have no idea when I'll be home."

"Okay. I'll bring the horses in and feed them."

"Thanks. Just watch out for Desperado. He's still not totally reliable, especially around men." She said goodbye almost abruptly, her voice strained with worry.

Miles called to Copper to follow him outside. The grinning dog dislodged her clinging pups and trotted after him. Whenever she went out with either of them, Miles wondered if the kids who had left her were hiding somewhere, watching to make sure their dog was being treated better than they were. The thought always made him clench his fists in impotent fury. What, if anything, were the police doing? Where were the social workers? Didn't a teacher or a pediatrician suspect anything? At least a dozen times a day he reached for the phone to call McLeod and demand a progress report. But after the way he'd dusted the guy off, he didn't think the constable would have much time for him. He didn't care, as long as McLeod found time to track down those kids.

After trying to calm himself by watching Copper roll in the grass and sniff around for a few minutes, Miles went to the barn. The old horses came in quietly but eagerly, in a group. Miles grinned at the way they sorted themselves into their own stalls and waited for him to bring dinner. After feeding them all, he paused at Houdini's stall, then, on impulse, let himself inside. The sad-faced old boy lifted his face from his feed bucket and sniffed the front of Miles's shirt, leaving behind traces of dirt and grain. Miles ran his hand down the horse's warm neck. Houdini nodded as if to ask for more, and when Miles scratched him around his ears, the horse closed his eyes and sighed.

"Lucky old man, aren't you?" he muttered to the horse. "You get to stay with Sasha, no matter what."

With a final pat, Miles went outside to tackle Desperado. He carried the full feed bucket into the paddock, the way Sasha did. The horse raced around, his hooves biting into grass and flinging mud. Miles stood quietly, waiting for the defensive beast to figure out his dinner was being served. When he did, Desperado snorted and tossed his head, approaching as if on his way to the guillotine instead of a meal. Miles extended his arms, showing the grain to the suspicious horse.

"C'mon, buddy. I'm here to feed you, not beat you," he said in a low voice, hoping he sounded as soothing as Sasha did. "You'll hurt yourself not trusting the right people," he added, wondering if he was talking to the horse or himself.

Eventually, Desperado met him halfway. The horse ate from the bucket after Miles set it on the ground several feet away from where he stood. But unlike the old horses, who kept their noses in their buckets, munching steadily, Desperado lifted his head with every mouthful, eyeing Miles warily as he chewed. Miles had the strange sensation of gazing into a distorted mirror.

Later, watching the news on TV, Miles picked at leftovers for dinner. Evening turned to night, and still Sasha wasn't home. He began to worry at ten. At eleven he was pacing the front porch, debating whether to call her pager number. What if she'd fallen asleep at the wheel on her way home? She could be alone and bleeding in a ditch somewhere, the way he had been the night she'd found him.

At eleven-fifteen the lights of Sasha's truck swept the yard. He was down the steps and ready to grab her tool kit before her feet touched the gravel driveway. Without a word she handed the heavy kit to him and shut the truck door by leaning on it. He slid his arm around her waist and led her to the house.

Earlier, he'd planned to say so many things to her when she came home. He was going to tell her he'd set up meetings with two different companies, to discuss investing in them. He was going to tell her about the fax he'd received from the private investigator in Tampa.

His concerns would wait. Sasha was exhausted, and all Miles wanted to do was take care of her. He could only hope that, unlike stallions, he had some long-buried instinct for nurturing.

Sasha leaned against Miles, grateful for his support. She did so much nurturing she forgot how nice it felt to be taken care of occasionally. Now she absorbed Miles's warm strength, breathed in his woodsy-musky male scent and allowed herself the luxury of being temporarily depleted of her own strength.

"You look like death warmed over," he murmured. "I've been pacing a trail in your carpets."

His words warmed her further. "It was a tough delivery. The foal's neck and one foreleg were bent back, so I had to wrestle with him, the mare and Mother Nature to straighten him."

"But you did it."

"Yeah. Poor little guy will be seeing a chiropractor for a while, but he's up and nursing."

"Good." His quick hug as they reached the door made Sasha feel the loss of his embrace even more. She followed him into the house. He paused at the kitchen door, setting her kit down. "Dinner, or just bed?"

Sasha shook her head. "Too tired to eat, too wired to sleep."

"Go take a hot shower. If that doesn't relax you, I'll give you a massage."

She smiled and nodded. "I better say good-night now, anyway, in case the shower does the job."

He dropped a light kiss on the top of her head. Sasha dragged herself up the stairs, then turned to see Miles watching her. The longing in his eyes made her forget her exhaustion. It mirrored exactly the longing in her soul.

Miles carried his glass of Scotch into the living room. The fire he'd lit hours ago had died down to embers, but the glow appealed to him. He pried off his boots and sprawled on the sofa, in a strange, restless mood he couldn't define. But he knew the cause.

From upstairs, Sasha's shower sounded like muted rain. He sipped his whiskey and imagined her tall, slender body under the hot water. Arousal gripped him, making him ache, making him curse. Not Sasha, but circumstances. The circumstances of the present that had propelled him into her life, and the circumstances of his past that would shut him out of her life.

With his empty glass balanced on his chest, Miles let his eyes drift shut. Now, imagining Sasha in the shower, he pictured himself there with her.

"Miles?"

It was Sasha, her voice slipping into his fantasy so gently it took him a moment to realize she was actually standing beside him, taking the glass from his slack grip. He opened his eyes and found himself looking directly into hers.

"Feel better?" he asked, unable to move, even to look away.

"Some. It's late. We should go to bed," Sasha murmured, and then sat beside his hip and put her hand on his chest. Miles's heart started to pound under the light pressure. Slowly she came closer until he was breathing in the sweet, fresh scent of her skin and feeling awareness pumping through his veins. Then her lips touched his.

Miles tried to stay passive, to simply accept her kiss without making any demands of his own. He tried, but the wet heat of the tip of her tongue on his lips lit a fuse he no longer wanted to control. His hands reached for her, holding her slender ribs with shaking reverence. Sasha's hair drifted around them like fragrant silk. When Miles arched up under her to press his mouth to hers, Sasha opened her lips to his questing tongue. The taste of her went to his head faster than a double shot of the finest single malt.

Blood surged to his loins, making him hard, making him ache to lose himself in the healing warmth of her body. Miles fought the raw power of his body's hunger, his soul's needs, forcing himself to give all choices to her. Easing her away, he sat up and locked his gaze on hers.

"Sasha?" was all he could manage to say.

"Yes, Miles, yes," she whispered.

"Are you sure?"

She gave him a hint of a smile. "Very."

She held out her hand. For the first time, Miles realized she was wearing a thick terry-cloth robe in a deep, forest green. The robe wrapped and tied around her slender body and reached almost to her ankles. Her feet were bare. Her hair fell around her shoulders like a dark silk cape. He wanted to untie the belt of the robe and slip his hands under the fine strands of her hair until it drifted over his skin.

Miles stood and took her hand in his. Silently they walked upstairs. When they reached her bedroom door, Sasha opened it and drew him inside. His impression was of softness, things that were feminine without being too frilly; oldfashioned with antiques and lace. Her scent filled the room, delicate, womanly. He followed her to the four-poster bed, trembling.

"Sasha, if you change your mind," he began, praying she wouldn't.

"Why would I?"

"Do we need—?"

"Under my pillow." Her smile told him that she knew his nerves were in an uproar. Then she touched his cheek.

It was enough to free Miles from his fog of disbelief. Fighting the urge to crush her to him and sink into her body for frantic release, he cupped her face in his hands and bent to kiss her. Her soft lips parted under his. She opened to his tongue and met his thrusts with parries of her own. Her sweet taste went to his head like fine cognac.

The first touch of her fingers on his chest made Miles start. Breaking the kiss, he watched her unbutton his shirt, smiling as her long, sensitive fingers shook. Then she spread her hands on his bare chest and he felt as if flames were sliding over his skin.

Taking her mouth in another deep, wet kiss, Miles lowered his hands from the delicate curves and bones of her face to trace the lapels of her robe. Down to the simple tie in the belt. One tug and it came open to her waist, freeing her to his touch. Miles wanted to rush, he wanted to take his time. He let his fingertips graze the warm, silky skin of her neck, her collarbone. Slowly he pushed the lapels apart to expose her shoulders. Sasha tipped her head back, breaking the kiss. The robe dropped as Miles's mouth left hers and found her throat. Her pulse beat under his kiss.

Miles lifted his head and looked down at Sasha's closed eyes. Her lashes fluttered, her lids opened. She met his gaze with her dark, steady, knowing eyes and smiled dreamily.

"Sasha, I feel as if I've never made love before," he confessed, his voice coming out hoarse.

"You haven't," Sasha whispered, still smiling. "Not to me."

Her easy acceptance touched him and scared him. Miles had no touchstone of reality except her, and he couldn't bear to let her down. "I want so badly to make this good for you, but I can't remember what kind of lover I was."

"That doesn't matter. I'm not someone from your past. It's only you and me now. Follow your instincts." Her smile widened. "I plan to follow mine."

At a loss for words, Miles simply nodded, then brushed her lips with his. His hands encircled her waist, then rose to cover her breasts. They were small, round, firm. The nipples hardened under his palms. Sasha gripped his shoulders and moaned quietly. He bent and replaced one hand with his lips, trailing kisses over warm, fragrant skin. He took her nipple into his mouth, teasing it with his tongue, alternately suckling and licking at the sweetness of her. Her fingers laced through his hair, encouraging him to continue.

"I like your instincts," Sasha murmured huskily, almost making him laugh with pure joy. "My instincts say we should lie down before I fall down." Miles lifted his head to look into her eyes. "They also say you are wearing far too many clothes."

Sasha's skillful fingers traced maddening patterns across his bare chest. He closed his eyes for a moment, savoring the contact, then tore his shirttails from his jeans and ripped the shirt off without undoing the last few buttons. Sasha sat on the edge of her bed. The robe pooled around her waist and covered her thighs, leaving her upper body bared to his greedy gaze. She had the athletic, perfect beauty of a classical statue.

Miles's hands went to his belt buckle, then, fumbling, he managed to unbutton the fly and remove his jeans. He stood looking down at Sasha, trembling, aching to bury himself in her body, yet wanting to draw out every second into minutes, turn minutes into hours, so it would never be over.

"You are so damn beautiful," he murmured, settling onto the bed beside her. "I'm almost afraid to touch you."

"Please, touch me," Sasha whispered. "I can't think of anything I want more right now."

"Neither can I," Miles agreed.

Threading his fingers through the silk of her hair, he cupped her head and drew her closer. Her mouth opened under his, her tongue welcomed his. When her bare breasts met his chest, he felt as if their combined heartbeats could start an earthquake. He held her like that for a while, feeling as if he were binding her to him simply by holding her. Finally he eased her up toward the pillows, then brought his free hand to the belt of her robe. With fingers that shook he freed her of the heavy cloth. Still kissing her mouth, he teased himself by delaying the moment when he could see all of her.

When he couldn't wait any longer, Miles drew his mouth from hers and slowly let his gaze drift over her long, lean form. Trembling, he traced the same path with his fingertips. Her skin was as smooth as polished marble, but warm and resilient with life. She lifted her arms to draw him down and he gave up the last vestiges of regret that he couldn't recall his past experience with other women. Sasha was unique. All that mattered was the present.

Sasha wrapped her arms around Miles's back and felt her body flow against him like water rippling over a rock. She absorbed his warmth and solid strength and held him tighter, needing to be even closer. His kisses grew hotter, harder, making her breathless. His hands swept over her skin, finding all the places that ached for his touch. His hardness nudged her thigh through his cotton briefs, and his readiness echoed her own. Impatiently Sasha reached down to his waist and struggled to slide his briefs off without breaking a kiss that seemed to have no beginning or end.

Finally Miles lifted his head and looked into her eyes. "Slow down, Sasha," he said through gritted teeth. "I'm too close to the edge right now."

"So am I," she whispered urgently.

She felt his control snap. He groaned and moved away to free himself of his briefs. Now his hard flesh sprang hot and ready against her thigh. Reaching up under her pillow,

Sasha found the condom wrapper she'd tucked there after her shower. As she stretched, Miles brought his mouth down on her breast. The warm, wet tugging of his lips sent shock waves down to her center.

Somehow, Miles took the flat packet out of her fingers, drawing his mouth from her breast long enough to remove the contents. While he took care of protection with trembling hands, Sasha trailed wet kisses over his upper body, smiling at his moans. When his fingers slid up her inner thigh to the heated place between her legs, it was Sasha's turn to moan. Miles parted her, explored her with slow, careful touches that fueled the inner fire that threatened to blaze out of control.

Then Miles was leaning over her, his lips caressing her exposed throat. They moved in an instinctively choreographed dance that brought his hips between her thighs. She reached down and wrapped her fingers around the thick shaft nestled against her and seeking entry to her body, then guided him. Slowly, slowly Miles eased into her. Sasha sighed as her body accepted his possession. She felt herself opening to him until he was deep inside her. She hugged him close and raised her knees to lock her ankles around his hips, urging him deeper.

For a timeless moment they stayed without moving. Being joined with Miles felt breathtakingly new and miraculously familiar. Sasha ran her hands over his back and shoulders, gliding over the light film of sweat on his skin, enjoying the tightly reined power of the muscles wherever she stroked. Miles caught his breath and his strong arms trembled as her fingers skimmed over his taut buttocks.

"Sasha!" he gasped. "I can't hold back."

"Don't," she whispered, lifting her hips to let him know she was as ready for him as he was for her.

With a low growl, Miles began to move inside her, rocking her, driving her higher with every thrust. Sasha met him with equal hunger, with equal need, letting the spiral of sensations tighten within her until she didn't think she could feel any more pleasure. With a subtle change of his movements, Miles showed her she could indeed feel more. She clutched at his broad back and cried out as unbearable pleasure set off fireworks behind her closed eyes. Before she could fully recover, Miles groaned fiercely and thrust wildly into her, sending her over the edge once again.

For a long, long time they stayed locked together. Miles breathed harshly against her neck. His body lay heavily on hers. Sasha reveled in every sensation, every point of contact between their heated bodies. She felt utterly sated and achingly alive.

"I must be crushing you," Miles muttered finally, kissing her neck, "but I don't think I have the strength to get up."

"Then stay," Sasha told him lightly, stroking his damp hair. *Stay,* she wanted to plead. *Don't ever go.* He might even be tempted, but that wouldn't be fair to him. Sasha couldn't impose her needs on him. Miles had to get back to his own life in order to fully reclaim his identity. He would stay until he had to leave. The way she felt about him wouldn't change because of that.

Long after he'd recovered enough strength to ease himself off her, Miles held Sasha close to his side. He didn't want to break the spell by moving, by speaking. He listened to her breathing, felt the soft pressure of her breast against his ribs and tried to sort out his thoughts.

Mostly, he thought he'd died and gone to heaven. He felt new, reborn, after making love to Sasha. No, *with* Sasha. Even without his memories of other women, he knew that what they'd just shared had been incredibly special. Way, way beyond sex. Not that he was ready to put a name to any feelings. Not with his memory out in left field and his life on hold while he wallowed in self-pity.

Miles knew damn well that he had to go back to Secret Island to pick up the pieces of his identity and put the puzzle of his life together. The longer he stayed here with Sasha, indulging himself with her compassion and her quiet strength, the less likely it was that he would get a grip on what had gone wrong in Florida four weeks ago. Miles had been dodging the questions of why he'd driven all the way into Canada, of what he'd been running from, or possibly to, and of why he'd chosen to cut himself off from almost all human contact. That last was a real puzzler, because the more time he spent with Sasha and her friends, the more he realized he *liked* being with people. Why would a man who liked companionship create a life-style in which he had no real friends?

All those unanswered questions, and only a few hints gleaned from bare bones of facts.

Sasha sighed and snuggled closer. Her lips pressed against his shoulder. Automatically, Miles tightened his hold around her and felt his body respond to the brush of her knee on his thigh. It would be so easy to bury himself in her body again, and bury his questions in his mind. But he owed her the little bits of truth he'd discovered, before he took advantage of her again.

Miles pressed a kiss into Sasha's fragrant, silky hair. "That fax this afternoon was from the investigator in Florida," he told her.

"Anything helpful?" Sasha asked, sounding casual. A part of him wanted her to be excited and curious, but Miles knew he needed her serenity to face his own stormy seas.

"It's a preliminary report on my early years. Nothing to hint at why I ended up driving to Canada."

Sasha stroked his chest, then ran her fingers up his neck to his chin, tempting him to forget everything but making love with her again. "Well?" she prompted.

"Seems I spent most of my childhood, until I was sixteen, in foster homes." She stroked his neck, then rested her hand on his heart. "Not all of them were up to your parents' standards. Several of the foster parents I was placed with have been busted for battering kids and giving substandard care. A couple of them bounced me back and forth like a hot potato, but they weren't charged with anything back then."

"Oh, Miles, I'm so sorry," Sasha murmured, kissing his shoulder.

Her pity stabbed his pride. "It doesn't have anything to do with you."

"That doesn't mean I can't be sorry that you were subjected to abusive treatment."

"I don't want you to feel sorry for me," Miles snapped, unable to put a lid on his sudden resentment.

Sasha wriggled out of his embrace to lean on her elbow and look down at him. "Is that why you waited until after we made love to tell me?" she asked, hitting the nail on the head. "It wouldn't have made a difference, you know. You don't have to test me."

Her gentle understanding made him want to rile her, to find out if she had any feelings beyond compassion. "Don't you ever get angry?" he demanded.

"Yes. And it's not a pretty sight. But it has to be over something that outrages me. I would have made love with you if you'd confessed you were actually a visitor from Mars."

He reached up to cup her cheek. Her dark eyes met his gaze steadily, with a hint of humor in their depths. "I feel like a visitor from Mars. The facts about my life pile up, and I can't relate to them. Does that make sense?"

Sasha smiled. "It does, if Peter's theory is right."

Miles snorted. "You mean, about trying to escape some trauma that turned me into a hermit?" She nodded. He snorted again. "That's the stuff you shovel in the barn, Sasha. I'm who I am. I just can't remember."

"Then why didn't you head back to Secret Island the minute you got out of the hospital? Why are you here, if you're a hermit at heart? Why are you so concerned about Copper's kids, if you're a selfish, ruthless bastard?" She shook her head. "I'm betting you weren't born to be a hermit or selfish and ruthless. Peter and I both think you withdrew from people to protect yourself."

"So does Peter have an answer for what happens if I remember my past? Will I stay like I am, or go back to being a hermit?"

"That depends on what you decide, doesn't it?" Sasha asked with that irritating calmness. "You have to figure out what you need and what you want."

"Right now I want to make love with you again, but I know you need to sleep."

She smiled and ran her hand down his chest, down his belly, down to his already aching loins. Her fingers closed around him, sending wildfire through his veins. "We can do both," she murmured, which was exactly what he'd been hoping to hear.

It wasn't until much later, with Sasha curled asleep in his arms, that Miles realized he'd bought into this fantasy that had to end. He couldn't keep taking Sasha's sweetness, her compassion, her strength without offering something of equal value to her. And he didn't have anything of equal value. One of the keys to his financial success, he recalled, was the phrase, "If it looks too good to be true, it probably is." With a sick feeling, Miles understood that the same warning applied to relationships. Eventually, Sasha would come to her senses.

Chapter Fourteen

Sasha gave in to her radio alarm slowly, unwilling to let go of the dream of lying snuggled in Miles's arms. As reality filtered into her brain she realized she was indeed curled against his very solid body. When Sasha finally opened her eyes, she found him looking at her, his expression much too serious for a man who made love the way he did.

"Good morning," she murmured, reaching up to touch her fingers to his mouth. "Why are you frowning?"

Miles looked startled. "I didn't realize I was. I guess I was worried you'd be having second thoughts."

The question didn't surprise her. "Should I be?"

"Yes, but I hope you aren't." His answer didn't surprise her, either. He gave her a crooked grin. "What's on your agenda for today?"

"Shower, feed the critters, breakfast and rounds. What about you?"

"Same as you until after breakfast. Then laundry, which I never did get around to doing the other day. I've got a meeting in Newmarket with one of the local companies I'm thinking of investing in. Do you want me to pick up something for dinner while I'm in town?"

The comfortable domesticity of the conversation made Sasha smile. "Mmm. That'd be nice. Better make it something flexible, in case tonight resembles last night."

He waggled his eyebrows and leered. "I hope it does."

Laughing, Sasha pushed out of his arms and slipped out of bed. She didn't think about her nudity until Miles said, "My God, you're beautiful!" Then she felt herself blush over every naked inch. "Is there room for two in your shower?" he added, sounding a little hoarse.

The warmth inside her increased even more when she realized what he was suggesting. "There's room, but there isn't time."

Miles reached across the bed to open her bedside table drawer and take out a shiny packet. Then he winked. "Sure there is. I'll help you feed the critters and make breakfast," he told her as he strode toward her, magnificently naked and already aroused. "There are some things that are worth making time for."

Minutes later, as he thrust into her, with the warm water pouring down over them and the tiles cool against her back, Sasha found herself agreeing that this was indeed something worth making time for.

By the time they were dressed and ready to feed the cats, dogs and horses, the animals were complaining noisily. Copper followed them to the barn until Pretty Polly flashed past and took a swipe at the unsuspecting dog's nose. Woofing indignantly, Copper turned and went back to wait on the front porch. Miles prepared the buckets of grain for all the pensioners, while Sasha got Desperado's breakfast. As she made her way to the stallion's separate quarters attached to the back of the barn, she could hear Miles greeting each of the other horses by name, chatting with them the way she did.

He would deny it, of course, but he was a very gentle, very giving man. All he needed was a chance to heal his soul. She couldn't give him back his memory, but she had given him that chance. In return, he'd given her the fireworks, the passion, the chance to fall in love that she'd almost lost all hope of finding. No matter what happened in the future, she would treasure that gift.

To her surprise and delight, Desperado greeted her with a low nicker and nuzzled her gently when she offered him the grain bucket. He allowed her to stroke him the entire time he was eating, and barely looked up from munching until his bucket was empty. Then he stood almost patiently, while she ran her hands down each of his legs, checking their condition, then lifting each worn, chipped hoof to inspect the state of his feet.

"What a wonderful fella you are," she told him as she let herself out of his paddock. "Maybe I should think about keeping you. What do you think?" Desperado snorted, then moved quietly away, swishing his black-and-white tail at the flies.

"He's right," Sasha said to herself. "Totally impractical. Much better for him to be with an Appaloosa breeder." She'd already spoken to two different breeders who could use the stallion to his fullest potential as a sire. It would be selfish for her to keep the horse just because he was starting to respond to her attentions. That would be like expecting Miles to stay forever, just because he was comfortable here.

More than a little shaken by where her thoughts were leading, Sasha hurried back to the house to pour juice and coffee while Miles cursed the aging toaster and shook cereal into bowls. Over breakfast, seeking a neutral topic, Sasha asked Miles about the businesses he was interested in. He spoke enthusiastically about both, one a specialized software company, the other a small manufacturer looking to expand. The spark in his eyes when he talked about the ways he could help the companies told Sasha this was one thing Miles was definitely not trying to escape from in his past. He might have started with a casual poker game, but this was clearly his passion.

Suddenly it was past time for her to leave for her first appointment. She accepted Miles's offer to clean up with a quick kiss that turned into a much longer one. Then she grabbed her medical kit and rushed out the door.

When Sasha returned at noon, she stopped first at the paddocks to feed the horses and make sure each one was okay. With those old-timers, it didn't take much to pull a muscle or a tendon, and spring was making them kick up their heels in undignified glee.

Desperado greeted her with a low nicker of pleasure and trotted to where she stood with his feed bucket. As he wolfed down the grain, loaded with vitamins and minerals, she spoke quietly to him. First she told him about the calls she'd made that morning, then she explained that he was going to be shown to prospective buyers soon, and he'd have to be patient and well behaved.

"You like being groomed, don't you, you devil," she murmured, smiling at the answering snort. "Some Desperado. You're turning into a lapdog. The next step is a bath. First I'll scrub you all over, and then I'll rinse you with warm water. You'll love it." Desperado lifted his head and flicked his ears, glancing past her, then dipping his head into the bucket again. It was enough to let her know she wasn't alone anymore.

"If he isn't interested, can I take his place?" Miles asked, laughter lurking in his low voice.

Glancing over her shoulder, Sasha met his smile and chuckled. "Sure, if you don't mind being soaped with a rubber currycomb, and rinsed with water from a hose."

"Hell, no. I figure that's part of the appeal." Miles stepped closer to the rail that separated them. Desperado gave him another quick look over the bucket, then went back to lipping up the remaining crumbs of his lunch. "I think he's decided I'm not the enemy, either," Miles added. "I came out earlier with some carrots, just to take a break, and he didn't try to take my head off."

Sasha smiled. "Bribery seldom fails with these guys. Although I had a pony mare once, when I was a kid, who was too smart to fall for bribes. When I showed her in conformation classes, I'd show her I had treats for her if she'd stand still like a good little girl. She figured out the first time that she wasn't going to get her treats right away, so she'd clamp her nostrils shut and refuse to smell whatever I was trying to use to bribe her."

Miles laughed softly, the sound warming her more than the sun beating on her shoulders. "Sort of cutting off her nose to spite her face?"

"In a manner of speaking." Carefully Sasha moved to Desperado's side and stroked his neck. He tossed his head and rolled his eyes, then heaved a sigh and relaxed. As she continued to touch him, letting him get used to the feel of human kindness, she murmured encouragement. "He's doing better than I expected," she confided to Miles, keeping her voice low and soothing.

"He'd have to be as thick as two planks not to appreciate the way you're touching him," Miles answered, his voice also quiet, a little husky, very intimate.

The memory of their morning shower made her pulse kick up and gallop. As if Miles were enjoying the same memory, his eyes darkened. He bent his head toward her, closing the distance between his lips and hers, until he was so close that Sasha had to shut her eyes to hide the hunger she was afraid would show too clearly. And then, when she could feel his breath whispering over her lips, Miles murmured, "I thought the morning would never end. I'm glad you're back."

Sasha's knees buckled. Miles's hands tightened on her shoulders, holding her up. With her eyes still closed, she made a soft sound of assent and waited for his kiss. His mouth brushed over hers, then he released her. Disoriented, Sasha opened her eyes and stepped back. Miles gave her a sheepish grin. He slipped one arm around her shoulders and drew her with him toward the house.

"Are you sweeping me off my feet?" she teased, hoping the answer was affirmative.

"I'd like nothing better than to carry you upstairs, throw you on a bed and make wild and crazy love to you. But—"

"If your knee is still too sore to lift me, I'll be happy to go under my own steam," Sasha told him.

Miles leaned in and dipped his head until he could capture her lips with his. The kiss was soft, sweet, playful and over much too soon. Slowly she raised her eyes to meet his.

"I was about to say you must be hungry," he corrected, his voice raspy.

Sasha smiled. "Ravenous," she assured him. "But not for lunch."

By the time they'd made their way back downstairs, Sasha barely had time to return a couple of phone calls to clients and gulp down her lunch. After giving Miles a quick, hard kiss, she bolted out the door to her truck. Five minutes later she was driving back to pick up her day-planner with her appointments, addresses and phone numbers.

"I'd lose my head if it weren't—" she started to say as she dashed inside. Then she saw Miles and halted abruptly. He stood in the open basement doorway, swaying, gripping at the open door. His laundry bag lay at his feet, an echo of the other day. She had to call his name three times before he turned to look at her. His face was ghostly white, and sweat beaded on his forehead and upper lip.

"Miles, what is it?" she gasped, her heart pounding.

"I . . . I just remembered . . . about basements," he answered hoarsely. "Why I can't go down the stairs." He gave her a sickly smile. "I don't have a basement at Secret Island."

She wrapped her arms around him and led him to the living room, where they could sit side by side on the sofa. "Tell me what you remembered. Don't lock it in. Don't shut me out."

Tremors shook his powerful body. Sasha held him close, trying to absorb some of them. His breathing came in ragged gasps. After a minute of silence Miles drew a deep, slightly steadier breath.

"I can't remember all the details, but I got enough to feel like I was reliving it." Miles paused. His hand closed around hers. She held on and waited. "It must have been when I was little, maybe three, four, five years old. Too young to understand what was going on, too helpless to do anything about it.

"There was a man. A big, ugly bastard. He had some connection with my mother, but I don't know what. I'm not sure I want to know. He liked to scare me. He also liked to cause pain, then warn me not to tell my mother or he'd hurt her, too. I can hear his voice, slurred and rough, threatening me. He must have been a drunk."

Sasha changed her position so she could see his face. His eyes were focused on a point behind her. Gently she touched his cheek with her fingertips. "Tell me about the basement, Miles."

Miles drew in a long, slow breath. "It was dark, with steep, creaky stairs that were open in the back." He looked at her long enough to add, "Like yours," with a quick grin. Then he looked away again. "This guy used to rough me up and lock me up in the basement, in the dark. Sometimes he'd tie my hands behind my back and loop the rope around my neck so I couldn't move without choking myself. I have no idea how long he'd leave me down there, but a minute like that must feel like eternity to a little kid."

Somewhere during his recital of this horror, tears had begun sliding down her face. Speechless, she pressed her hand to his cheek. After a moment he swallowed hard, then turned to press a kiss into her palm.

"Hey, it's way in the past," he said gruffly. "It's not a great piece of memory to get back, but this probably means the rest of it will start coming back. And the only downside is that I have to use the Laundromat in Newmarket." He flashed her a grin that had to be mostly bravado.

"It's nothing to joke about, Miles," Sasha protested.

He pulled away from her and stood. His golden eyes flashed sparks. "What would you rather I do? Wallow in it? Run to Peter and lie on his couch whining? It's bad enough I turn into a cringing five-year-old when I try to go down your basement stairs. I'm a grown man, Sasha. Not a little kid. Not a mistreated horse. Don't treat me like one of your rescue projects. *I've* got to get a handle on this and deal with it. Building a house without a basement was one solution. Doing my laundry in Newmarket for a few more days is another. I don't want you feeling sorry for me."

Sasha stood slowly, stunned by his anger. Stunned and hurt. She'd been so sure he knew her well enough to know she didn't pity him.

Miles stood beside her. "Sasha, I really am dealing with this," he said gently. "You better go. I've already made you late."

Unable to speak, Sasha nodded curtly and turned away before Miles could see the fresh tears spill down her cheeks. These tears weren't for him, however. They were for the fragile link between them that was so close to breaking.

The instant Sasha turned away, Miles wanted to kick himself. He wanted to call her back and apologize for being such a bastard, but she was gone before he could think of something to say that would convince her that he didn't mean to hurt her. Hell, he couldn't even remember what he'd just said. It had been like a dam bursting. First that Stephen King horror of a memory flashing through his head. Then his anger, hitting him like a tidal wave.

Unfortunately, he'd taken his anger out on the only person he wasn't actually mad at.

If Miles had an ounce of sense and decency, he'd call Peter and tell him he needed to talk. Instead, he went to his phone in Sasha's office and dialed the number of the private investigator. A few minutes later he hung up, satisfied that the investigator would start digging in the right direction. Then he called Eleanor Dobbs for an update on the business he'd left in her hands. Cheerfully she filled him in and made notes on his instructions.

Miles should have felt better when he finished talking to Eleanor, but he didn't. He still felt like a class-A, brass-plated jackass for yelling at Sasha. He wouldn't see her until she came home in the evening and he decided to run out now and pick up flowers—something really spectacular—while he was doing his damn laundry.

By the time Sasha came home that evening she seemed to have forgotten about his explosion, but the cream-colored roses made her glow with such pleasure that Miles phoned the florist the next morning and placed an order for roses to be delivered again in a week. After all, he might not be around to bring them himself.

That evening Sasha lay across Miles's lap, reading while he watched an espionage movie. When the phone rang he answered, then handed the receiver to her.

"Hi, Doc, it's Barbara Dugan. Was that the handsome mystery man I've heard about?"

Laughing, Sasha sat up. This didn't sound like an emergency call. "What can I do for you, Barbara?"

"Well, I've been talking with Al and we decided we'd like to replace old Silver on the petting farm. Would you be willing to part with Houdini? He's got such a great story. Kids love that kind of happy ending. And we kinda miss having a horse around the place."

"Houdini would be in horse heaven at your place," Sasha told her. "He'll love all the attention. When would you want to get him?"

Miles got up and walked out of the living room. Sasha didn't think anything of it until she'd finished making arrangements with Barbara. She looked up to find him glowering at her from the doorway, his arms crossed over his chest.

"How can you do that?" he demanded. "How can you let that poor old guy go somewhere else? This is his home."

His vehemence startled her. She started to get up, then sank onto the couch and gaped at him. He scowled back.

"I beg your pardon," she finally said stiffly. "Are you hollering at me for sending Houdini to a better home?"

"I thought you cared about him."

"I *love* Houdini! That's why I'm willing to let him go to people who can give him more attention. The Dugans have a petting farm, and kids come to visit almost daily. Those kids go crazy for a chance to pet a horse, and Houdini loves kids. It's ideal for him, and I know he'll never be mistreated. They're wonderful people, and responsible animal owners. I've been their vet since I started practicing. Their last horse died in his sleep at the age of thirty-one, which is well over a hundred people years.''

Miles didn't look convinced. "What about you?"

His question puzzled her. "What about *me?*"

"Won't you miss him when he's gone?"

Sasha stared up at him, wishing she could read his thoughts in his eyes. "Yes, I'll miss him," she said. "But I'll let him go because I love him."

Miles shook his head, but, to her relief, came back to the sofa and sank down beside her. Immediately she went into his arms. For a long while he was silent. Sasha assumed he'd gotten interested in the movie again, but when they were going upstairs to bed, he said, "It still doesn't make sense. What's the point of loving Houdini, if you send him away?"

She turned and wrapped her arms around his waist. Tipping her face up toward his, she smiled to cover the aching sadness she felt whenever she thought about his impending departure. "Sometimes that's the point of loving."

She thought he might continue the discussion, but he only stared down into her face for a long moment before groaning and crushing her closer. His hands sifted through her hair, then cupped her head as he bent and kissed her. This was a kiss like none other. Sasha clung to his strong shoulders and absorbed the rough desperation of his mouth on hers. She knew what was driving him, and whatever assurances she could give him, she would.

Miles lifted the hem of her sweater and drew it off over her head, then, with trembling hands, he traced the lacy cups of her bra. His fingers trailed fire over the skin of her neck and chest, turning her bones to liquid. By the time Miles had reached around her back to unhook her bra, she was trembling with the effort to stand.

Sasha managed one lame tug at his T-shirt before he ripped it off and tossed it away. A second later, he had pulled her into his arms again. Her bare breasts met the hard, warm wall of his chest and she lifted her face for his kiss. The expression in his golden eyes made Sasha want to cry. She knew he was thinking that each time they made love could be the last time. She knew, because that was what she was thinking, too.

Without warning, Miles flicked off the lights, then scooped Sasha up and carried her to the bed. She looped her arms tightly around his neck and when he set her down, she pulled him down with her. Somehow he managed to kiss her mouth, her neck, her breasts, and work her jeans down and off her legs at the same time. Then he reared back and stared at her, his eyes a little wild in the dim light.

"I can't get enough of you," he said, his voice harsh. "All I have to do is smell your scent on something you wore and I get hard. It's like a compulsion."

"I know," she whispered. She got to her knees so she could look into his eyes. "I feel like a mare in heat around you."

Miles groaned, a low, feral sound, and tore at his jeans. He kicked them away, then knelt in front of her on the bed, his body powerfully aroused. She ran her fingers down his chest, following the centerline of dark, silky curls down past his navel, teasing at his thick shaft, smiling at the way his breath caught. A moment later her own breath caught at the feather-light brushing of his fingertips on her beaded nipples.

"If I were a stallion, what would I do?" Miles asked in a rasping whisper. Sasha felt her eyes widen. "Tell me, Sasha." She tried to speak, but her voice stuck in her throat. Miles leaned close and kissed her lips softly. "That's okay. I think I can figure it out," he told her.

And then his hands were stroking all over her, making her tremble in anticipation. He touched her everywhere except between her legs, where she was damp and hot for him. When he drew her down so she rested on her hands and knees, his hands touched her gently, telling her wordlessly that she could stop him at any time. Like a mare in season, all she wanted was the joining of their bodies. Feeling him behind her, she shifted her hips.

Miles reached under her pillow, then trailed kisses over her back and shoulders as he quickly took care of the condom. He lifted her hair and pushed it to one side, then leaned over her. She felt his thigh brush hers, felt his hardness resting on her hip, felt his body surround her. His teeth closed gently on the back of her neck and a shudder ran through her as his fingers slid between her thighs. His caresses brought her higher and higher, until all she could do was gasp his name.

And then he knelt behind her, his belly against her bottom, his hands clasping her hips. He entered her slowly, with far more tenderness than any stallion ever used to claim his mare. Sasha felt Miles deep inside her, felt as if there was no part of her that he wasn't touching. With every stroke he branded her as his. She closed her eyes and saw fireworks.

When they finally collapsed together, Miles gathered her close and held her tightly. A long, long while later he kissed the side of her neck and murmured, "This being a stallion is a tough job, but I like the perks."

Miles came back bursting with enthusiasm from his morning meeting with the owner of a small publishing company. A black pickup truck he didn't recognize sat in the yard. The logo on the driver's door had a picture of a black-and-white horse standing in a horseshoe. Framing the picture were the words, D. Eckley & Family, Champion Appaloosas, Mount Albert, Ontario.

Sasha had mentioned that there were breeders interested in Desperado, but she hadn't said any of them had been invited to nose around when no one was home. Frowning, Miles strode toward the paddock. As he came around the corner he saw a young woman standing beside the fence. Desperado, the rogue, was slurping at her hand through the bars. Mindful of the stallion's tentative grasp of social graces, Miles slowed his pace and called a greeting quietly so he wouldn't startle either the horse or the woman.

The stallion's head rose and his ears pricked forward at the sound of Miles's voice. The woman turned toward him, then wiped her hand on her jeans and smiled, revealing a mouth full of braces. He reassessed his impression of her age to about seventeen.

"Hi. I'm Candy Eckley. Are you Mr. Reiss?"

Miles smiled, both at her mistake and at her guileless expression. "Miles Kent. Doc Reiss is out on calls. Is there something I can help you with?"

"My dad said Desperado is for sale. We looked at him earlier this year, when Mr. Hogg still owned him, but no one could handle him." An earnest frown puckered the girl's face. "Daddy promised I could breed my mare this year, and I wanted to see Desperado again before I brought her to another stallion." Her expression cleared. "I can't wait to tell him Desperado is such a sweetheart now."

"Don't underestimate him," he warned. "Sasha says he may never be totally reliable."

Candy nodded. "We wouldn't try to break him to saddle. We'd only use him as a stud." She smiled. "Can you tell Doc Reiss that Daddy will call her for an appointment, so not to sell him before we get a chance to make an offer? Here's our card."

Miles took the card. He wanted to tear it up, but he stuffed it into his shirt pocket and muttered something about relaying the message to Sasha later in the day. Candy Eckley thanked him profusely, crooned a long string of baby talk to Desperado—who lapped up the attention without any apparent twinge of conscience, the traitor—then returned to her father's truck with a jaunty wave.

Seething, Miles stomped to the house. How could Sasha sell Desperado? She'd worked so hard with him, and risked her neck too many times. Now that the damn beast was finally trusting enough to eat out of her hand, she was planning to sell him to strangers! It was Houdini and her grandfather's hunters all over again. And the cats and the puppies. The woman had a peculiar way of showing she loved something, if she was so willing to let it go. Not that he was any expert on love, but he figured that if you loved something, letting go was the last thing you'd want to do.

By the time he'd reached the porch, some of the edge of his anger had dulled. He didn't even really have a clear idea of *why* he was so angry.

Copper greeted him with her entire body wagging. He stopped to play with her and the pups for a few minutes. Their eyes were open now, and they were clumsily tumbling all over each other and their mother. Stroking their silky coats and laughing at their antics erased the remainder of his anger. Perhaps Sasha was right. Even if she wasn't, it was her business.

"Where are your owners, Copper?" he asked her. The dogs ears lifted and her head tipped to the side as if she were considering the question. "They loved you and let you go, didn't they?" The dog grinned as if she understood. He shook his head. "But that was different. They couldn't fight for you any other way, could they? Sasha was taking care of Houdini and Desperado just fine, even if she wasn't riding the hunters. It doesn't—"

The ringing of the phone saved him from further philosophical discussions with the panting dog.

"Hi, Miles. It's Donna. My kids said they saw a couple of notices about a lost dog that could be about Copper."

"Where?" he demanded.

She gave him the cross streets, then added, "They were on their bikes and didn't stop to read the posters, so it could be a wild-goose chase."

After thanking her, Miles hung up, then started to dial the number McLeod had given Sasha, which was taped to the wall beside the kitchen phone. Then he reconsidered. What if it was a fool's errand? He and McLeod weren't exactly good buddies. He didn't want to call the constable unless this was a firm lead.

The only thing to do was check out the posters himself.

Chapter Fifteen

Miles raced outside and revved the rental car much too hard. He managed to get his anxiety under control by the time he pulled up at the first intersection Donna had given him. Sure enough, there was a crudely lettered poster on the utility pole, but it was torn and barely legible. What was left of the note said, "Dog lost. Gol . . . male. . . . e soon. Kids miss . . . swers to Co . . ."

"Close enough for rock 'n' roll," Miles muttered, then steered the car to the second intersection Donna had told him about. There was nothing but paper bits hanging on to staples scattered over the surface of the pole, as well as the other poles in the immediate area, as if someone had recently torn off all notices.

Cursing under his breath, he decided to cruise the nearby streets. If there had been two posters, there must be more, he reasoned. He couldn't call McLeod on the strength of a couple of scraps that might not refer to Copper at all.

But none of the utility poles in a three-mile radius bore a poster advertising for Copper's return. Disgusted, Miles drove into a gas station to phone Sasha and tell her why he wasn't there at lunchtime. As he got out of the car next to the phone booth, he noticed a gaunt, pale woman in a worn dress tacking a paper to the utility pole at the curb. Two scruffy, raggedly dressed children, a young boy and younger girl, stood to one side, their faces too wary for such young kids. They had to be Copper's owners, he thought with a surge of adrenaline. Their sadness tugged at his heart.

Their faces tugged at his memory. He saw a brief flash of an image. Several kids, about the same age as these kids, dirty, hungry and scared, huddled together. With a shudder of anger Miles pushed away the memory. The past didn't matter when the present was so urgent. He had to do something to rescue Copper's kids and their mother.

Casually Miles approached and read the paper. "Dog lost. Golden retriever female. Pups due soon. Kids miss her. Answers to Copper." At the bottom of the hand-printed notice was a phone number repeated on strips that could be torn off.

"Lost your dog, huh?" Miles said, hoping he sounded friendly and sympathetic, rather than threatening.

The woman flinched and shuffled a step back. The little girl clutched at the boy's shirt and stuck her thumb in her mouth. The boy slowly looked up at Miles. His fearful expression faded slightly when Miles smiled, making him wonder if the boy had seen him through the windows when he'd left Copper on Sasha's porch. Guardedly, the boy nodded.

"I haven't seen her," he told the youngster, "but I'll take your number just in case."

The trio simply stared at him until he'd taken one of the strips of paper from the notice. Then the mother backed away and turned, pushing the children toward the next utility pole. Miles strolled to the pay phone, then fumbled through the weather-beaten directory until he found the number for the Ontario Provincial Police. The voice on the other end told him McLeod was off duty, but would be in later in the day.

"Tell him it's about the dog and the kids," he said after leaving his name. He also left the phone number of the sad little family.

As he spoke into the phone, Miles covertly watched the three walk to the third utility pole in front of the gas station. When he finished leaving his message for McLeod, he hung up, then reached for another quarter to phone Sasha. The mother and kids retraced their steps to the edge of the gas-station parking lot. Miles froze, his attention fixed on the trio. The woman shoved the little girl into a battered old car parked across the street. The boy climbed in after his sister, and the woman shut the door. After two tries, the car started, sending up a cloud of black exhaust. Miles held his breath as the car drove past him and out to the narrow side road.

Acting strictly on impulse, Miles jumped into his car to follow the woman home. He would phone Sasha later. If he could give McLeod an address for the creep who beat the woman and her kids and killed their other dog, they'd be one step closer to getting free of him. After reliving some of his own memories, he felt even more the urgency of helping anyone in the same circumstance to escape.

Following the woman was harder than he'd anticipated. The old car crept along, doing well under the speed limit. The two-lane country road ran nearly straight, and at midmorning it was almost empty of traffic except for their two cars, forcing him to drive very slowly in order to hang back. Finally she signaled, the light blinking dimly behind the tape holding the taillight in place. He slowed enough so she wouldn't see him turn behind her. The side road was unpaved and rutted. The woman drove even more slowly. Impatiently Miles forced himself to stay well back until he saw her turn down a gravel driveway barely accessible through densely overgrown bushes on both sides.

He decided to be prudent and park the car on the shoulder of the road, where it was hidden by those wild bushes. Leaving the doors unlocked but pocketing the keys, he got out of the car and crept toward the ramshackle house practically invisible from the road. He told himself he was looking for a house number, so he could give McLeod an exact address, but he knew he couldn't just drive away after that. Not if those sad-eyed kids and their worn-out mother were in danger. The police might not understand, but he knew Sasha would. Somehow, she'd become his conscience since the accident had wiped his memory clean. If she were with him, she'd do the same. Hell, he'd stuck around at Sasha's farm on the excuse that he wanted to make sure the kids were okay, so here was his chance. Maybe it was his way of helping the helpless child he'd been himself. Whatever his rationalization for butting in, there was no way he could back out until he knew the kids and the woman were safe.

Using the bushes for cover, Miles made his way toward the house. The weathered structure listed slightly, the porch sagged, several windows had been covered with plastic or cardboard, suggesting that they'd been broken. The yard resembled a junkyard, with rusting car parts and farm machinery scattered in weed-invaded piles. For a disorienting moment Miles felt as if he'd been here before. Then he realized he must be picturing the house where his childhood tormentor had locked him in that nightmarish basement. With a shudder he shook off the memory and edged closer to the house.

Suddenly the front door flapped open. A tall, thin man in ragged overalls started to step out onto the porch. Abruptly he turned and strode back inside. There was a muffled crash from inside, as if a piece of furniture had been smashed. A man's voice, raised in unintelligible shouting, followed. More crashing, mingled with the sounds of dishes breaking, and more of that furious snarling. Then the man appeared again, his fingers closed around the woman's upper arm in a grip that Miles knew would leave bruises.

From his hiding place among the bushes, Miles heard the woman's voice, her words indistinct, her tone whining. Another snarl from the man, then the sound of a car door slamming. A moment later the other car door slammed, and the car groaned to life. Miles ducked farther back into the bushes and prayed the man would be too preoccupied to notice Miles's white rental car parked on the shoulder in front of the house. His prayers were apparently answered. The car tore backward down the driveway, spitting gravel within inches of Miles' feet. Through the leaves and branches, he saw the car speed backward into the gravel road, turning rapidly away from his rental car. Miles suspected the driver hadn't even glanced in his rearview mirror.

The scene Miles had witnessed seemed so familiar that for a moment he felt as if he were watching a movie he'd seen before. Then he remembered, in a flash of clarity that stole his breath. Eleanor Dobbs! He'd witnessed her ex-husband trying to kill her and had subdued the animal until her son, Jonathan, also badly beaten, had been able to phone the police. The bastard had decided to kill them, rather than allow Eleanor and their son to leave him. Eleanor had been permanently disabled, and Miles had hired her as his office assistant, even though she didn't know how to type and he had hardly enough income for himself.

So, now at least he remembered why Eleanor and Jonathan thought they owed him something. But if he'd done all that for them, why did he sense some lingering guilt, as if he hadn't done enough? Was there someone else in his past he should have tried to save? Or had he fulfilled the legacy of violence and hurt someone the way he had been hurt?

Overhead, a crow cawed. The raw sound shook him out of his thoughts and reminded him that those two sad ragamuffins were still in the house. After all that snarling and smashing of furniture and plates, they must be scared stiff. And they were much too young to be left alone, even for a few minutes. Kids could get into trouble without realizing it. He'd check on them, then call McLeod from the house. Not for the first time, he wished Sasha was with him. He could use her calming influence if the kids panicked at his presence. After all, he figured, one big guy looked a lot like another when a kid was small and battered.

Glancing around to make sure no one was watching, praying the mother and her creepy boyfriend would stay away long enough for him to make sure the kids were okay, Miles snuck up to the house. The porch stairs rocked under his feet, and the floor creaked with each step. The screen door sagged on its hinges. The inside door stood open. Cautiously he walked into the front foyer. The smell of garbage and stale smoke hit him immediately. He looked around the dark rooms of the first floor, appalled by the litter of ashtrays, beer cans and junk-food wrappers. There was little furniture, and what there was sagged raggedly.

The upstairs rooms were little better. Miles stayed there only long enough to make certain the kids weren't in any of the rooms or closets. Puzzled, he went back down to the front hall. Where could they be? Maybe outside. There was a dilapidated garage behind the junk piles. He'd check there as soon as he was sure they weren't hiding in the house.

"Kids!" he bellowed, hoping he wasn't going to scare them further. "Where are you? It's okay. I'm a friend from the farm where you brought Copper. I want to help you. Okay?"

He paused, straining his ears for any answering sound. Nothing. He drew another breath to call again, and heard a faint sound from somewhere in the house. In the kitchen? He moved as quietly as he could, listening for the noise so he knew which way to go. There it was again. Muffled thumping. And muffled, high-pitched calls for help.

Suddenly he knew where the kids were.

More than ever, Miles wished Sasha was with him. He needed her strength now, as much as the kids trapped in the basement did.

Filthy and exhausted, Sasha ducked home for a quick change and an early lunch. She fed the horses, refilled the cats' water bowls and let Copper out. Miles wasn't around, but she found the note he'd left about the Appaloosa breeder, along with Dan Eckley's card. She grabbed an apple, then brought the apple core out to Desperado, who lipped it gently from her palm.

"Well, at least I've succeeded with you, old boy," she murmured. "But Miles is not a horse. And I knew from the start that he would have to go home to get back the rest of his memory. It was just too easy to love him, too easy to fool myself."

She sighed and gave the horse a final pat. Whatever happened between her and Miles, she'd always have the sweetness of loving him, and memories that were hers to treasure.

Miles flung open the stained and peeling door to the basement. A dim light from deep inside cast eerie shadows. The children's cries suddenly stopped. He knew instinctively that they were holding their breath.

"It's okay, kids. I'm a friend," he called down to them. "You can come up now. You're safe. I'm going to get you out of here. Copper and her pups are waiting for you."

Their only answer was a renewal of thin, high whining. Miles stood in the doorway, fighting nightmare visions, fighting nausea. He drew in a breath of the foul air and called again for the kids to come upstairs.

"We can't," a reedy, very shaky voice finally replied.

"Sure you can. There's no one here but me, and I'm a friend. I'm taking care of Copper, too. She had her pups. Six of them. Come on upstairs and I'll bring you to the farm so you can see them yourselves. Okay?"

"We can't. We're stuck."

"Stuck?"

The whimpering intensified, punctuated by shushing. Miles didn't have any idea in what way the kids were stuck, but he knew he was going to have to go down into that basement and get them unstuck. There was no way to know when the mother and her vicious boyfriend would be back. He couldn't count on having enough time to call the cops. Anyway, if the cops were going to arrest the creep brutalizing them, the kids didn't need to see that.

None of which made the first step easy.

Praying that some of Sasha's strength had rubbed off on him, Miles clutched the sticky doorframe and concentrated on steadying his shaking knees. One step down. Two steps down. By the time he'd made it halfway he was sweating like a pig and fighting not to black out. He couldn't afford to pass out and get himself caught trying to rescue the kids. Whatever memories this musty black basement was trying to trigger were memories he could do without.

Blindly he shuffled his foot from creaking step to creaking step until he reached the uneven dirt floor. The musty smell gave way to the rank stink of sewage and garbage. And there, in the middle of the low-ceilinged basement, cringing on the floor beside one of the support beams, sat the two ragged kids. Even in the dim light he could see their eyes were wide with fear, and their dirty faces streaked with tears. For a moment he was looking into a mirror deep within his soul. Then the image changed to Sasha's gently smiling face, and he knew he was finally free of the demonic hold of this memory.

"It's okay, kids. I'm here to help you. Now, what's this about being stuck?" Then he looked closer and his heart sank.

Sasha drove up her driveway faster than usual, eager to see Miles and feel his arms around her. Instead of Miles's rental car sitting in its usual spot in her yard, she found a white OPP cruiser, Donna's truck, plus a blue station wagon and a gray sedan she didn't recognize. Heart pounding at the horrific possibilities, she raced up the porch stairs and burst into the front hall. Her work boots thudded to a halt at the sight that greeted her when she looked into the living room.

Miles sat on the sofa, a small blond child snuggled in his arms. One of his arms cradled the child. His free hand stroked the tumbled curls and narrow little shoulders. She gaped at the scene, only snapping her jaw shut when Miles met her eyes and smiled.

Stunned, Sasha sagged against the doorjamb and took in the domesticity of the pair on the couch. Miles looked so right, holding that child close to his chest. There was a tenderness in his smile that touched Sasha's heart deeply. Whatever had happened, Miles looked like a man ready for the future. As she came into the room she wondered if she had a place in that future. She hoped so, but she wouldn't prompt him. His decisions had to be made based on what was best for him, not for her.

Walking across the living room, she saw a woman she didn't know sitting at the dining room table with Dave McLeod and a female OPP constable. Their voices created a low, steady murmur. None of them looked up when she passed by.

She sat on the arm of the couch and looked at the child Miles held. A little girl, maybe three, maybe four, with her eyes closed and her thumb in her rosebud mouth. Her blond hair looked freshly washed. "Playing Papa Bear looks good on you," Sasha whispered, the words going straight from her heart to her lips, totally bypassing her brain. Her face flamed at the possible implications.

If her comment bothered Miles, he didn't let on. He grinned briefly, then looked at her with grave eyes. "These are Copper's kids. I found them chained to a beam in their basement." Sasha gasped in horror. "Their mother's boyfriend has been doing that for a while. They've both got infected sores on their ankles."

"Dear God!" she whispered. "No one with an ounce of humanity would do that to an animal, let alone a child!" Then she focused on something else he'd said. "You rescued them from their basement?" He nodded. She smiled, knowing words weren't necessary.

"When I got them here, I called McLeod. Then I got hold of Donna and Doris. I figured the kids could use someone maternal to fuss over them, and I wanted witnesses that I hadn't inflicted any of their injuries when I cleaned them up. They both brought kids' clothes. And McLeod brought a woman cop and a social worker."

That explained the cars she hadn't recognized. "Where are Donna and Doris now?"

"In the kitchen with Kevin, admiring the pups. This is Lucy." His eyes flashed with anger. "Do you know, when I asked her name, she said it was Brat, because that's what that scumbag Elmore Hogg calls her. Poor baby thought it was her name."

"Did you say Elmore Hogg?"

"Yeah. You know him?"

"I know his brother, Darrel. He's the creep who wanted to destroy Desperado."

Miles nodded. "Right. The Eckley girl mentioned him. I didn't make the connection then. Looks like evil runs in the family. Apparently Elmore's been lying low after a little prison escape a couple of years ago. McLeod said there are enough charges against Hogg to keep him tied up until these two are grandparents. They're in there now—" he jerked his head toward the dining room "—trying to figure out how to convince the kids to go with the social worker." He smiled. "They both pitched a fit about leaving Copper again. They say they want to stay here."

Sasha slid onto the couch and put her hand on Miles's strong, warm arm. Love for him flooded through her. "You're wonderful. What about the mother?"

Again, anger chilled the warmth in his golden eyes. "She's not totally innocent, although she's been battered pretty badly. The cops charged her with a list of things including failure to provide the necessities and accessory, because of Hogg. I doubt she'll get the kids back too soon. McLeod and his partner were both here when she told us it was the kids' fault that Hogg had kept them chained, and she blamed them for his arrest. He was her meal ticket, since she couldn't keep a job long enough to support herself and the kids."

Tears stung Sasha's eyes. "Miles, you really are a hero." She leaned toward him and brushed her lips over his.

"I couldn't have done it without you," he murmured.

She shook her head. That didn't make sense. "I wasn't even there," she protested.

"Sure you were. I told myself you were with me every step of the way into that basement."

His words sent a rush of warmth through her and left her speechless. But her mouth did work well enough for another soft kiss.

"Hi," a little voice said under her chin. Sasha looked down from kissing Miles to meet the huge blue eyes of little Lucy. "Can you be my new mommy?"

The next week and a half were so packed with activity that each night Sasha found herself falling into a deep sleep the moment she fell into Miles's welcoming arms. He must have been equally exhausted, because each morning they awoke in virtually the same embrace, barely moving all night. Mornings, however, proved that the spark of desire still burned between them. No matter how busy her schedule would be, no matter how many impossible things she had to finish in too little time, she started every morning with a smile.

First there was round after round of testimony to fit into the normally unpredictable and full days of foalings, breedings and routine barn calls, as well as the purchase examinations and emergencies that had to be worked into other appointments. The Children's Aid Society and the police were vying for control of the case, with the charges against the unrepentant mother and Elmore Hogg mounting daily.

Dave McLeod dropped by for coffee one evening. Although both men still acted like rival stallions, she was pleased that Dave seemed to have a new respect for Miles.

"So, in addition to escaping from prison, battering and forcibly confining his girlfriend's kids," Dave told them, "Elmore and brother Darrel were running a small but profitable business in stolen dogs and horse trailers. Darrel has a few convictions for assault and battery and sexual assault. A real wholesome family."

Sasha shuddered.

"What about the kids' mother? Is there a chance she'll plea bargain and get the kids back in this lifetime?" Miles demanded, his voice so harsh that Sasha wanted to touch him, soothe him.

Dave shook his head. "Doubtful. The mother has charges against her related to harboring Elmore, as well as negligence of the kids. Then there's the matter of a small cache of illegal and unregistered firearms in the basement, which would have been a parole violation if Elmore had waited in prison long enough to be eligible for early release."

The Children's Aid Society had temporarily assigned Kevin and Lucy to foster parents in the area. With Dave's help, Sasha and Miles were given permission to visit, and went every evening to see the confused and frightened pair. Sasha had asked the case worker what her chances of becoming the kids' legal guardian might be. The discouraging news was that her chances as a single woman were pretty slim.

In all, Sasha reflected on Friday night as she struggled to stay awake long enough to shower, this was proving to be an incredibly stressful time. The certainty that Miles was planning to leave soon stretched her nerves to the limit, but she couldn't find the courage to confront him with her feelings. His nightly phone consultations with the private investigator in Florida left him distracted and distant. No matter how many files and faxes Eleanor or the investigator sent him, his memory hadn't returned. Not since he'd remembered saving Eleanor and her son.

Physically and emotionally exhausted, Sasha stood under the warm water and rinsed the day's accumulation of horse and dirt out of her hair. When she opened her eyes, Miles stood on the other side of the glass shower doors. Slowly she slid the door open and let herself enjoy the sight of his magnificently aroused naked body. Then she met his eyes and smiled. A second later he was under the shower with her, his mouth on hers, his hardness already nestling against her belly.

"Where do you get the energy?" she gasped when he released her mouth.

He chuckled. "I sneak a handful of oats and vitamins when I feed Desperado. I figure what's good for one stud has to be good for another."

Her answering laugh turned to a soft moan as his slick hand covered her breast and his thumb rubbed over her nipple, sending sparks to her core. Then his hand slid down her side to cup her between her thighs. His mouth caught hers again, his tongue easing between her lips as his finger eased apart the folds between her legs. All she could do was cling to him and let him drive her higher until her climax wrung a small cry from her and buckled her knees. He caught her and rocked his pelvis against hers, teasing them both with the promise of joining their bodies.

"Sasha, you make me crazy!" he gasped. "I have no memories, but I swear, no other woman could make me feel like this."

"We can make our own memories, Miles. We don't have to compare this to anything to know it's special," Sasha murmured, longing to tell him how she felt but unwilling to put any strings on her love.

He hugged her tighter and groaned. "Let's get out of here and make some more memories!"

Memories! Miles looked down at the woman cradled in his arms. Memories weren't enough. He wanted to make a life with Sasha. A life with a future, not just a past. But he couldn't, not until he regained his memory. Until then he would be incomplete, a hollow shell, with too little to offer her. He might never be the kind of man she deserved, but he'd never find out if he stayed here, hiding from the truth.

Sasha's fingers traced erotic patterns on his shoulder and arm, then drifted to his chest, scattering his thoughts. Her touch sent shivers over his skin. As lightly as the brush of a butterfly wing, she feathered the hair on his chest, then followed the line that bisected his belly. His breath stopped when her fingers fluttered over his sex, then wrapped gently around him. He felt as if he'd stepped off a cliff into open air, free-falling without a net. Each time they made love it was like this, as if he began and ended with her touch.

"Hmm. You seem to have something in common with Desperado," she murmured, sliding her fingertips over him.

He laughed despite the way she made him writhe. "You really know how to stroke a guy's ego."

Her low chuckle sounded very smug and a little wicked. "I always suspected that's where the male ego lived."

Without warning she pushed him onto his back and bent over him. He felt her damp, silky hair swirl over his chest and hips, and then felt the hot, wet touch of her mouth. Sensations gripped him, lighting fires in his chest, sending flames to his loins, nearly lifting him off the bed. It was heaven, but it wasn't enough. Before she could take him past the point of choosing, past the point of stopping, he reached for her and drew her up to him.

Sasha clung to him, her mouth soft and open above his, her body pliant against his. It wasn't enough.

"I want you," he muttered, unable to put his fierce hunger into better words. *"I want you!"*

He rolled over so that once again she lay beneath him. Freeing one hand, he covered her small, firm breast and teased the already pebbled nipple. She sighed and murmured something against his lips. He smiled, then drove his tongue into her mouth, savoring the sweetness there. His sex pressed into the firm hollow of her belly. Sasha's long, slender legs wrapped around him, pulling him closer. He ached for her, but he didn't want this to end too soon.

"Miles, don't tease," she breathed. "I want you inside me. Take me, damn you!"

Her words nearly undid him. For a moment he forced himself to freeze, to hold perfectly still, to regain the control that was slipping away. He wasn't ready. She wasn't ready, although she thought she was. It wasn't time to let this end.

He drew a deep breath and pressed a soft kiss to her lips. Then he eased lower until he could trail kisses down her neck, along her collarbone, down to one breast, then the other. Her skin tasted sweet, so sweet. He took one nipple into his mouth and smiled at her low moan of pleasure.

Her fingers combed through his hair, following him as he worked kisses down her belly. The sweetly musky scent of her invaded his senses when he nuzzled at the dark curls between her thighs. A need to possess her gripped him, so elemental, so primal that he nearly growled at the power raging inside him. Whatever happened later between them, he wanted Sasha to know, *now,* that she was his, and he was hers.

With trembling hands he cupped her bottom and opened his mouth over her heated flesh. Her gasp reached him through the sound of his own ragged breathing. The taste of her was like some magic elixir, making him drunk, making him need more. Every stroke of his tongue wrung tiny cries from her. Wanting to pleasure every part of her, he reached up and covered her breasts with his hands. The sound of his name on her lips drove him to push her higher, even though he heard her urging him to join her.

He wanted so much from her, but all he could do at that moment was to give, and give, and give. With his hands and his mouth he brought her over the edge of sensation, then rolled her over onto him and drew her down onto his aching manhood. The ripples of her pleasure urged him deeper. Sasha tilted her head back, letting her hair drift over his thighs, then looked down into his eyes and smiled. In the instant before his own climax tore his soul from his body, he called her name like a prayer.

Chapter Sixteen

Sunday morning after chores, Sasha and Miles brought Kevin and Lucy to visit Copper and the puppies. After a tearfully joyous reunion they went to a local pancake house for brunch, along with Sam and Maggie. It broke Sasha's heart the way Kevin ate hunched over, with one arm curved protectively around his plate, as if expecting to have his food taken away at any moment. And Lucy refused to eat unless she was sitting in Sasha's lap, clutching the new stuffed dog Miles had given her.

Back home, Miles seemed more preoccupied than usual. He wouldn't talk about the children, or even about the weather. Without a word he went upstairs to the guest room he no longer slept in. An hour later, when Sasha finished printing out the last of her monthly invoices, she found Miles in the dining room. He'd spread all the photographs on the big table and was standing over them, staring, but she wondered if he saw them at all. His beautiful hazel eyes were so troubled when he looked up at her that she knew she was facing the beginning of the end.

Determined to be brave, she approached and selected a photo at random. It was an eight-by-ten color shot of a low, sprawling house with more windows than walls, its exterior nearly engulfed by tropical vegetation. She looked up to find Miles watching her. She smiled, although her heart felt as if it were breaking.

"I still can't remember it," he muttered, his tone bitter. He waved his hand to encompass all the photos. "I can't remember enough. Every day I take these out and look at them, and all I can remember is walking on the beach picking up seashells. I can't remember Eleanor Dobbs in the fancy wheelchair she says I bought her."

Sasha looked at the photo of a plump, smiling woman in a flowing, wildly patterned caftan, sitting in a high-tech wheelchair, in front of a desk holding a computer and a fancy-looking phone and fax machine.

"She's worked for me for over ten years, but all I can remember is dragging her husband off her when he tried to kill her with a baseball bat."

It was a memory he hadn't revealed until now. Sasha shuddered. Miles pointed a finger at a photo of a tall, slender young man wearing wire-rimmed glasses, jeans and a T-shirt, standing in front of a four-wheel-drive car parked by a beach. "That's her son, Jonathan. Eleanor told me I set up an educational trust for him, but I don't remember doing it. Nothing rings any bells, damn it! Nothing!"

Despite the anger that flashed in his eyes, Sasha reached out and took his hand in hers. "Give it time, Miles. Whatever memories your mind doesn't want to be remembered must have buried themselves very deeply. They won't necessarily surface just because you want them to."

Miles snorted, but he squeezed her hand. "You make it sound like my memories are separate entities from me. Parasites, or aliens." He gave her a crooked grin. "My memories are part of me, Sasha, and I've been playing the coward too long."

"You're leaving now," she said softly, the words striking her heart like hammer blows. She'd always known he would have to go. She'd known from the first tug at her heart that she'd have to let him go. But for a while it had seemed possible that he'd find a way to stay. Dear God, it hurt to face it!

He nodded. "My past isn't here, with you, and the longer I hang around trying to fool myself, the farther away my past is going to get. I rack my head and feel like I'm trying to hold water in a net." He caressed the back of her hand with his thumb. His eyes searched hers. "It will help if you understand."

She smiled, hoping to look brave, but it felt like a very sad smile from the inside. "I do. I've always known you'd have to go back if you want to find your past."

"It's there, all right. Buried with my mother." At Sasha's smothered gasp, Miles's lips thinned. "Eleanor faxed the bills from the hospital and the funeral home to me while we were at brunch. My mother was buried two days before I took off running. The investigator tracked down her history, too. Turns out I hadn't seen her or heard from her until the last investigator found her dying in a hospital less than an hour from my island."

"Oh, Miles, I'm so sorry," Sasha whispered, her heart aching for his loss, for his frustration.

"Don't be," he snapped, releasing her hand. He turned half away from her, but she could see the anger, *feel* the anger burning in him. Confused, she touched his shoulder, seeking to comfort as well as to question his reaction. Miles shrugged off her touch. She waited. When he turned to look at her again, his eyes flashed and his jaw clenched.

"Tell me," she urged gently. "Tell me why you're so angry."

Sasha reached out to touch his arm, but Miles moved away. "I don't know, damn it! All I know is what the investigator told me. She was a hooker, and the bastard who locked me in the basement was one of her boyfriends. She had a series of them. Parasites, all of them. Living off her. The courts took me away. She'd get me back. Then *she'd* send me back to foster services. When I was fourteen she disappeared for almost twenty years." He turned and looked at her, his face a tight mask of anger and hurt.

Sasha opened her mouth to express her sorrow and empathy, but Miles lifted his hand to stop her. "It's okay. I don't really remember any of this. Apparently, whenever I got sentimental, I'd hire an investigator to find her. They all struck out, until a week before she died. I paid the hospital bills. I arranged the funeral. And I can't remember a thing. Twenty years to find her, and I can't remember one word, one gesture, nothing."

He let out a deep breath, his shoulders sagging as if under some tremendous weight. Sasha longed to tell him that whatever his mother had been, whatever she'd done, took nothing away from the man he was today. She longed to tell him she loved him, no matter who he was, or thought he was. She longed to tell him to stay with her and let her help his wounded spirit heal.

Instead, she remained silent, because Miles had to make his own choices, had to reach his own conclusions, had to heal himself. All she could do was support his decision to leave, and pray that someday, once he'd regained his memory, he'd come back to her—if, but only if, there was a place for her, as she was, in his life.

"I have to go back there, Sasha," Miles said. "I have to retrace my steps until I find out who I am. I can't keep going like this. I feel like I'm wearing someone else's clothes, but I don't know whose."

Sasha nodded. All along she'd known this moment would come. Miles couldn't stay here with her when he felt so strongly that he needed to reclaim his past. He didn't belong here, and there was no place for her in his life, a world away from hers. It was for the best, for Miles as well as for her, but that didn't make it any easier to say goodbye. Perhaps they should have resisted the strong attraction between them, but she would always treasure being his lover, even for this precious short time.

"I've talked to Peter a few times in the last couple of days," Miles told her. "He warned me that when I get my memory back, I may lose whatever I have of my time with you. It's called a fugue state. Sasha, I don't want to forget a second of the time I've spent with you, but I can't go on like this."

The pain was too great. Sasha had to stop him from saying any more, or she'd start to cry. "I understand, Miles. When are you planning to leave?"

His eyes mirrored her regret. "This afternoon." Dear God, so soon? Sasha fought back the sting of tears as he added, "I'll drop off the car at the airport and take off around three."

The airport was over an hour away, and he'd have to be there early to return the car and buy his ticket. That meant he'd have to leave almost immediately. She swallowed hard before she trusted herself to speak. "Do you need any help packing?"

He raked his fingers through his dark hair, mussing it even more. Sasha held back the impulse to go to him and smooth the errant locks off his forehead. "No, thanks. My things are already in the duffel. I'll leave the extra computer stuff with you, since I've got everything I need at home. I've already cleaned up your hard disk, so you won't have to worry about my files cluttering up yours."

So soon, and so ready to go, she thought, too stunned to thank him for the ironic thoughtfulness of erasing all trace of himself from her computer's memory.

For a moment anger threatened to choke her. Then she looked at Miles and realized how carefully they'd avoided making promises, how scrupulously they'd kept that unspoken bargain. Her anger faded to sadness. There was no other way. She'd never intended to fall in love with him. Miles had never intended to stay with her. Neither of them had entertained the fantasy of her going with him. If she didn't love him, it would be so much easier to let him go.

Abruptly, Miles strode back to the dining room table and began gathering up the photos into a haphazard pile. Sasha picked up several, squared their corners and handed them to him. He took the photos, then looked into her eyes.

Tell me you would stay if you could, Sasha pleaded silently, but she wouldn't say the words that might make him question his decision. What was right for him wasn't necessarily right for her, but she would cope, as always, with loving and letting go. It was one of the things she did best.

Miles dropped the pile of photos onto the table and took her shoulders in his big hands. "Sasha?" he murmured. When she didn't look up at him, he kissed her forehead and said her name again. Still she couldn't meet his eyes. She couldn't bear him to see how much she wanted to plead with him not to go.

He trailed gentle kisses all over her face and murmured her name until his lips found hers. Sasha tasted the finality of bittersweet regret in his kiss.

Miles held Sasha carefully, afraid that if he let himself get too close he would crush her, trying to absorb her into his soul. Her lips gave softly under his. She tasted so sweet. If he didn't let her go now, he might never. The need to stay right where he was and say to hell with his past rose up in him like a tightening spiral. It would be wrong, but he wanted her beyond right or wrong.

Somehow, he broke the kiss. Sasha looked up, her dark eyes glistening. "It's okay, Miles. You've always been honest with me. We both knew you were here to heal, so you could go back to your own life. Anyway, whatever your past was like, you need to consider the future."

Tell me to stay, he pleaded silently, unable to form the words, afraid she didn't want him to.

"You gave me so much, Sasha. I don't have anything to offer. I can't think about the future—hell, I can't even think about the present—until I find the past."

She blinked rapidly, and Miles knew he'd never forgive himself for hurting her. "And when I do, there's no guarantee I'll be anyone you want to know. The more I find out, the less I like."

Sasha smiled. "That's because you don't see yourself the way I see you." Then she stopped smiling. "I can't tell you who you are. You have to find that out for yourself."

Tell me you could love me, anyway, he wanted to say, but it wouldn't be fair. "What if I never get my memory back? What if I never find out who I really am inside?"

Sasha placed her hand on his chest. He felt his heart beating under her palm, felt the heat of her hand seeping into him like good whiskey, warming, soothing. "Then forget the past. Look here—" she pressed her hand against him "—for the truth. Create yourself the way you want to be. Use the opportunity to start over."

Miles shook his head. "No one exists in a vacuum. I need to know *why* I lived like a hermit before I can decide what to do about it. I need to know what I was running away from."

Tell me to come back, he bargained in his mind, *so I can leave with a clear conscience. Give me something to live for.*

"Then you have to go back," Sasha said softly, dashing his last hope. "You know better than anyone what's best for you."

Suddenly her serenity infuriated him. Miles dropped his hands and stepped back, losing the contact of her hand on his heart.

"I better go," he muttered.

Sasha nodded. "I'll be in the barn," she told him as casually as if he were going to the grocery story instead of out of her life. "I have to get Desperado cleaned up. That Appy breeder is coming this afternoon to look at him." She gave him a quick little smile and turned away without a backward glance, sending his temper skyrocketing.

"Damn it!" Miles bellowed. She turned back as if he'd slapped her. Her lips parted, but he was too angry to stop the words from pouring out.

"How can you say you care about that poor beast, then sell him to the highest bidder? What's with you, Sasha? Do you only care about the ones who leave? You're so used to loving and letting go, I don't think you know how to hang in for the long term. It might not be in his best interests to leave, but it sure makes you look good to let him go. Altruistic. Self-sacrificing. Very noble," he sneered.

Sasha gasped and stepped back, but the shock and hurt in her eyes couldn't compare to the pain in his heart when Miles realized the truth of his own words. It wasn't the damn stallion he was shouting about. It was himself. Himself and Sasha.

"You're a coward, Sasha. An emotional coward," Miles shouted.

Sasha's chin lifted. Her dark eyes flashed. "That's not fair."

"Sometimes life isn't fair," he snapped back, chafing because he knew she was right and he was too angry, too hurt, to back down.

Without another word Sasha turned and walked away. Miles heard the front door shut, more softly than he would have closed it. Cursing himself for lashing out at her that way, he gathered his photos and made his way upstairs to throw the rest of his things into his duffel bag. Princess lay sleeping in the open bag. Lifting her out, he realized he was even going to miss the arrogant feline who used his clothes for a nest.

This wasn't the way he'd pictured his leaving, he thought as he loaded his duffel bag into the rental car. In fact, he hadn't thought about the actual leaving. Sasha's farm had become home, instead of the place he called home but couldn't remember. The catch was, Sasha believed he didn't belong here.

As Miles slammed the car trunk shut, he was struck by a painful irony. Somehow they'd gotten their original positions crossed. From the start, Sasha had counseled him to use his memory loss to make himself over from scratch. He'd argued that he needed to reclaim his past before he could think about a future. Not once did she even hint that she might want him to stay, with or without his memory. No pressure to influence his decision. No emotional blackmail. Exactly what he'd told her he wanted: no commitment.

Miles climbed into the car and turned the ignition key. For the last time he drove down the long gravel driveway. He didn't dare go to the barn to say goodbye, to Sasha, to the horses and cats. It had been hard enough to give Copper and her pups a final pat and say goodbye to Lucy and Kevin over the phone. Now that he'd hurt Sasha so badly, it would be cruel to force her to say goodbye again. Cruel and point-less, since her silence made it clear she didn't want him to come back once he got himself sorted out.

Almost on automatic pilot, Miles drove south on Wood-bine Avenue, past the horse farms and plowed fields, past the sod farms and the golf course. He realized how green and fertile everything around him had become in four—al-most five—weeks. Above the two-lane country road, two hawks circled. Red-winged blackbirds fluttered up from ditches beside the gravel shoulder and balanced on the util-ity wires. Impulsively he lowered his window to let in the sounds and the fresh smells.

At Davis Drive he turned toward the entrance to the 404. He stopped for the red light and looked at the crisscrossing of entrances and exits at the end of the highway below. Crossroads, he thought. He was at a crossroad in his life, too, and like the highway, one direction seemed to stop too soon, but there were alternative routes.

The light turned green. Miles pressed on the gas pedal and steered toward the highway entrance. As he took the tight curving ramp a little too fast, his tires squealed a protest. Suddenly that sound brought back the memory of another time he'd driven a little too fast, on his way to the hospital where he'd just discovered his mother lay dying.

From Desperado's paddock Sasha heard Miles driving away, but couldn't bear to watch his car disappear down the lane. Instead, she risked her toes, at the least, to stand close to the stallion and wrap her arms around his neck. His muscles were warm and firm. He smelled comfortingly earthy, and, bless him, he stood patiently, as if he under-stood her sorrow.

"I'll miss you, old boy," she murmured, but she knew there were no words to express the ache Miles had left be-hind. Desperado snorted softly, making her smile weakly.

"It's for the best," she told him, fighting the sting of her tears. "You need a proper home, a place where you know you belong." And so did Miles.

This time his snort sounded decidedly skeptical, and felt emphatically damp. Laughing and choking back a sob, Sasha stepped away from the horse and wiped the spit off her arms and jeans. As she did so, she glanced at her watch. Oh, God! Miles would be halfway to the airport, and Desperado's buyer would be at the farm any minute! She'd better busy herself getting the horse ready. Maybe work would distract her from the urge to throw herself into a stall and cry her eyes out.

Ten minutes later, as she was leaving the house after splashing cold water on her face in a vain attempt to erase signs that she'd been crying, a black pickup truck pulled into the yard. A man in his mid-forties climbed down from the driver's side, and a woman who looked to be in her late teens hopped down from the passenger side. Both wore jeans and T-shirts. The man wore a straw cowboy hat shoved back on his head. The pair walked toward the barn.

"Hello!" Sasha called out. They stopped. "Mr. Eckley? I'm Sasha Reiss."

"Call me Dan," the man boomed back. When Sasha caught up with them and shook hands, he added, "This is my daughter, Candy."

"Hi, Candy," Sasha said, extending her hand and striving not to feel uneasy. There was nothing wrong with the Eckley family, or their horse-breeding operations. She'd checked them out before making this appointment. She wasn't going to take any chances on another Darrel Hogg. Desperado had had enough bad experiences to last a lifetime.

When he saw them approaching his paddock, Desperado snorted, wheeled and bucked, then trotted around with his tail flagging and his neck arched proudly. Since his bath the day before, he was gleaming white with shining black spots. As if he knew he should make a good impression, he reversed and showed his paces in the opposite direction, then trotted to the fence and stuck his nose out to be petted. Candy obliged, earning a sloppy kiss across her palm.

"I saw this fellow a few months ago at that swamp Hogg calls a farm," Dan Eckley told her. "Candy said he's like a new horse, but I had to see him for myself. You've worked a miracle with him."

"I'm thrilled that he's for sale again," Candy added with a bright smile. "If I were in your shoes, I'd never let him go."

Sasha's answering smile froze. She felt as if a fog had lifted from her brain—and her heart. Why was she giving up this magnificent animal who had grown to trust her? Who had begun to thrive under her care? Who had shown her as much affection as he knew how to give?

Why, in fact, did she feel compelled to let everyone and everything she loved go? Why wasn't she keeping Desperado?

Why hadn't she told Miles she loved him and wanted him to come back once he'd faced his past?

Was Miles right, was she an emotional coward? Had she been strong to let Miles go, or afraid to risk asking him to stay?

"I'm sorry, Dan, Candy. I really did intend to sell Desperado when I spoke with you. But the more I think about it—"

"I'll double your asking price," Dan interrupted her to say.

She shook her head. "It isn't the money. It's the horse." *And the man.* "I've decided to keep him." *Please, God, I hope he'll want to come back.*

The man eyed her suspiciously. "You aren't going to geld him, are you?"

"Certainly not! Not with his bloodlines and conformation."

"Well, if you aren't going to sell him, how about giving us an exclusive on his stud services for this season? Since we came out here in good faith and all."

Sasha chuckled as an enormous sense of relief washed over her. "No problem. Have your lawyer draw up a contract and send it to me." She offered her hand to Dan and Candy. "I hope you don't think I'm rude, but I just realized there's something very important I have to do immediately. Will you excuse me?"

The instant the Eckley truck started, Sasha revved her own engine and followed them down the driveway, fidgeting while they waited for a dump truck to bump and bang its way past. Then she had to wait for a car going the opposite way to pass her driveway. "C'mon, c'mon," she muttered as the car approached. To her irritation, the white sedan slowed, then blocked her entrance. Furious with the driver, whom she couldn't see, Sasha leaned on her horn.

The driver's door opened. She lowered her window to give him a piece of her mind. A man stood up on the far side of the car. Numbly, Sasha's mind registered what her heart was afraid to believe.

"Going somewhere?" Miles asked, leaning on the roof of his rental car.

Her fingers fumbling with the door latch, Sasha finally opened her door and nearly fell out. A heartbeat later Miles stood in front of her. Her pulse raced, suffusing her with heat as she looked up at him.

"Did you forget something?" she asked in turn.

Miles flashed a devilish grin. "Isn't that where you came in?" he murmured. Then, before his small jest registered, he said, "Actually, I remembered something. In fact, everything."

Without stopping to think of the consequences, Sasha threw her arms around his neck. "Oh, Miles! I'm so happy for you!"

His hesitation took long enough that she started to pull away. Then his arms went around her and held her closer, so that her breasts snuggled against his solid chest and his hips cradled hers. For a long moment he simply held her. Then he let out a deep breath.

"It's a mixed blessing," Miles told her. "Most of my memories are worth forgetting. I'd had this fantasy that my mother had been searching for me, and we would have one of those fairy-tale reunions. I used to tell myself that one of her evil boyfriends had carried her off, forcing her to abandon me."

He sighed heavily. "Turns out when I found my mother, she didn't exactly welcome me with open arms. She told me I had been the worst mistake of her life and she wished I'd never been born. After she died I went to her funeral. I was the only one there besides the minister, and after the way she'd rejected me, I felt as if my reason to live had been yanked out from under me. I got into my car and drove, because I think better when I drive. And I drove all the way into Canada, and stayed at a bed-and-breakfast out in the countryside."

Miles stopped speaking and Sasha waited patiently for him to go on. Instead, he ran his big hands over her back, then found the end of her braid and released the elastic. Sasha clung to him as he unbraided her hair, their closeness allowing her to feel his growing arousal, which matched hers. But just when she was about to tell him to finish his story after they made love, he spoke again.

"It's so ironic, Sasha. You've been telling me to start over and not worry about remembering my past. And I've been insisting I had to get my memory back before I could go on."

He paused to press a kiss to her forehead, but it was long enough that she murmured, "What's ironic about that?"

"I sat around that bed-and-breakfast for two days, sulking. And finally I realized that who my mother was didn't matter. I didn't have to wallow in arrested development and live like a hermit. Hell, I'd started with nothing and ended up with a small fortune. I got in my car to head for home and start over, then nearly wiped out any chance of having a future."

Miles lowered his head and took Sasha's lips in a long, sweet kiss that filled her with yearning. When he broke the kiss, he pulled her close and sighed.

"I never wanted to hurt you." He tightened his arms around her. "But I was so sure I had to leave to get my memory back."

Sasha pushed away enough to look up into his eyes. "I know that. You didn't have to come back to tell me."

"No," he interrupted in a low growl. "I came back because I couldn't stand leaving." Miles drew back and looked into her eyes. She slid her hands up to his powerful shoulders and gazed back, smiling in answer to his rueful grin. "The last thing I remember thinking before I woke up wrapped around a tree was that I wanted to find a woman I could make a life with. Next thing I knew, my mind is a blank slate and there you were. The only catch was, I was too stupid to recognize you. Until now." He took a deep breath. "I've decided to stay."

"Stay?" Sasha echoed. "Here?"

"Here." Miles pulled her hips closer to his and rocked her slowly against him. "Given my clean record and all the bucks I've pumped into the Canadian economy already, I won't have any trouble getting landed immigrant status." He tipped his head to one side as if weighing a decision, but there was a definite glint in his golden eyes. "Of course, it won't hurt if my wife sponsors my application."

Sasha felt the blood leave her head. "Wife?"

Miles grinned. "If you'll have me." His grin faded. "I know it's fast, but I love you so much it hurts to think of not being with you." He brushed a kiss across her lips. "What do you say, Sasha? Think you can do as much with this reprobate as you did with Desperado?"

Suddenly the day seemed brighter. Sasha smiled. "It looks like I'm keeping both of you," she told Miles, "but only Desperado gets to perform stud service to outside mares."

Miles grinned wickedly. "Only one mare this stallion is interested in, and I intend to mate for life."

His low, husky voice sent shivers of anticipation up Sasha's spine, but she couldn't quite shake practical matters. "What about your business? And your home?"

"This isn't the horse-and-buggy era, Doc. I've got my fax machine and modem. I'll just have to put an extra phone line in your house, and I might have to travel occasionally. I've got some ideas for Secret Island, as a retreat, maybe. But I'd like to take you there first, for our honeymoon. How soon can we plan a wedding?"

She smiled at his impatience, which perfectly matched her own. "Let me think. This is May, so my parents are in Italy. They'll be in England for June. We need some time to do this right. Can we wait until July?"

"Barely."

Miles bent and kissed her thoroughly. When her knees buckled, Sasha wound her arms around him and simply held on. His hands roamed her back and her bottom, drawing her closer, sending unmistakable messages to her rioting nerve endings. "Oh, God, I want you!" he breathed, then took her mouth again.

Miles broke the kiss slowly, his hand on her breast kneading, giving pleasure, promising more. "The house or the barn?" he growled.

"The barn is closer," she whispered. But when he took her hand she stood her ground, tugging him to a halt. "Wait," she said, trying to keep a straight face. "I'm afraid I forgot something."

Miles whirled and gaped at her. *"What?"* he bellowed.

She smiled. "I forgot to tell you I love you."

He grinned. "I know just the cure for that kind of amnesia," he told her as he led her toward the barn.

Epilogue

Sasha stood beside the Jeep wagon and watched her husband carefully take their two-day-old son out of his car seat. She smiled at the sight of the tiny bundle cradled so tenderly in Miles's large, strong hands. As he handed Matthew to her, their eyes met for a long, tender moment. A precious moment, since it was likely to be their last alone for a while.

She snuggled her sleeping son against her shoulder and breathed in his sweet baby scent. Then she turned to walk the few steps to the nearby pasture, where three mares grazed beside three striking Appaloosa foals. In his high-walled stallion paddock, Desperado lifted his head and nickered, as if welcoming them home.

"I think the significance of this introduction will be lost on Matt," Miles murmured as the mares and foals approached.

Sasha grinned. "Never too young to start living and breathing horses."

Miles grinned back. "Or too old."

"It was your idea to buy the mares and expand the barn," she reminded him.

He sighed and slipped his arm around her. "Chalk it up to male bonding," he explained. "I couldn't bear to see that poor stallion pining for female company when I have my mate right here."

His quick kiss might have turned into one that lingered, except for the slamming of the front screen door and a cry of, "They're here! They're here!" from Lucy. With Kevin close behind her, she raced across the yard toward them. "Sasha! Miles! We want to see the baby!"

Miles released Sasha and crouched to catch Lucy in a hug. As always, something warm and soft expanded within him when the little girl threw her skinny arms around his neck and held tight. Kevin, still more reserved, hung back until Miles reached out and drew him into the hug. When they let go of each other, Miles stood and lifted Lucy so she could see Matt.

"He's pretty," she declared. "Is he gonna call you Mommy and Daddy?" She turned those wide, heart-melting blue eyes toward him, then looked at Sasha, who nodded. "Can *we* call you Mommy and Daddy, too?"

Deeply touched, Miles hugged the child and looked at Sasha for guidance. She smiled, and he could see that her dark eyes sparkled with tears. A quick glance at Kevin showed that the boy was standing with his head tipped down, gazing up through his lashes at Sasha. When she extended her free hand toward the boy, Kevin hesitated, then rushed to her side, where she held him with her hand on his shoulder.

"We'd love it if you call us Mommy and Daddy," she answered, her voice husky with the emotions Miles saw shining in her eyes.

"Yay! I'm a big sister!" Lucy crowed. She wiggled for Miles to let her down. "I'm gonna tell Gran and Gramps and Auntie El'nor and Uncle Jon'than!" she called before charging off toward the porch where Sasha's parents and

Jonathan Dobbs stood beside Eleanor in her new portable wheelchair, watching and smiling.

"I guess that means I'm Matt's big brother, eh?" Kevin asked hesitantly. Miles nodded, watching the boy carefully for signs of his hidden feelings. The poor kid had been through too much already, and still didn't seem to know how to trust or just plain enjoy life. "He's gonna be too little to play with for a long time, huh?"

"For a while," Sasha agreed. "But you'll be surprised at how fast he grows up. And Miles and I can't think of anyone who would make a better big brother than you."

Miles watched the hope glow in the boy's eyes. The kids had been with them for almost a year, slowly healing under Sasha's tender, loving care. With the help of a sympathetic judge, Miles and Sasha had been named the children's legal guardians shortly after their mother had been convicted of a number of crimes. The kids never spoke of her, or of Elmore Hogg, and Miles hoped they'd be able to leave their bad memories behind forever. If he and Sasha had any say in the matter, Lucy and Kevin would never have to worry about security, safety or love.

Miles looked up at the sound of crunching gravel to see Lucy running toward them, with Sasha's parents following at a more sedate pace. Copper and her not-so-runtish daughter Penny bounded joyously around the little girl. Lucy barreled into his legs, looked up and said, "Hi, Daddy! Hi, Mommy! Hi, baby Matt. It's cake time." Then she slipped her little hand into his.

Miles rested his hand on Kevin's head and waited for his in-laws to join them. When they were all together, he looked from one to another, from his beautiful wife and the miracle of a son they'd created together, to her warm and generous parents, to the two children who reminded him so much of himself.

"Now that I've got you all here," he said, a little surprised to find his voice choked with emotions, "I'd like to thank you all for the best gift anyone could ever give a man."

Sasha met his eyes and gave him that special smile that touched even the coldest, darkest part of his soul and warmed him to the core. "And what's that?" she asked softly.

"A new life," he answered.

* * * * *

Silhouette®

SPECIAL EDITION

COMING NEXT MONTH

#973 THE BRIDE PRICE—Ginna Gray
That Special Woman!
Wyatt Sommersby couldn't help but be attracted to the passionate Maggie Muldoon. When her free-spirited nature resisted Wyatt's tempting proposal of marriage, it left Wyatt wondering—what would be the price of this bride?

#974 NOBODY'S CHILD—Pat Warren
Man, Woman and Child
Feeling like nobody's child compelled Lisa Parker to search out her true parents. It brought her face-to-face with J. D. Kincaid, a man whose emotional past mirrored her own, and whose tough exterior hid a tender heart....

#975 SCARLET WOMAN—Barbara Faith
Years ago, Clint Van Arsdale watched as his brother eloped with Holly Moran, a girl from the wrong side of the tracks. Now Holly was a widow—yet despite the pain of a shared past, Clint could no longer escape their undeniable attraction.

#976 WHAT SHE DID ON HER SUMMER VACATION—
Tracy Sinclair
Melanie Warren's vacation jaunt unexpectedly landed her in an English country manor. When the very proper and very sexy David Crandall invited her to become nanny to his adorable twins, she just couldn't turn him down....

#977 THE LAST CHANCE RANCH—Ruth Wind
Life's hard knocks forced Tanya Bishop to leave her son in the care of strong and sensible Ramon Quezada. Returning home to reclaim her lost child, she didn't count on falling under Ramon's seductive spell.

#978 A FAMILY OF HER OWN—Ellen Tanner Marsh
Jussy Waring's lonely heart longed for that special kind of family she'd only heard about. When Sam Baker came into her and her young niece's life, would she dare hope that her dream could finally come true?

MILLION DOLLAR SWEEPSTAKES (III)

No purchase necessary. To enter, follow the directions published. Method of entry may vary. For eligibility, entries must be received no later than March 31, 1996. No liability is assumed for printing errors, lost, late or misdirected entries. Odds of winning are determined by the number of eligible entries distributed and received. Prizewinners will be determined no later than June 30, 1996.

Sweepstakes open to residents of the U.S. (except Puerto Rico), Canada, Europe and Taiwan who are 18 years of age or older. All applicable laws and regulations apply. Sweepstakes offer void wherever prohibited by law. Values of all prizes are in U.S. currency. This sweepstakes is presented by Torstar Corp., its subsidiaries and affiliates, in conjunction with book, merchandise and/or product offerings. For a copy of the Official Rules send a self-addressed, stamped envelope (WA residents need not affix return postage) to: MILLION DOLLAR SWEEPSTAKES (III) Rules, P.O. Box 4573, Blair, NE 68009, USA.

EXTRA BONUS PRIZE DRAWING

No purchase necessary. The Extra Bonus Prize will be awarded in a random drawing to be conducted no later than 5/30/96 from among all entries received. To qualify, entries must be received by 3/31/96 and comply with published directions. Drawing open to residents of the U.S. (except Puerto Rico), Canada, Europe and Taiwan who are 18 years of age or older. All applicable laws and regulations apply; offer void wherever prohibited by law. Odds of winning are dependent upon number of eligibile entries received. Prize is valued in U.S. currency. The offer is presented by Torstar Corp., its subsidiaries and affiliates in conjunction with book, merchandise and/or product offering. For a copy of the Official Rules governing this sweepstakes, send a self-addressed, stamped envelope (WA residents need not affix return postage) to: Extra Bonus Prize Drawing Rules, P.O. Box 4590, Blair, NE 68009, USA.

SWP-S795

He's Too Hot To Handle...but she can take a little heat.

SILHOUETTE

Summer Sizzlers

This summer don't be left in the cold, join Silhouette for the hottest Summer Sizzlers collection. The perfect summer read, on the beach or while vacationing, Summer Sizzlers features sexy heroes who are "Too Hot To Handle." This collection of three new stories is written by bestselling authors Mary Lynn Baxter, Ann Major and Laura Parker.

Available this July wherever Silhouette books are sold.

As a *Privileged Woman,*
you'll be entitled to all
these *Free Benefits.*
And *Free Gifts, too.*

To thank you for buying our books, we've designed an exclusive FREE program called *PAGES & PRIVILEGES™*. You can enroll with just one Proof of Purchase, and get the kind of luxuries that, until now, you could only read about.

*B*IG HOTEL DISCOUNTS

A privileged woman stays in the finest hotels. And so can you—at up to 60% off! Imagine standing in a hotel check-in line and watching as the guest in front of you pays $150 for the same room that's only costing you $60. Your *Pages & Privileges* discounts are good at Sheraton, Marriott, Best Western, Hyatt and thousands of other fine hotels all over the U.S., Canada and Europe.

*F*REE DISCOUNT TRAVEL SERVICE

A privileged woman is always jetting to romantic places. When <u>you</u> fly, just make one phone call for the lowest published airfare at time of booking—<u>or double the difference back!</u> PLUS—

you'll get a $25 voucher to use the first time you book a flight AND <u>5% cash back on every ticket you buy thereafter through the travel service!</u>

SSE-PP3A

*F*REE GIFTS!

A privileged woman is always getting wonderful gifts.
Luxuriate in rich fragrances that will stir your senses (and his). This gift-boxed assortment of fine perfumes includes three popular scents, each in a beautiful designer bottle.  Truly Lace...This luxurious fragrance unveils your sensuous side. L'Effleur...discover the romance of the Victorian era with this soft floral. Muguet des bois...a single note floral of singular beauty.

*F*REE INSIDER TIPS LETTER

A privileged woman is always informed. And you'll be, too, with our free letter full of fascinating information and sneak previews of upcoming books.

*M*ORE GREAT GIFTS & BENEFITS TO COME

A privileged woman always has a lot to look forward to. And so will you. You get all these wonderful FREE gifts and benefits now with only one purchase...and there are no additional purchases required. However, each additional retail purchase of Harlequin and Silhouette books brings you a step closer to even more great FREE benefits like half-price movie tickets... and even more FREE gifts.

L'Effleur...This basketful of romance lets you discover L'Effleur from head to toe, heart to home.

Truly Lace... A basket spun with the sensuous luxuries of Truly Lace, including Dusting Powder in a reusable satin and lace covered box.

Complete the Enrollment Form in the front of this book and mail it with this Proof of Purchase.